THE DUKE'S DAUGHTER

SASHA COTTMAN

Chapter One

By every measure of her own behavior, Lady Lucy Radley knew this was the worst.

'You reckless fool,' she muttered under her breath as she headed back inside and into the grand ballroom.

The room was a crush of London's social elite. Every few steps she had to stop and make small talk with friends or acquaintances. A comment here and there about someone's gown or promising a social call made for slow going.

Finally, she spied her cousin, Eve. She fixed a smile to her face as Eve approached.

'Where have you been Lucy? I've been searching everywhere for you.'

'I was just outside admiring the flowers on the terrace.'

Eve frowned, but the lie held.

Another night, another ball in one of London's high society homes. In one respect Lucy would be happy when the London social season ended in a few weeks; then she would be free to travel to her family home in Scotland and go tramping across the valleys and mountain paths, the chill wind ruffling her hair.

She puffed out her cheeks. With the impending close of the

season came an overwhelming sense of failure. Her two older brothers, David and Alex, had taken wives. Perfect, love-filled unions with delightful girls, both of whom Lucy was happy to now call sister.

Her newest sister-in-law, Earl Langham's daughter Clarice, was already in a delicate condition, and Lucy suspected it was only a matter of time before her brother Alex and his wife Millie shared some good news.

For herself, this season had been an unmitigated disaster on the husband-hunting front. The pickings were slim at best. Having refused both an earl and a viscount the previous season, she suspected other suitable gentlemen now viewed her as too fussy. No gentleman worth his boots wanted a difficult wife. Only the usual group of fortune-hunters, intent on getting their hands on her substantial dowry, were lining up at this stage of the season to ask her to dance. Maintaining her pride as the daughter of a duke, she refused them all.

Somewhere in the collective gentry of England there must be a man worthy of her love. She just had to find him.

What a mess.

'You are keeping something from me,' Eve said, poking a finger gently into Lucy's arm.

Lucy shook her head. 'It's nothing, I suspect I am suffering from a touch of ennui. These balls all begin to look the same after a while. All the same people, sharing the same gossip.'

'Oh dear, and I thought I was having a bad day,' Eve replied.

'Sorry, I was being selfish. You are the one who needs a friend to cheer her up,' Lucy replied. She kissed her cousin gently on the cheek.

Eve's brother William had left London earlier that day to return to his home in Paris, and she knew her cousin was taking his departure hard.

'Yes, well, I knew I could sit at home and cry, or I could put on a happy face and try to find something to smile about,' Eve replied.

Eve's father had tried without success to convince his son to return permanently to England. With the war now over and

Napoleon toppled from power, everyone expected William Saunders to come home immediately, but it had taken two years for him to make the journey back to London.

'Perhaps once he gets back home and starts to miss us all again, he shall have a change of heart,' Lucy said.

'One can only hope. Now, let's go and find a nice quiet spot and you can tell me what you were really doing out in the garden. Charles Ashton came in the door not a minute before you and he had a face like thunder. As I happened to see the two of you head out into the garden at the same time a little while ago, I doubt Charles' foul temper was because he found the flowers not to his liking,' Eve replied.

❧

It was late when Lucy and her parents finally returned home to Strathmore House. The Duke and Duchess of Strathmore's family home was one of the largest houses in the elegant West End of London. It was close to the peaceful greenery of Hyde Park, and Lucy couldn't imagine living anywhere else.

As they came through the grand entrance to Strathmore House she was greeted by the sight of her eldest brother David seated on a low couch outside their father's study. He was clad in a heavy black greatcoat and his hat was in his hand.

'Hello David; bit late for a visit this evening. I hope nothing is wrong,' said Lord Strathmore.

'Clarice?' asked Lady Caroline.

'She's fine, sleeping soundly at home,' he replied.

Lucy sensed the pride and love for his wife in her brother's voice. He had found his true soulmate in Lord Langham's daughter.

David stood and came over. When he reached them, he greeted his mother and sister with a kiss. His dark hair was a stark contrast to both Lady Caroline and Lucy's fair complexions.

He turned to his father. 'Lord Langham's missing heir has been found, and the news is grave. My father-in-law asked that I come and inform you before it becomes public knowledge. A rather horrid business, by all accounts.'

'I see. Ladies, would you please excuse us? This demands my immediate attention,' Lord Strathmore said.

As Lucy and Lady Caroline headed up the grand staircase, he and David retired to his study. As soon as the door was closed behind them, David shared the news.

'The remains of Thaxter Fox were retrieved from the River Fleet a few hours ago. His brother Avery, whom you met at my wedding ball a few weeks ago, has formally identified the body. Lord Langham is currently making funeral arrangements,' David said.

His father shook his head. It was a not unexpected outcome of the search for the missing Thaxter Fox.

He wandered over to a small table and poured two glasses of whisky. He handed one to David.

'Well, that makes for a new and interesting development. I don't expect Avery Fox had ever entertained the notion before today that he would one day be Earl Langham,' Lord Strathmore replied, before downing his drink.

'Perhaps, but he had to know the likelihood of finding his brother in one piece was slim at best. From our enquiries, it was obvious Thaxter had a great many enemies,' David replied.

'Including you,' said the duke.

David looked down at his gold wedding ring. It still bore the newly wed gleam which made him smile.

'He and I had come to a certain understanding. If he stayed away from Langham House and Clarice, I would not flay the skin off his back. No, someone else decided to make Thaxter pay for his evil ways.'

The Langham and Radley families held little affection for the recently deceased heir to the Langham title. After Thaxter had made an attempt to seize Clarice's dowry through a forced marriage, both families had severed all ties. Thaxter had disappeared not long after.

David would do everything in his power to protect Clarice. With a baby on the way, he was fully prepared to stare down the rest of the *ton* if it meant keeping his wife safe. As the illegitimate, but acknowledged, son of the duke, David had overcome many of society's prejudices in order to successfully woo and wed Lord Langham's only daughter.

'Unkind as it sounds, I doubt few at Langham House will be mourning the demise of the eldest Mr. Fox,' his father replied.

'No.'

Chapter Two

'You have a visitor, Mr. Fox,' the Langham House butler announced.

Avery quickly rose from his seat. As he took the small, cream-colored calling card from the silver tray, the butler scowled. He was clearly unused to his deliveries being met half-way.

'Thank you very much,' Avery said. The butler scowled once more.

The practice of never openly thanking staff sat uncomfortably with Avery. Was it any wonder the French had risen up and over-thrown the ruling classes? While he couldn't see such a bloody and violent uprising happening in peaceful, verdant England, it still left him considering which side he would be on if it ever came to revolution.

He didn't feel he belonged among the *ton*. He doubted he ever would. While Lord Langham and his family had welcomed him cordially, Avery had a deep-seated suspicion that they were only showing their social faces to him. They certainly didn't trust him. At no point during any of his visits to Langham House had he ever been left alone.

Oh Thaxter, what did you do to these people?

He looked at the elegantly printed card and smiled.

'Send the major in, please.'

'Major?' Lord Langham asked.

'Yes. Major Ian Barrett. He was my commanding officer in the 2nd Battalion, 95th Regiment of Foot. His family were most generous to me after I was wounded at Waterloo,' Avery replied.

As soon as Ian Barrett entered the room, Avery stood stiffly to attention.

'At ease, Fox; neither of us is in the army any longer,' Ian said. He offered Avery his hand.

Ian turned to Lord Langham, and before Avery had a chance to make formal introductions, he reached out and gave the earl a hard slap on the shoulder.

'Frosty!' he laughed.

Lord Langham chuckled. 'I'm never going to live that down, am I? How are you?'

Ian nodded. 'Well. Though I hadn't realized you and Avery were related.'

'Only distantly; we were the last of the line when it came to suitable heirs,' Avery found himself replying.

He immediately regretted his words when he saw the disapproving look on Ian's face.

'How is your brother? Lord Langham asked.

Ian screwed up his face.

'Albert has his good days and his not-so-good ones. Unfortunately, the not-so-good ones appear to have become the norm.'

Avery recalled the odd occasion he had seen the Earl of Rokewood during the years he lived at Rokewood Park, the Barrett family estate in Northamptonshire. Usually it was just a glimpse of his back from another room, but he had once set eyes on the man properly. They had encountered one another late one night in the library at Rokewood Park.

The sunken, haunted eyes of the earl had drawn him in. Avery's stammered apology for disturbing the house's owner was met with the merest of nods from a man who carried himself as if he were made of glass.

Lord Langham turned to Avery. 'I was at school with both Lord Rokewood and Ian. I spent a summer in my youth at Rokewood Park; marvelous place.'

Avery nodded. 'Yes.'

Rokewood Park had been Avery's salvation. He owed a lifelong debt to the Barrett family for taking a non-commissioned officer into their home. After the war, he had nowhere else to go. His own family home had long ceased to exist.

'So, what brings you to London, sir?' Avery asked.

'Oh, this and that. When I read the notice of your brother's death in this morning's papers, I thought I should come by and pay my respects. I assumed you would be in residence here. I am sorry for your loss, Avery,' Ian replied.

Silence hung in the room for a moment. Ian knew enough of Avery's traumatic childhood to know he would not be beside himself with grief. Lord Langham's response was consistent with the social veil which everyone seem to adopt when Thaxter's name was mentioned.

Once the funeral was over, Avery intended to get to the bottom of his late brother's life. To discover as many of his evil secrets as he could. Whatever damage Thaxter had done in the short time he had been Lord Langham's heir, Avery was determined to make restitution. To restore something of his family's name.

He stifled a snort. Why he should care for his father's good name was beyond reason. His father and brother had cared little for him. He had no memory of his mother. Yet despite all these years estranged from his family, it mattered to him.

'Thank you,' he replied.

'If you like, I will leave the two of you alone to catch up on old times. My son-in-law, David, will shortly be back from the city and he and I need to discuss business matters for an hour or so,' the earl offered.

Lord Langham shook hands with Ian and left the room. Of course, the earl would allow them time alone; Major Barrett would make certain nothing was stolen from the room while he was present.

'Well, you have had an eventful few weeks since you left us, Avery,' Ian said, taking a seat.

Eventful! More like a bloody nightmare.

'Yes, I had thought to start to look for employment, but it looks like I will have my hands full in dealing with Thaxter's legacy,' he replied.

Ian sighed. 'You always said he was a bad one. God rest his soul. Any idea as to what happened?'

Avery fiddled with the glove on his left hand. He wore it to hide the angry scars he had earned on the battlefield at Waterloo.

It had only been two days since the river police had dragged Thaxter's body out of the river, but already he was uncomfortable with the whole business of condolences. The sooner his brother was buried, the better.

'From what I understand, my brother made a lot of enemies over the past few months. He ran up a significant amount of debt, which he was unable to repay,' Avery replied.

The fact that Lord Langham had left his heir to the mercy of what appeared to be murderous debt collectors spoke volumes about how far Thaxter had become estranged from him. The Langham family had closed ranks against the outsider and left him to his fate.

Earl Langham's nephew Rupert, his original heir, had died the previous summer, and after a long search Thaxter Fox had been discovered as the next in line to inherit the title. With Thaxter now also dead, Avery stood in his brother's place as heir to the title and fortune. He dreaded the day someone bowed and called him Lord Langham.

'Nasty business, but it appears Fate has once more stepped in and given you a position with honour,' Ian said.

Avery shook his head.

As he saw things, there was no chance of him ever restoring his personal honour. He had killed another man and personally gained from it. From that place, no man could return.

Ian shifted in his chair. 'You cannot blame yourself for what happened. It was war. Many things happened on the battlefield

Avery frowned. Had things changed so much in England that no-one wore black to a funeral, especially the members of the deceased's family?

Clarice smiled at him as she took a seat in the front pew next to Lucy. David reached over and shook Avery's hand.

'Thank you for coming,' Avery said.

As the priest began the funeral service, Avery kept his mind diverted by staring at the stained-glass window high above the altar. The image of St James in his layered crimson robes, holding a staff, stared down benevolently at him. It was odd that he felt at home in this place, as he couldn't remember the last time he had been inside a church.

❦

From where she sat in the front pew, Lucy stole the occasional glance at Avery Fox. His hair, which she decided was on the light side of sable, had been flattened by his hat. The offending hat sat next to him on the seat. Inwardly she smiled. The men of her social class all knew to give their hair a ruffle after removing their hats, but Mr. Fox, it would appear, was not used to the custom. It was an awkwardness which she found charming.

She also noted the pair of black leather gloves Avery wore. Casting her mind back to their first meeting at her brother's wedding ball, she recalled that Avery had worn only one glove that night, on his left hand. She had made discreet enquiries with Clarice as to this odd habit.

'He was injured during the final onslaught at Waterloo. I haven't seen his hand, but I expect he keeps it covered so as not to show the scars. Papa tells me they are quite unsightly,' Clarice said.

She looked up and saw Avery's gaze was fixed upon her. For a moment, she was captivated by his emerald-green eyes. He blinked. It was a simple action, but it had an immediate effect on her. A flush of red heat filled her cheeks and she quickly moved back in her seat, her heart racing.

She sat and pondered her unexpected response to a simple blink. Had she lowered herself to the level of flirting at a funeral?

I can't be that desperate to capture a man's attention, can I?

Ashamed of herself, she made certain for the rest of the service that she sat so as to keep Avery blocked from her view. Lord Langham, seated between them, fortunately did not appear to have noticed anything was amiss.

❦

After the service Thaxter Fox was buried in the small church graveyard. The bells tolled out the number of years of Thaxter's life: thirty-one. Silence finally descended on the graveyard as the death knell came to an end.

Standing beside the grave, along with the other male mourners, Avery pondered his rapidly changing circumstances.

After visiting the undertakers to formally identify Thaxter's body, the earl had taken Avery back to Langham House. Thereafter followed a long evening of whisky and toasts to dearly departed friends. Sipping the finest Scottish malt whisky, Avery had forced himself to show the outward signs of grief for his brother.

If he were honest, there were a dozen men he had grieved over more than Thaxter. Old pains and injustices could not be overcome through the simple act of dying. He, for one, could never forgive his brother.

Lord Langham cleared his throat at the graveside.

'I trust you will understand why my family will not be going into full mourning with you, Avery. We buried my wife some three years past and while I came out of mourning a year or so ago, Clarice has only recently begun to wear colors again. I will not ask it of her to wear blacks again so soon. David has agreed that the men of the family shall wear black armbands for a month, and Clarice shall wear a black rose pinned to her dress. I trust that meets with your approval,' Lord Langham said.

Avery looked down at his own set of mourning clothes. David had kindly lent him a black suit and it fitted him surprisingly well.

He stifled a wry grin: black was his favourite color; he could wear it every day and not be concerned. He certainly didn't miss the rough wool of his old green regimental uniform and its very uncomfortable high hat.

'Social appearances must be kept,' he muttered under his breath.

It began to rain and the priest hurried through the graveside service.

'Ashes to ashes, dust to dust.'

The rest of the mourners, though few in number, each picked up a handful of the soft graveside soil and tossed it on to the lowered coffin. They walked away, some giving Avery a final offer of condolence, while others departed silently.

Finally, he was left standing alone beside his brother's grave.

He picked up a handful of dirt and for a moment stood looking at it, sorely tempted to spit on it. He looked toward the churchyard gate, and saw Lord Langham and Ian Barrett sheltering under a tree, waiting. He gave them a nod.

In the long years since he had fled his home, he had made every effort to be a better man than his father and brother. Until that fateful day on the battlefield at Waterloo, he'd thought he had succeeded.

He threw the dirt on to the coffin. He would not embarrass either gentleman by showing what he truly thought of his brother.

'Goodbye Thaxter; sleep well,' he said, and turned from the grave.

A small wake was held at Langham House, attended almost exclusively by the Radley and Langham families. Ian Barrett stayed for just one drink. As he had other business matters to attend to whilst he was in London, Avery accepted his apologies with good grace.

'It was kind of you to come all this way, sir; I know you don't make it up to London that often, so I appreciate your coming today,' he said, shaking the major's hand.

'Yes, well, considering the delightful young lady I have met today, perhaps I should change that habit for a new one,' Ian replied. He nodded in the direction of Lady Lucy.

'Yes, she is rather pretty and she has been kind to me,' Avery replied.

He had caught her looking at his hands during the funeral service and wondered how much her brother David had told her of him. It didn't take much for a casual observer to note that Avery favored his right hand over his left.

He turned away from Lucy.

Ian raised an eyebrow.

'So how long do you intend to mourn your brother?' he asked.

Ian knew the full story of Avery and Thaxter's relationship and why Avery had falsified his age in order to join the army a full two years before he was eligible. Avery shrugged his shoulders. The idea of a month with a black armband didn't appeal to him greatly, but he suspected with his elevation to earl-in-waiting, his every move would be scrutinized by London's elite.

'It's a pity I couldn't come back to Rokewood Park with you,' Avery replied.

He knew it was impossible. He had a new role to fulfil. New responsibilities which he could not in all good conscience avoid by hiding away in the countryside.

'Well, perhaps next time you are over Northampton way, you could call in and see us. Best of luck, Avery. Lord Langham is a good man; I think you will do well. And don't be too hasty in dismissing those who might be the kind of friend you need in the *haute ton*. Lady Lucy Radley is very well connected. Not to mention unwed.'

❦

Lucy had caught Ian Barrett and Avery Fox looking in her direction and knew instinctively they were talking about her. She was in two minds as to whether she should go and talk to Avery once she saw Ian Barrett making his farewells.

The effect Avery had had on her during the funeral left her

Chapter Three

'I want you to move in here,' Lord Langham said.

The wake was now over, the mourners all gone, and Avery was seated on a high-backed leather Chesterfield sofa in Lord Langham's private sitting room.

Avery shook his head.

'I'm perfectly fine where I am, across the river. If I need to journey up here to see anyone, I can cross over at Westminster Bridge. If it's urgent I shall pay sixpence to the watermen and they can row me across.'

He prayed he would never have to urgently cross the Thames; for one he didn't like the dangerous waters, and two, the few coins he had in his possession were rapidly dwindling. At this juncture, he didn't feel comfortable in asking Lord Langham for funds, but he knew the subject would eventually have to be broached.

Lord Langham frowned.

'It's not the done thing, Avery. My heir should be resident at Langham House. How am I to teach you how to carry on the estate after I am gone if you are on the other side of the Thames?'

Whether he meant it or not, Avery caught the disapproving tone in Lord Langham's voice when he mentioned the south side of London.

Not that his room at the Queens Head on Black Prince Road was anything to behold. It certainly wasn't as elegantly furnished as Langham House. A single, narrow wooden bed and a small wash-stand were the only pieces of furniture in the room. In the time, he had been in London, he had spent most of it in search of Thaxter. He returned at night to the public house in Lambeth only to wash and sleep.

He sighed.

Now that Thaxter had been found, and buried, he was at a loss. He had little in common with the likes of Lord Langham and his family. He was an outsider. A fortuitous interloper, nothing more.

Lord Langham put a fatherly hand on Avery's shoulder. He flinched at the touch.

'Sorry,' the earl said, and quickly withdrew his hand.

'Old habits,' Avery replied.

He wasn't going to mention that the only time his own father or brother had laid a hand on him during his childhood was with either a belt or a clenched fist.

Adding to his discomfort was the knowledge that the offer to move into Langham House had not been extended to Thaxter. Whatever his brother had done to offend the Langhams must have been grave indeed. Henry Langham did not strike Avery as a man caught up in the inconsequential details of life.

'I know you have spent most of your life alone, Avery, but it won't help your transition into London society if you stay away. As a soldier, you must have learnt much of the rules of engagement. The *ton* is little different. The best adage to live by is to know thy enemy. And surround yourself with friends.'

Avery nodded. 'Yes, yes, of course.'

'There is one other very important reason for you to take your place among us. You will in time need a wife,' Lord Langham added.

Avery's breath caught in his throat. A wife was near to the last thing on his mind.

'Even your brother had accepted the need for a suitable partner for his future role. Though the way he went about trying to woo a potential spouse left a lot to be desired. You, on the other hand, I am confident will have more success.'

He met Lord Langham's gaze. Was now the time to press for more information on the deeds of Thaxter Fox? To get to the truth of the matter?

He straightened the front of his jacket and considered his position. He finally had a bargaining chip at his disposal and he intended to use it.

'I will move to Langham House if, once I am here, you disclose all that happened between your family and my late brother. It is obvious that Thaxter did not hold your good favor at the end. If I am to live under your roof there should be no secrets between us,' he replied.

Lord Langham hesitated briefly. Avery gritted his teeth, determined to get his way.

'Agreed, but I must also add a condition. If I tell you what happened between your brother and my daughter, you must never breathe a word of it to another soul. Only a handful of people know about it, and it must stay that way. I will not have Clarice hurt.'

Avery offered his hand in agreement.

❧

The following morning, he paid the last of his rent for the room at the Queens Head and left. His brown leather army bag was slung over his shoulder; within it were contained his meagre possessions, including his old army rifle.

Halfway across Westminster Bridge, he stopped. Looking out over the Thames, he indulged in the simple pleasure of letting the river breeze ruffle his hair.

As he stood looking back down the Thames, the Houses of Parliament on his right, the top of Lambeth Palace in sight on his left, he sensed he had reached another major turning point in his life. As a member of London's high society, he doubted he would get many opportunities to venture back to drink at the riverside pubs.

Pity.

His life had been a short series of identifiable milestones, all revolving around the one thing he held dearest to his heart: his honour.

The first time he had attempted to run away from home, his father beat him to within an inch of his life. As the wounds slowly healed, he vowed never to take up the family trade. Thievery and skullduggery were not how he wanted to live his life.

All throughout the long years of his army service he had used honour to judge each situation in which he was called to make a decision. If a course of action was dishonorable, he would find another way to handle matters.

On the murky river below he could see two of the familiar black waterman boats passing one another. The cries from the crews as they hurled good-natured, foul-mouthed insults across the water had him laughing. London certainly had a flavor all of its own.

He pushed away from the stone wall of the bridge and gave one last backward glance to the southern side of London before continuing on his way toward the West End. In his pocket jangled a few coins the Langham household butler had pressed into his hands when he left Mill Street late the previous night.

'His lordship would like you to make a suitable arrival at Langham House. He asked that you arrive in a well-set hack rather than on foot,' the butler had said.

Social standards and expectations were to be the norm from now on. As of this day he belonged elsewhere.

Outside the hallowed halls of Westminster Abbey, he hailed what he hoped would be an acceptable hackney coach and gave the driver his new address. As he climbed inside and settled back against the leather bench seats he felt his heart beating strongly. A dryness in his mouth confirmed his thoughts. He was nervous. All his training and years living rough in the army had not prepared him for the elegant ballrooms and homes of the parish of St James.

He was back to where he was when he ran away from home. An inexperienced, green boy.

'Sit still and observe quietly,' he muttered, repeating the words of his first rifle sergeant. By watching what others did and said, he could learn their ways.

'And perhaps not make a complete and utter fool of myself.'

Once he was alone in his new suite at Mill Street, he closed the door behind the Langham House footman. The man's offer to unpack Avery's bag had been well received, but politely declined. When he dug in his pocket for a coin to tip the man, it was quickly explained that this was not how things were done in private homes.

A chuckle escaped his lips as he put the bag down on top of the enormous four-poster bed. At least the footman had the decency to laugh about Avery's awkward social skills and make the newest member of the household feel more at ease.

His gaze roamed over the gold-and-black checked silk counterpane. Looking up he saw that the fabric of the draped canopy matched. He had never seen a bed so big. It could easily sleep five people. His theory was quickly proved by the pile of six pillows stacked at the bedhead. Running his hand over the fine bedcover, a wicked thought captured his mind. Having at least one other person in this bed would be a godsend.

Preferably naked and most definitively female. How long had it been since he had felt the soft, warm touch of a woman? His body began to harden at the thought of the gentle laughter which came when he placed hot, teasing kisses on the nape of his lover's neck.

The girls in Portugal had been friendly, but complicated. Always asking when he would come to supper and meet their brothers. A few extra coins in their hands and talk of their numerous *brothers* would miraculously disappear.

The English girls of the village close to Rokewood Park had been far more obvious in their desires and demands. A roll in the hay, a kiss afterwards and no eye contact if they passed you in the street had been their hard and fast rule. He would give anything right now for one of those women to knock on his bedroom door and bring relief to his lustful needs.

'You are not lord of the manor just yet. I doubt Langham would appreciate you bringing a lady into this house to share your bed,' he cautioned himself.

An image of Lady Lucy Radley sprang to his mind. The memory of her blush-reddened cheeks as their gazes met in the church had him swallowing deep. Her pale pink lips had held the promise of soft, sensual kisses. He longed to bury his face in her long blonde tresses.

'Steady on, Fox; she is a duke's daughter. You just caught her off-guard. Don't go thinking anything more of it. She is not for the likes of you.'

He forced himself to put away all notions of amorous pursuits, for the time being at least. There were other, more pressing matters to command his attention.

He opened the battered travel bag and took out his spare linen shirt, and a few other odd, well-repaired pieces of clothing. He took his army rifle, still wrapped up in a regimental jacket, and placed it safely under his bed. Keeping his rifle close by was one old habit which would die hard.

At the bottom of the bag he retrieved the last item, a small, nondescript grey bag. He stood holding it in his hand.

This second bag was a fairly recent purchase. It blended in perfectly with the bottom of the larger bag. While Avery very rarely let his travel bag out of his sight, he found comfort in the added protection this simple act of camouflage afforded. Any rogue rifling through his belongings would more than likely overlook the dull, grey, sock-like thing at the bottom of his travel bag.

'Come on then, let's have a look at you,' he muttered.

The expansive bedroom window allowed the room to be bathed in sunlight. Another sharp contrast to the tiny, windowless room in which he had been sleeping under the rafters at the Queens Head.

From out of the bag, he pulled a pocket watch. A ray of light caught the gold cover of the watch and cast a glint. He smiled lovingly at it. His imagination whispered that the handsome time-piece had likely once been owned by someone who lived in such a fine house as this.

'I promise you no more chilly attics,' he murmured. He lay the watch down on the bed.

A knock at the door roused him from his thoughts. He quickly threw his spare shirt over the watch and called. 'Enter.'

Lord Langham's smiling face appeared around the door.

'All settled?' he asked.

Avery nodded. He did not have a lot of things to unpack or get settled.

'Good. In that case I was wondering if you would indulge me and allow my tailor to attend you. We cannot have you getting about in borrowed clothes any longer.'

Lord Langham strode into the room followed by a stout, middle-aged man with a length of thin fabric in his hand. Behind the man several household footmen carried large boxes covered in striped fabric. The man pointed to a spot on the floor near the French doors and the boys deposited the boxes before withdrawing from the room.

'This is Mr. Swain. Mr. Swain, Mr. Avery Fox.'

Mr. Swain bowed low. It was clear he knew who Avery was.

'Mr. Fox. A pleasure to meet you. I hope I may be of service to you today and in the future,' he said. He stood back and placed his hands by his sides, an expectant look on his face.

Avery scowled. He had never dealt with a tailor before; what was he supposed to do?

Lord Langham cleared his throat. 'Mr. Fox has had a long military career; he is not used to having the services of a gentleman's tailor.'

He turned toward Avery. 'Mr. Swain will need to take your full measurements, so you will have to remove your jacket.'

Lord Langham wandered over to a nearby chair and made himself comfortable. Avery slowly removed his jacket and lay it on the bed over the spare shirt. The pocket watch remained hidden from sight.

The second Mr. Swain stepped forward and put his hands on Avery's waist, he knew it was going to be an interesting afternoon.

He looked at Lord Langham, seeking reassurance that having this man's hands all over him was what was supposed to be happening.

Henry Langham sat chuckling in the chair.

'You wait till he measures you up for new trousers, Fox. I bet five pounds you hold your breath when he takes your inside leg measurements.'

Mr. Swain took the measuring tape from around his neck and went silently about his business. When he did get to the point where he had Avery standing, legs akimbo, while he ran the measuring tape around his thigh, Avery began to feel faint.

'Done,' Mr. Swain finally announced.

'Excellent,' Lord Langham said.

'Is Friday soon enough, milord?'

Lord Langham nodded. 'Yes, I think we can hide Mr. Fox away from society for a few more days.'

The tailor made his bowed farewells and left. Avery stood staring at the door, a deep scowl between his eyebrows. Why was he being hidden from society?

'Relax, young man. Mr. Swain will have the basics of your new wardrobe ready by Friday, then you can start to circulate. The season is coming to a close, but it will do you good to make at least a few appearances in the next few weeks. Selective ones, of course, in the circumstances,' Lord Langham said.

Avery picked up his jacket and considered the black armband he had hastily sewn around the left arm. David had assured him he was fine with Avery sewing it to the jacket when he lent it to him. Lord Langham still wore his piece of mourning cloth on his sleeve, but it was only held on by pins, almost as if it were a mere afterthought to social propriety.

'Take your time to relax and find your way around the house this afternoon. Later in the week we shall sit and discuss matters of business and what role you might like to play in the running of the estate.'

Lord Langham left Avery to his own devices for the rest of the day. David made a brief appearance later that morning, promising to spend time with him in the forthcoming days. Lady Clarice and the dowager Countess Langham were nowhere to be seen.

Avery spent the afternoon lying on his back, enjoying the soft comfort of the big bed in his room. He found himself whistling to overcome the silence of the house. He rolled over and ran his right hand across the silk cover. Soft and sensual to the touch, it tempted him into taking off the black leather glove which he permanently wore on his left hand.

As his fingers settled on the soft, cool fabric, he looked at the series of deep slashes which ran from his middle fingers to his wrist. They presented a sharp contrast to the expensive elegance of the bedclothes.

He frowned. The hand was stiff and only afforded a limited range of movement. No amount of bespoke clothing, or money for that matter, could make him whole again.

❧

Avery's first evening at Langham House provided his first real insight into not only the relationship between his late brother and the Langham family, but more importantly, how the Langham family viewed his presence.

At dinner, he dined only with the Dowager Countess Langham. Lord Langham sent his apologies due to a prior engagement, while David and Clarice were dining with Lord and Lady Strathmore.

When he entered the room, Avery fully expected Lady Alice to turn her nose up and ignore him. He was soon wishing she had. No sooner had the first course been served than Lady Alice began her interrogation of him.

'So, Mr. Fox, you were in the army?'

'Yes, Lady Alice, fifteen years all told.'

'And you were injured at Waterloo?'

'Yes, Lady Alice. I was lucky to survive.'

And so, it went on. For two solid hours, the silver-haired dowager countess grilled him about his life. By the time the footman served an overly sweet dessert wine, Avery had begun to wilt under the constant questions.

Thank god, she wasn't on the side of the French during the war.

'Well. Thank you for a most illuminating evening, Mr. Fox,' Lady Alice announced.

She signaled to a nearby footman, who hastened over to pull out her chair. Avery quickly put down his wine glass and rose from the table. He came to her side, handing her the walking stick she had propped against the table.

Taking the walking stick, she flinched when Avery put a supportive hand under her elbow. She looked up at him and for an instant he could have sworn he saw fear in her eyes.

The look was gone as soon as she blinked. A tight smile came to her lips.

'Thank you, Mr. Fox,' she said.

'I should very much like for you to call me Avery, Lady Alice. If that is to your liking. It does seem a little overly formal to address me in such a way under your own roof,' he replied.

She considered his words and then nodded.

'Avery it is. Good night, Avery; welcome to Langham House.'

She hobbled out of the room, leaving Avery with a handful of servants to wait on him alone.

He resumed his seat at the table and finished the last course of flavored ices and fruit. The first olive branch of friendship had been extended to Lady Alice, and he was pleased that she had accepted it. Less comforting was that she had not reciprocated the gesture, but he consoled himself that it was to be expected.

'Small steps,' he whispered into his wine glass before draining it. His offer to the servants to leave him to his own company was met with a polite refusal. He tried not to read too much into the curious situation. Likely it was just a normal part of the social rules. Members of the family must always have servants on hand at their beck and call.

He sighed. With no-one else home and lacking the funds to venture out, he faced the prospect of a long, boring evening alone.

'Is there a library in the house?' he asked the ever-present footman.

Within minutes he was standing in Lord Langham's well-stocked private library. Hands on hips, he whistled his appreciation of the magnificent collection. Towering shelves literally groaned under the weight of heavy tomes. He had never before seen so many books in the one place. He walked around the room, slowly perusing the collection. As he ran his finger along the spines of book after book, an appreciative smile formed on his lips. The Langham family not only read widely, but they had similar tastes to his own.

'It's just like finding King Solomon's treasure,' he muttered to himself.

Finally, he chose a collection of Wordsworth's poems. Book in hand, he strode over to the footman.

'Is it all right if I borrow this to read in my room?' he asked.

The footman shifted uneasily on his feet. Avery could see from the look of concern on the young man's face that whatever his instructions for the evening had been, they had not included Mr. Fox asking to remove books from the library.

'Forget about it. I would hate to get you into trouble over a book,' he said.

Turning on his heel he walked back to the bookcase and returned the book to the shelf.

'Excuse me, Mr. Fox, but I'm sure it would be acceptable for you to sit and read the book in here. I can build up the fire and have one of the other lads bring you a brandy,' the young man replied.

Avery retrieved the book and was soon ensconced in a comfortable chair by the fire, a warm brandy keeping him company.

The following morning Avery rose early, as was his lifelong habit. He quickly washed and dressed and stepped out into the hall. An hour of reading before breakfast was central to his plans for the day.

As he closed the door to his room, a footman rose from a nearby chair and bid him a good morning. As Avery passed by, the footman fell in step behind. Instantly, Avery stopped and spun around. A rush of hot anger raced up his spine.

'Is Lord Langham up and about this early?' he asked. Knowing he was not trusted enough to move about the house without a footman shadowing his every move, had his blood on the edge of boiling.

'I believe so, Mr. Fox,' the footman replied.

'Take me to him.'

Avery concentrated on his breathing as he knocked and entered Lord Langham's study. He shot a warning glance to the footman who had followed him. Fortunately for all concerned, Henry Langham was a perceptive man and upon rising from his large oak desk, quickly dismissed the nervous footman.

'I won't bother wishing you a good morning Avery, because from the look on your face, it is not,' Lord Langham said.

Avery felt the tremble in his fisted hands as he struggled to contain his wrath. A movement to his right caught his eye. David Radley got to his feet from a chair near the fire. David looked at Lord Langham, who silently shook his head.

David Radley had shown only the utmost courtesy to Avery in all their encounters, but at that moment Avery hated him. David was the one afforded an early morning meeting and coffee, while Avery, the heir to the title, was left to wander the house like an ill-welcome guest.

Ill-welcome indeed.

'What can I do for you Avery; you look particularly vexed?'

Avery forced his rage down. A good soldier never fired a shot in anger.

'I was wondering why you invited me to come and live here,' he bit off.

Lord Langham scowled, clearly perplexed by the question. 'I asked you to come and live with us because you are my heir. Someday all this will be yours,' he replied.

'Are you perhaps having second thoughts? That you somehow made a mistake? I think it might be best that I leave this house until the time comes that I have a right to be here. When I will be welcome,' Avery replied.

The pain of personal insult had taken him by surprise. Had the tension of wondering if he would ever see Thaxter alive again finally caught up with him?

Lord Langham crossed the floor.

'What has happened? I thought you and I were in agreement on this arrangement?' The look of concern on his face was genuine enough to give Avery hope.

'You and I also agreed to discuss the circumstances as to why your family fell out with my brother. Circumstances which I suspect have a major bearing on why my every step is being shadowed in this house. Why I cannot borrow a book from the household library and read it in the privacy of my own room. And why you have a footman posted outside my bedroom door.'

He sucked in a huge lungful of air and covered his eyes with his gloved hand. He was so close to tears he could barely stand himself.

'Oh,' Lord Langham replied.

Avery removed his hand, only to find himself staring at a clearly troubled Henry Langham. 'I am sorry, Avery. I gave no such orders for you to be so closely scrutinized. I suspect my mother may have been a little too heavy-handed in her instructions to the staff. Rest assured I shall speak with her as soon as she comes down for breakfast.'

The image of Lady Alice from the previous night at dinner formed clearly in Avery's mind. A most troubling one.

'What did my brother do? Your mother was fearful of me last night when I tried to assist her. For a moment, I think she thought I was Thaxter – familial similarity and all that,' Avery replied.

David cleared his throat. 'Perhaps it is time Avery was made fully aware of matters.'

Lord Langham nodded and pointed Avery toward one of the chairs arranged in a semi-circle in front of the fireplace. All three took a seat.

'What we tell you now must never leave this room. The only

other people who know the truth are my mother and Clarice. I ask that you do not make mention of it to either of them. They have both suffered enough,' said Lord Langham.

'My wife is with child, Mr. Fox and I will not have anything said to her which could cause her distress,' David added.

The sudden formality with which David addressed him caused a slow-burning fear to heat the pit of Avery's empty stomach. Lord Langham pursed his lips and sat silent for a time.

What had Thaxter done to the women of this family?

'A short time ago David asked for my permission to court Clarice. Due to reasons which I will not go into, I refused. After that I sent Clarice and her grandmother home to my estate in Norfolk. Unbeknownst to either David or myself, Thaxter followed them to Langham Hall.'

David took a cup from a nearby tray and after filling it with coffee, handed it to Avery. Though David held the cup steady and met Avery's gaze, the air was thick with tension.

'Thank you,' Avery said.

David remained seated forward in his chair, his body rigid.

'When your brother arrived at Langham Hall he attempted to force Clarice into marrying him,' David said.

'When you say force her to marry him, I take it you mean . . . ?' Avery replied.

He tasted the burning bile which had risen up from his stomach and into his mouth.

'Yes.'

'Oh god,' Avery whispered as the truth of his brother's wickedness hit him. Thaxter had always been a vicious bully, but even Avery had never thought him capable of rape. Memories of the last time he saw his brother alive quickly flooded his mind.

Fists and foul curses rained down upon him as Thaxter held him down for yet another violent thrashing.

He puffed out his cheeks as he forced the air from his lungs. Yes, Thaxter had been capable of such villainy.

'Fortunately, Clarice managed to escape and the staff at Langham Hall held Thaxter prisoner until I arrived,' David added.

'But Lady Alice cannot think I pose that kind of threat to the womenfolk of this house. You would not have allowed me within the front door if that was the case. What else did he do?' Avery replied.

'Just the matter of a significant amount of priceless heirloom silverware your brother had stuffed into his bag before David managed to recover it. We were not so fortunate with a number of other pocket-sized but extremely valuable items here in London,' Lord Langham replied.

Avery took a sip of the hot, bitter coffee before setting his cup down. He rose from the chair.

'I'm . . .'

The word sorry was on the tip of his tongue and there it would stay. He'd be damned if he would apologize for something Thaxter had done. It wasn't as if he was here as the representative of the Fox family. A family who had treated him far worse than the Langhams. At least the earl's family didn't visit him in his bed at night and attempt to throttle him.

'What my brother did was reprehensible and from the manner of his demise I would suggest he has paid for his evil ways with the only thing of value he truly had. Thank you for the coffee and please give my regards to the rest of your family.'

He turned and headed for the door.

'So, shall we see you at breakfast?' David asked.

'I shall pack my things and be out of the house within the hour.' Avery replied.

'Why?' Lord Langham cried.

'Because, my lord, I have been judged by my brother's actions. A foul villain I have not seen since I was thirteen. You did not grant me a fair trial, just an unjust sentence. And that, my lord, I cannot abide,' he replied.

'Please Avery, you cannot leave,' Lord Langham said, rising from his chair.

'Please stay,' David added.

Lord Langham now stood between him and the door. Avery shook his head, as a droll smile threatened at his lips. He did not need to mention that he could best the older man if he truly wished to leave the room.

'We agreed that you would come and live here and I would explain to you about your brother. I have stuck to my side of the bargain. Now you need to keep to yours.'

Avery gave a curt nod in agreement. He had to give Lord Langham his dues; he had read Avery perfectly well. To others the exchange would signify little, but to Avery it was crucial. He now had in his possession the information he so desperately needed. Added to that was the fact that both senior males of the household had asked him to stay.

He considered his mission a success.

Thank god, he didn't call my bluff. Lord knows where I would be sleeping tonight.

'One more thing,' he said.

'Yes?'

'Books. I want to be allowed to borrow books from your library and read them in my room.'

Lord Langham chuckled, relief evident on his face. 'My dear boy, I will buy you the contents of Hatchards bookshop if you so wish it. Now, if you are done with your list of demands can we please go and have some breakfast? I am positively famished.'

Avery followed David into the breakfast room. Lord Langham stopped and handed them both a plate.

'Eat up, my lads; we have a full day ahead of us,' he said.

While the earl had an impassive look on his face, the light in his eyes betrayed him. He was delighted to have such a group seated at his breakfast table. He hastened to the other side of the table and brushed a kiss on his daughter's cheek. Avery politely turned away and began to fill his breakfast plate from the buffet. As he turned back he caught sight of Lord Langham hurriedly whispering in Lady Alice's ear.

All manner of breakfast delights was laid before him. The aroma of the cornucopia filled his nose. A whole baked salmon surrounded by roasted potatoes and onions caught his eye. Another serving dish held mushrooms, bacon and freshly fried eggs, his favourite breakfast food. It was difficult to choose what to leave off his plate, so in the end he took a little of everything.

With his plate piled high Avery took a seat at the table. Across from him Lady Clarice was pushing a piece of dry toast around her plate. She gave him a small wave of her fingers as David took the seat next to her.

'My sweet, go back to bed; you know mornings are the worst,' David said.

'Soon,' she replied.

Lord Langham cleared his throat and the breakfast table fell silent.

'Before you do, my dear, I would like to say a few words of welcome to our newest family member. Avery, the road which has led you to our door has been a long and interesting one. I sincerely hope that from this day forward you know that this is your home. That you are a part of our family. Welcome.'

'Hear, hear,' David said. He raised a coffee cup in salute.

Lady Clarice managed a weak smile. Lady Alice clicked her tongue. All of them in their own way welcomed him to their family.

'Thank you,' Avery replied, as a lump formed in his throat.

Chapter Four

'Nice jacket, not too sure about the waistcoat. I think it's a tad colorful,' Lady Alice remarked.

Avery grinned as he took a seat at the breakfast table on the following Saturday morning. His waistcoat was a solid dark blue in color, with the most sedate leather buttons the tailor could find. He looked down at his new ensemble, pleased with his smart clothes. It had taken over an hour for him to dress this morning. The choices presented by his extensive new wardrobe had nearly defeated him.

He knew he should be ashamed of the fact that he had tried on every piece of clothing in the privacy of his room, but he couldn't help himself. Excitement bubbled in his stomach. Avery, who had never owned more than one jacket at any point in his entire life, now owned nine of them. They would make a dandy out of him yet.

'Will you be venturing out today?' Lady Alice asked.

He nodded. Lord Langham had kept his word and set up an account at Hatchards bookshop for him. He couldn't wait to get to Piccadilly and be on their doorstep when they opened for business. He planned to spend most of the morning carefully selecting his first purchases. It was a close call as to which he was more excited about, the clothes or the books.

'After an early visit to Hatchards bookshop, I am meeting Ian Barrett for lunch. He is going to show me some of his favourite places in town.'

David and Lady Alice shared a conspiratorial grin.

David smiled. 'Good luck to you, Avery; just don't get too deep into your cups at those favourite places. Remember Lord Langham is hosting a dinner here tonight for some guests. He hasn't held a dinner party since his wife died, so tonight is important for all of us. It's his way of giving you his blessing as his heir.'

'So, who exactly is coming tonight?' Avery asked.

Lord Langham had been scant on the details when he'd mentioned it to Avery the previous evening. The earl was absent from breakfast due to an early-morning appointment with a parliamentary committee.

'Close friends and family. My parents. My brother Alex and his wife Millie. A few other selected guests. Oh, and my sister Lucy. I'm looking forward to it. I hope you are too,' David replied.

Lady Lucy Radley.

How odd it was that Avery had thought of her at least several times a day since the funeral. Those thoughts had usually involved her being in various stages of undress. He curled his toes up inside his shiny new boots. It wouldn't pay to show any response to the mention of her name, especially not in front of her brother or the ever-perceptive dowager.

He picked up his coffee cup and took a sip.

She was not for the likes of him, he silently reminded himself.

When Avery stepped out the front door of Langham House a little while later, it was with an uncharacteristic spring in his step. He was dressed as a true English gentleman. A doff of the hat from the Langham household driver added to his newfound confidence.

It was a perfect late summer morning, and he knew he should be out walking, but the temptation to take one of the Langham household carriages was too strong. He slowed his steps and strode purposefully toward the elegant black carriage which bore the Langham coat of arms in gold on the side of the door. He gave the Langham House footman a considered nod as he climbed inside.

If only the lads in his old army unit could see him now. He chuckled softly to himself as he settled back against the red leather seat for the short ride. Knowing them, they would probably bare their arses in the street if he passed them in his gilded cage.

The thought of his old friends gave him pause. After the battle and his long recuperation in the countryside, he had no idea where any of them were now.

Chelsea Royal Hospital would hold more answers regarding those injured or pensioned off after the war if he so desired. But the thought of setting foot inside its austere walls was a prospect he didn't relish.

And what if he was able to locate the former members of his company? As far as he was concerned, he had forfeited the right to stand alongside his former brothers in arms and share their battle honour. There would be no rejoicing in the memories of heroic deeds.

He clenched his right hand and willed himself to think of something else. Anything but *that* day on the battlefield.

The carriage turned into South Audley Street, heading for North Row. Calling upon a lifetime's experience of locking painful memories into small mental boxes, he brought his mood back.

He had the eagerly awaited lunch with Ian Barrett to look forward to, coupled with the prospect of new books. Tonight, Lord Langham was hosting a dinner party in his honour. He had every reason to be happy.

'Count your blessings, Lieutenant Fox. For once try to enjoy yourself,' he muttered.

&.

'It's been an age since we had a private family dinner,' Lucy remarked.

Her father helped her down from the family town carriage.

'We dined with your uncle and aunt last week,' the duke replied.

She screwed up her nose. Dinner with the Bishop of London and his wife was never an evening of relaxation for her. As a small child, she had thought the bishop went and told God all the naughty things she had done. Family events at the Old Deanery often had her sitting quietly in the corner praying that the bishop had not caught up with her latest exploits.

'I know, but this is with the newest part of our family.'

And her latest assignment.

In the days since she had seen him at the funeral, Lucy had found her thoughts turning often to the person of Mr. Avery Fox. She was resolved in her decision to assist his entrance into the world of the *ton* in whatever way she could.

'He is so unlike his late brother, you wouldn't think they stemmed from the same bloodlines,' she said.

When she'd made mention of her plans to Eve, a strange look had crossed her cousin's face.

'Just be careful how you go about things, Lucy. Mr. Fox is still a stranger to you. You don't know for certain that he is different from his brother. I have heard some very unsavory rumors regarding the activities of the late Thaxter Fox. Avery may just be more cunning,' Eve replied.

Little had been shared outside of Lord Langham's immediate family regarding Thaxter's conduct earlier that summer, but the manner of his death had been enough to cause a great deal of speculation among London's elite.

Lucy knew Eve was right in cautioning restraint, but as was often the case, she couldn't help herself. Every stray cat or dog that wandered into the grounds of the family castle in Scotland could be guaranteed of finding a home courtesy of Lady Lucy Radley. Everything and everyone belonged somewhere. And to someone.

'He is all alone in the world, Eve; I am just trying to be a friend.'

'Be careful, Lucy.'

Inside the elegant entrance to Langham House, she quickly

spotted Avery standing beside Lord Langham as the earl greeted his guests in turn. Lucy waited patiently at the end of the line of family members. Watching as Lord Langham welcomed each of his guests, she noticed that the Langham household were no longer in mourning attire. Gone were the black armbands Lord Langham and her brother, David, had worn at Thaxter Fox's funeral. Clarice was resplendent in a pale green-and-cream striped gown. Even Lady Alice, a stickler for protocol, was dressed in a muted mulberry silk gown.

Her heart went out to Avery. Newly resident at Langham House, he must surely be mortified at the clear social snub this presented. She carefully watched his every move, but he displayed no sign of distress. Her chosen protégé had learned the first lesson of the *ton*. Never show your true feelings.

Also gone from him were the borrowed clothes. His attire now displayed all the marks of a quality tailor. His formal evening jacket and breeches were cut to perfection. His silver waistcoat hugged his body. The white of his shirt fairly gleamed in the candlelight. Even his cravat had been expertly tied. The transformation from the poorly dressed stranger she had first spied at David and Clarice's wedding ball was startling.

There was also a complete lack of mourning pieces on his clothing. She wondered who had decided to end the family mourning after such a short period. His hands were covered by formal white evening gloves.

As she watched him, a secret smile came to her lips. For every move Lord Langham made, Avery mirrored it a short time later.

Astute man.

Instead of spending years trying to obtain and polish his social skills, Avery was simply learning from the behavior of those around him. It spoke of an intelligent mind, something she always found attractive in a man.

Her heart sank a little. Perhaps he didn't need her help after all. With his clever mind and ruggedly handsome face he would effortlessly cut a swathe through the *ton*.

And then he spoke. That interesting combination of northern

English accent and European clip once more captured her imagination.

'Lady Lucy,' he said.

She blinked hard with the sudden realization that he was addressing her personally.

'Mr. Fox,' she replied.

'It is good to see you again,' he said.

'You look very smart this evening Mr. Fox. I must compliment you on your new wardrobe; Lord Langham has been generous,' she said. Her gaze continued to roam appreciatively over his well-turned-out figure, only stopping when she got to his handsome face.

As his expression turned to one of disappointment, panic gripped her. Had she just insulted him by making mention of his new clothing?

Stupid girl, you had to throw that in his face. Of course, he has new clothes. Why did you have to mention that he could not have afforded them himself? Why couldn't you just say he looked smart?

'Thank you, Lady Lucy, but I am certain it is I who should be making note of your lovely evening gown. The lilac suits you, as do the Scottish pearls of your necklace,' he replied.

Lucy gave a silent prayer of thanks that he did not mention the black rose pin she had worn especially for him. Remembering their exchange at Thaxter's funeral, she could only hope Avery kept true to male form and had forgotten it.

'And that beautiful rose pin; I remember it from when we met at St James' church,' he added.

Oh.

The gentle blush which had been on Lucy's face now burned bright red. She held her breath, hoping it would dampen the fire which flamed her whole face and cheeks, but to no avail.

Avery held out his hand, and she shyly accepted it.

'It was very considerate of you to continue to wear black for my brother, but I assure you it is no longer necessary. Of course, if you do remember him with fondness then you are quite within your rights to do so as his friend.'

The last thing Lucy would have ever considered herself to be was a friend of Avery's odious brother. Thaxter had been openly rude to both her and Millie in public. Tragic though the circumstances of his death had been, she had not shed a tear in the church. She had worn the brooch purely as a gesture of friendship for Avery. Now she felt ill at ease. It was apparent Avery held little affection for the memory of his brother. She made a mental note to slip the brooch off at the first available opportunity.

David had made enough veiled remarks about Thaxter's standing within the Langham household for her to understand the lack of regard in which the late Mr. Fox had been held. Her brother's face wore a look of strained wrath on the odd occasion that Thaxter's name had been spoken in his presence since David had returned to London with Clarice. She suspected something unfortunate had occurred at Lord Langham's Norfolk estate between David, Clarice and Thaxter, but whatever it was, no-one was talking. What had transpired at Langham Hall was a closed matter.

She half turned away before stopping. Now was the perfect time to engage him in conversation. To find out more about this intriguing man.

'Mr. Fox, I cannot quite place your accent. I know from speaking to your late brother that your family hails from Whitby in Yorkshire, but there is something else in your speech. Pray tell where else have you lived?'

It was a bold move, but since they were at a private party it was acceptable for social strictures to be somewhat more relaxed.

She caught the quizzical look on his face.

'Whitby? Yes of course,' he replied.

A thrill ran down her spine. His reaction to his supposed place of origin had her mind racing with possibilities. Could Thaxter have lied about his family's origins? And if so, why would Avery continue with the fabrication?

Eve was right. The Fox family were strangers. The man standing before her had a hidden past. And yet his intriguing accent had her struggling for breath every time he spoke.

'I spent many years in Portugal, serving in His Majesty's army. I hadn't realized how much of an accent I had picked up during that time until I returned to England. I hope it does not displease you,' he added.

A mysterious past, years spent on the continent and breathtakingly handsome to boot. There certainly wasn't anything displeasing to her about Avery Fox. She put a hand to her chest. Her heart was racing.

'So, have you been out and about in town since you moved to Langham House? The west end of London has many interesting shops and museums,' she said.

A gentle smile crept to Avery's lips. She had rescued them both from a potentially awkward situation by deftly changing the subject.

'Actually, I haven't made it to any of the museums, but I did manage to acquaint myself with Hatchards bookshop earlier today. I purchased several books which should keep me busy for a week or so,' he replied.

A self-confessed bibliophile, Lucy gasped with delight.

'Is it not the most incredible place you have ever visited? I must admit I practically live there.'

He nodded. 'For someone who had never set foot inside a bookshop before today, I found it a truly magical place.'

For a brief moment, they stood smiling at one another. They had something in common, and with that a tiny bud of friendship blossomed.

A gong sounded for dinner, cutting into their conversation. One by one the other guests paired up. Husbands and wives together, Lord Langham and his mother. Lucy gritted her teeth in an effort to suppress her excitement at being paired with Avery. As the only two people left without partners, it was only correct that they would walk into dinner together.

She watched as he observed the other couples before offering her his arm. With a gracious smile, she accepted it.

As guest of honour for the evening, Avery by rights should have sat near the head of the table, but as it was an informal gathering,

Lord Langham did not press his guests to take their seats strictly according to protocol.

Lucy quickly scrambled to find a seat opposite Avery.

While they sat and waited for the first of the courses to arrive, Lord Langham encouraged Avery to recall a little of his life in the army. Lucy was pleased to see that the earl was at pains to help Avery better acquaint himself with the rest of the small gathering.

'I spent nearly all of this century so far abroad, serving with His Majesty's forces. It was only two years ago that I was returned to England,' he said.

'And where did you serve, Mr. Fox?' Lucy asked.

He put his wine glass down and considered her words. 'Portugal, Spain, Belgium and a little of France. But Portugal mostly,' he replied.

'Did you get to see much of Portugal? I remember travelling there as a young man when I undertook the Grand Tour. Lisbon is a wonderful city,' Lord Langham replied.

Lucy sat silent, remembering her place. It was inappropriate for a young lady to press a gentleman regarding his private life. All the same, she found herself enjoying the conversation.

As the light from the candelabra in the center of the table cast a golden glow on Avery's face, she studied him. He was newly shaven, and from the lack of blood nicks on his neck and chin it was clear Lord Langham had furnished his heir with his own private valet. Gone was the rough army shave she had noted during their previous encounters.

Pity. It did give him that rugged, world-travelled look.

For a moment, she stopped listening to Avery's speech. As her gaze roamed over his face, memorizing every beguiling detail, a small voice in the back of her mind pointedly asked at which particular moment she had taken up the close study of Mr. Avery Fox.

'I didn't get to spend much time in Lisbon itself; I was based in the mountains for most of the time. My unit had its base near Sintra, not far from the Castle of the Moors,' Avery replied.

'Yes, the ruins are truly inspiring. I particularly liked climbing up to see the monastery to Saint Jerome. I was fortunate enough to be a guest of the Dutch Consul at the Seteais Palace for several weeks at one point and got to spend quite a bit of time visiting the various ruins,' said Lord Langham.

Sintra. Lucy had seen books with beautiful color plate drawings of the ruins of the royal palaces high in the mountains. How romantic it must have been to actually live in those mountains, to see the ruins up close. She pictured Avery, sitting quietly, enjoying a glass or two of port and some cheese under the shade of a leafy tree, while taking in the wonderful view of the sunlit valleys which spread out below him for miles. An elegant and inspiring tapestry of life.

'Magnificent mountains, but very rough terrain. It rained almost every day, so we spent most of our time trying to keep dry. In winter, we had snow which lay up to six feet deep on the ground for months at a time. The horses had a terrible time trying to pick their way along the narrow mountain tracks. The only creatures that seem to enjoy living up at that altitude are the mountain goats. Fortunately, they were very slow when it came to the chase, so they made for good eating,' Avery replied.

Lucy silently chided herself.

Foolish chit. Of course, his life has not been one of idle leisure and pursuits. He was a soldier.

While Lord Langham had visited Portugal as a well-pampered guest, his new heir had lived the hard life of a poorly paid soldier.

'Did you get time to draw while you were there?' Clarice, seated nearby, asked.

Lucy scowled. Avery was her particular subject of special interest. Her sister-in-law's knowledge of such private details of his life caught her off-guard.

'How did you know I draw?' Avery asked.

'Thaxter mentioned it once to me. Said you were quite proficient with pencil and paper,' Clarice replied.

The table fell silent.

Across from him, Lucy watched as a pained look of surprise appeared on Avery's face. It was clear he had not expected his brother to have made any form of pleasant remark when it came to him.

He picked up his wine glass and after studying it for a moment, took a large mouthful. His eyes were cast down as Lucy watched him slowly swallow the wine.

'I'm a painter myself,' Clarice added.

His head shot up.

'Pardon?'

'Landscapes, mostly, though I have tried the occasional portrait. The picture behind you is one of mine,' she said.

The rest of the seated guests looked up and took in the skillfully painted scene of a lake and surrounds. Avery rose from his chair and crossed the floor to the painting, standing with his back to the rest of the guests. His shoulders rose and fell as he sucked in deep breaths.

Lord Langham came and stood by his side.

'She is rather good. I'm very proud of Clarice's work.'

Avery nodded.

From where she sat nearby, Lucy overheard Lord Langham speak low to Avery.

'I'm sorry, we didn't mean to embarrass you. I know you had a hard life at home and the army must have been a tough stretch for such a young lad. The last thing any of us ever want is for you to feel uncomfortable among us.'

'Thank you. You have been nothing but kind to me. It was hearing my brother even acknowledged my existence that came as a bit of a shock. I'm sorry if I caused any offence,' Avery replied.

They resumed their seats at the table just as the first of the evening courses arrived. Lucy barely looked at her bowl of onion soup; her appetite was the least of her concerns.

Her mind was concentrated on how she could help Avery transition into his new life among London's elite. If she could help it, he would never feel like an outsider.

She picked up her soup spoon and absent-mindedly twirled it about in her fingers. Across from her, she saw Avery check his cutlery and pick up the same implement. She smiled softly as a moment of realization dawned.

She had been racking her brains to discover ways to help him, and the answer had presented itself. She could be of excellent use to Mr. Avery Fox. Having lived her entire life amongst the *ton*, she knew exactly how a gentleman should conduct himself when in the company of ladies. Stifling a self-satisfied grin, she sipped her soup from the side of the spoon, being careful not to make any noise. To slurp one's soup was vulgar, to say the least.

Avery followed suit.

She sat back in her chair and studied him further, reveling in this unexpected development. Yes, she had to help him. Who knew what trouble those deep sea-green eyes could find themselves in if she didn't?

It is the proper thing for a young lady to do.

A sharp elbow in her ribs from Millie, seated next to her, broke the spell.

'The salt. Will you please pass the salt?' Millie whispered.

'Sorry.'

She handed Millie the salt without taking her gaze from the gentleman opposite. Millie cleared her throat and out of the corner of her eye, Lucy saw Millie's napkin fall to the floor. She watched as her sister-in-law bent down and picked it up, waving away an attentive footman who attempted to assist.

'Ladies retiring room now, Lucy,' she muttered as their gazes met.

As soon as the door of the ladies room was closed behind them Millie rounded on her.

'What the devil are you playing at?' she demanded.

'What do you mean?'

Millie harrumphed. 'Mr. Fox is what I am mean. You haven't taken your gaze off him all evening. The poor man must be dying of embarrassment, having to watch you make eyes at him.'

Lucy stared at her sister-in-law as she struggled to form a coherent response. One which would not include her having to tell an open lie. She knew Millie could read her like a book.

The truth was, a soft spot had indeed formed in her heart for Avery. While praying it was only pity for him being all alone in the world, she was beginning to suspect it was not.

'I just thought he might need some help in joining society,' she replied.

The raise of a singular eyebrow told Lucy that Millie was not buying her story.

'And you, an unmarried woman, thought you might be the perfect candidate for the job? Lucy that is utter madness. Apart from the fact that you barely know the man, how do you expect to be able to spend any sort of time with him without starting all manner of salacious rumors?'

Lucy sighed. She hated it when Millie was right.

While Millie crossed to the washstand and fixed up her hair, Lucy considered the situation. She had now admitted to herself that she liked Avery. And knowing her own true nature, there was every chance she might begin to feel something more for him. She also knew that getting her heart broken at this particular juncture would signal the final disaster in her London season.

While her two brothers had managed to find themselves suitable brides this year, she was staring at her second *annus horribilis*.

Millie returned and gently took hold of Lucy's hand.

'I don't want to discourage you completely from thinking Mr. Fox could be a possible husband, but I want you to think seriously about it. Take your time. I hoped you would have learned from your encounter with my brother.'

Lucy winced. It had always been a remote possibility that Millie wouldn't have discovered the truth about the disastrous kiss in the garden between Lucy and Charles Ashton.

Memories of that night still burned in her mind. Her tearful entreaty to Charles, begging him to show her what it was like to be kissed, had been followed by unmitigated disaster. His initial reluctance had been made worse by the lack of effort he put into the endeavor when he finally relented.

There had been no earth-shattering passion in the touch of his lips. No sudden and overwhelming release of her heart's desire.

The term 'cold fish' had immediately sprung to mind and she had told him so in no uncertain terms.

If Charles had been angry that night, his fury had been more than matched by the hurt to Lucy's pride. He had made her feel a worthless fool.

'Not that I would have ever suggested you should have chosen Charles to be your very first kiss. He doesn't have much experience with young, unmarried ladies of our class, if you get my meaning. I somehow suspect his future bride will not be an inexperienced debutante, and as for Avery Fox, you can be certain that he has even less idea of how to handle a lady of your status and experience. Just be careful,' Millie cautioned.

Millie, of course, was right. While Lucy had spent the better part of the evening staring at Avery Fox, she really knew very little about him.

But I was helping him and he seemed to like it. How much trouble could that get me into? Besides, how else am I to get to know him?

'All right, I shall behave and not stare at him so much, but please allow me to make my own choices and mistakes when it comes to my future,' Lucy replied.

Millie stood silent for a moment.

'Of course, it was presumptuous of me to tell you how to live your life. But I beg of you, take it slowly. Avery Fox is still very much a stranger to us all. Make it your business to find out a little bit more about him. On second thoughts, dear sister, make it your business to find out everything about him. That way, if you do come to the conclusion that he *is* a suitable husband, you will be making an informed choice.'

A nervous whimper escaped Lucy's lips. When had the business of finding love become such a calculating endeavor?

While Millie was now her sister-in-law, she was lost to Lucy as her closest friend. Gone were the long afternoons sitting in Lucy's bedroom sharing secrets and laughter. At parties and balls, Alex now commanded Millie's attention and time. With Clarice now married to David and with child, Lucy felt more and more alone.

Only Eve seemed to understand the depth of Lucy's yearning to be a well-loved wife.

She wanted passion. Although perhaps not passion as fiery as Millie and Alex's marriage; their rows were fast becoming legendary within the family. One minute they were holding hands like love struck children, the next they were staring daggers at one another. But Lucy hungered for love none the less. Her own parents' marriage was the golden ring she had her heart set on. It wasn't impossible to find a man who understood love, was it?

Millie put a comforting arm around Lucy.

'I'm sorry, I don't mean to be harsh with you. It's just that I'm worried you will go and do something reckless. At least I knew Alex wanted me when I played the high-stakes game of love. Don't risk your heart and happiness over someone who may not be a sure bet,' she said.

Lucy's mind was still in a state of turmoil when she returned to the dining room. As she took her seat, Avery gave her a friendly smile. She nodded serenely in reply, her heart sinking when he glanced down at his plate, his disappointment evident.

All the ground she had made with him earlier in the evening evaporated before her eyes. She chanced a glance at Millie, but she had turned away and was speaking to her husband.

Another course arrived and she sat quietly with her hands folded in her lap.

Polite but not intrusive.

Across the table Avery cleared his throat. Not loudly, but just enough for it to be apparent he was trying to gain her attention. She picked up her glass of wine and took a sip as those either side of her continued with their conversations. No-one touched their food.

Drawn by Avery's plea, her gaze drifted across the table. As it fell on his hands, she sighed. His white-gloved hands were softly settled one on top of the other. She looked up and met his eyes. Unaware of the correct knife and fork to use for the fish course, he was waiting for her to give him his cue. Waiting for her direction.

Much as she respected Millie's words of advice, Lucy decided she was going to trust her instincts. She picked up the correct fork and held it up just long enough for him to see it and take note. The warm secret smile they shared thrilled her to her toes. She tucked happily into the buttered sole.

She didn't recall much of the rest of the evening. Lord Langham made a heartfelt speech in which he mentioned his late wife. Clarice cried, and when David touchingly kissed his wife's forehead, Lucy felt an overwhelming rush of emotion.

Some toasts were made, welcoming Avery into the Langham family, and David gave a short speech thanking his father-in-law for being such a generous host.

It was only when she was tucked up warm in her bed at Strathmore House that Lucy recalled the brief words of appreciation that Avery made at the end of the evening's formalities. His exact words escaped her memory, but it was the tension that she felt in him as he spoke which remained in her mind.

Humble words of gratitude were not the usual in her rarefied world. In Avery, she knew he truly meant it when he said he looked forward to being part of a family. That a man who had a roof over his head and people whom he could call friends was truly blessed.

She rolled over in her bed, surprised to find hot tears had sprung to her eyes. How lonely he must have been all those years. To know he had no-one in England who awaited his return. No-one who cared.

'Well, you shall have friends, Mr. Fox. Friends who do care for you, friends who . . . oh dear!'

She quickly sat up in bed, unable to stem the tears. With her hand clutched to her bosom she felt the loud thump of her heart pounding in her chest.

Her heart knew it was in deadly peril.

For now, she would do everything to make sure their relationship remained platonic. She would not make a fool of herself again. Wiping away the tears she pondered the situation.

It was clear now that Avery did not intend to mourn his brother. As such Lord Langham would likely have him out in society within days. With his smart new clothes and well-kept appearance, he would make quite the impression at fashionable events.

Events at which other young unmarried misses, and their mothers, would also be in attendance. There were plenty of other young ladies still firmly on the shelf at this stage of the season. And plenty with the perceptiveness to see the newly elevated Mr. Fox as manna from heaven. He wouldn't stand a chance against them.

With her brother Alex, the future Duke of Strathmore, firmly off the market, the future Earl Langham was now the most eligible bachelor in London.

She threw back the bedclothes and leapt out of bed. Quickly moving across the floor to her writing desk, she pulled out the chair, lit a candle, took a piece of paper and began to write. If she was going to help save Avery from the scheming, matchmaking mamas, she needed a plan.

Avery, as a former military man, would no doubt appreciate her tactics. He of all people would understand the need for a sound strategy.

When she was done with Mr. Avery Fox, he would be the epitome of English gentlemen. He would know exactly which fork to use at dinner without a second thought. He would blend perfectly in with the crowd. He would be her crowning achievement. Only then would he be equipped to make the right choice as to whom he wished to marry.

'Except for his accent. I shall not make him change it. It is perfect as it is,' she vowed.

She hummed quietly as she wrote, oblivious to the chill of the room as the fire slowly died.

Chapter Five

'Now remember what I told you.'

Eve looked at Lucy and gave her a conspiratorial grin.

'Yes. But don't forget what you promised me. You will take your time. No foolish tricks to make him like you,' Eve replied.

Lucy brushed a kiss on her cousin's cheek.

'Sweet cousin, as I have told you, I do not have Mr. Fox in my sights for anything in the least romantic. He is simply a private project of mine to help ward off the boredom of the remaining weeks of the season. When I am done with him, I shall walk away and not look back.'

Lucy pointedly ignored Eve's less than subtle snort.

She had shared just enough of her plans with Eve to get her agreement to visit Langham House this morning.

'If that is the case, then why does it feel that our visit to Lord Langham's home should be accompanied by hounds? You are hunting Avery Fox down in his new abode,' Eve said.

'Nonsense; we are simply visiting Clarice and enquiring as to her health,' Lucy firmly replied.

Lucy had bet on the newer of her two sisters-in-law being home this morning and sent an earlier calling card. While Clarice had looked well enough at the dinner party two nights earlier, Lucy was prepared to take a chance on her not venturing from home in the early hours of the day.

'I'm sorry I won't be able to accompany you to the shops today, dear girls. You will have to excuse me, but I am still very much indisposed most mornings,' Clarice said.

Seated with her hands held tightly together, the bags under her eyes and a green pallor revealed the depth of Clarice's current struggle with morning sickness. She smiled at them both, but said nothing more. By society's rules, neither of the two unwed misses should have any knowledge of such things.

Lucy privately begged to differ.

David and Alex, who were both out for a mid-morning ride in Hyde Park, would likely have conniptions if they discovered Lucy had spent a whole rainy afternoon thumbing through the pages of the *Kama Sutra* which India-born Millie had given her. The erotic pictures within the book left little to the imagination.

'That's perfectly all right; Eve and I just wanted to come and see you. I especially wanted to thank you for the lovely dinner we had the other night.'

A tray of sweet buns and a pot of tea were served by a footman. Clarice didn't bother with any of the food.

The three ladies sat back in their chairs and were soon deep in conversation about the family's seat in Scotland.

'You will love Strathmore Castle; my father says it's the best castle in all of Great Britain,' Eve said. Lucy nodded in agreement.

Clarice waved away the sweet bun Lucy offered her.

'Thank you, no., I'm struggling to keep anything down this morning. And speaking of Scotland, David and I have been discussing the journey north for the past few days. I'm sorry, but it is likely we won't be coming up until Christmas. David needs to spend time at our estate in Bedfordshire, and I'm certainly not well enough to travel that sort of distance.'

If Christmas it was, so be it. As long as they were all together as a family.

'Hogmanay will be wonderful, Clarice; no-one does it as well as we do. All the members of the Radley family venture up from London. And everyone from the village comes. The party lasts well into the next day. We even have fireworks which light up the side of the mountain,' Lucy said.

Clarice rose gingerly from her chair.

'Excuse me, will you, my dear friends?' she whispered and quickly left the room.

'Is she, all right?' Eve asked after Clarice had left the sitting room.

'Yes; Mama says the first few months are the worst,' Lucy replied. She put down her cup of tea and surveyed the room.

I wonder if he is at home this morning.

She felt the sharp sting of guilt. How could she be thinking of Avery Fox when poor Clarice was so terribly indisposed?

I am a horrible person.

Eve reached over and tapped Lucy on the arm.

'I doubt there is anything you or I could do for poor Clarice, so why don't we see if your Mr. Fox is at home?'

Lucy huffed. 'He's not my Mr. Fox! Besides, I don't think we should; it wouldn't be polite. What happens if we meet Lord Langham? What do we say if he finds us prying about his house?'

The idea was both delightful and wicked in its prospect. Compelled by the opportunity which had suddenly presented itself, Eve rose quickly from the couch and headed out into the hallway. Lucy followed closely behind.

Stealing along the hallway, stopping every so often to examine one of the many paintings which decorated the walls, they soon came upon an open door. Poking her head inside, Eve squealed with delight.

'Oooh, the house library!' Eve cried and raced into the room. She immediately headed for the nearest bookcase and began examining the books on the shelves. If there was one person who loved books more than Lucy, it was her cousin.

Lucy followed more sedately behind.

'Remember, always gently and with respect,' Lucy said, quoting their paternal grandmother.

Eve laughed and brandished a book in the air.

'Yes, Grandmother,' she laughed.

'Wise words of caution,' a male voice replied.

Lucy turned and her breath caught.

Seated – well, to be more accurate, lazily strewn across a long leather couch – was the subject of their search: Mr. Avery Fox.

Lucy took in his glorious body in an instant, exercising her increasingly well-honed appreciation of the male form.

Dark hair, a long ponytail tied at the nape. Though it was tied neatly, it was loose enough to show a hint of disregard. A dark grey jacket worn over a pure white linen shirt. No cravat. At the top of his shirt she saw the merest hint of chest hair. Long legs clad in black trousers, which clung tightly to his thighs. Polished boots completed the look.

Unable to tear her gaze away, Lucy stood mesmerized. She had seen a hundred, nay a thousand men wearing such attire, but never before had she reacted in such a way. A hot spike of desire coursed through her body. She shivered with its thrill.

Oh gosh.

'Mr. Fox. Good morning to you. Forgive me, I did not see you,' she said, catching herself. A hot blush burned on her cheeks.

She blinked as he unfurled his long muscular legs and rose from the couch, dipping into an easy bow.

'You have to forgive me Lady Lucy, I am prone at times to forget my manners. Too many years living a soldier's life, I'm afraid,' he said.

'Please sit, Mr. Fox; we are the ones who have interrupted your peaceful morning,' Lucy replied. She looked at the book he still held in his right hand. Then, seeing the glove on his left, she quickly averted her gaze.

'I'd have thought you might be a touch too old for *Gulliver's Travels,*' she said, casting about for something to say.

In the corner of the room, Eve snorted. Avery's hand dropped instantly, leaving the book to hang loosely by his side. Lucy regretted her words.

Stupid, stupid girl.

He shrugged his shoulders. 'I suppose I am, but I have never got around to reading it until now, so I thought I should. The bookseller recommended it most highly. It is rather good,' he replied.

'I read it when I was ten,' Eve added. Lucy wished at that moment her cousin would disappear into thin air. Instead she made her way over to where Lucy and Avery stood and grandly offered Avery her hand.

'Since my dear cousin won't introduce us, I'm Evelyn Saunders,' she said.

As Avery took her hand and bowed, Lucy felt an overwhelming desire to pinch Eve.

'Mr. Fox; I have heard so much about you,' Eve teased. Lucy ground her teeth in frustration.

Avery made a step toward the door and Lucy let out an involuntary gasp. He was leaving. 'Oh, please don't go on account of us. We are just waiting for Clarice to come back downstairs. And *Gulliver's Travels* is one of my favourite books,' she stammered.

Eve looked from Lucy to Avery and clicked her tongue. She withdrew her hand.

'I shall go and see how Clarice is faring; I can see three is a crowd'.

She headed for the library door.

Lucy held her breath at Eve's clumsy attempt to play matchmaker. She hoped Avery had missed the note of intent in her cousin's words.

'Thank you dearest Eve; that would be lovely, we shall see you back here soon,' Lucy replied. She prayed Eve would have the good sense to stay away. She needed time to casually discuss matters with Avery before making him an offer of assistance. If she appeared too eager, he might well be frightened off.

'Fine then, off I go,' Eve announced as she left the room.

A watchful look appeared on Avery's face.

Curses. How do I get him to stay now?

'So, how are you settling in at Langham House?' Lucy asked.

He sighed. 'It can be a little overwhelming at times, but Lord Langham and the rest of the household have made every endeavor to make me feel welcome. After the difficult circumstances surrounding my brother's untimely death, it is more than one could expect of them.'

Lucy nodded. Thaxter Fox, hateful man, was the farthest thing from her mind. She motioned toward the couch. 'Please; you don't need to keep standing on my account.'

She hastened to sit down in a nearby chair. With luck Avery would resume his seat. If her luck then held, he wouldn't realize that being left alone with her was a serious social indiscretion.

Now all she needed was for Eve to play her part and keep Clarice busy.

Think, Lucy. Say something interesting and intelligent.

'I hope you had a pleasant evening the other night. It must be nice having family around you once more.'

He frowned at her remark. On the long list of topics, she could have chosen to discuss, she sensed family was close to the bottom.

'Sorry,' she said.

Avery resumed his seat opposite her. 'No, it's quite all right. And yes, it is nice to have family around me, even if we are rather distant relations. I take it from what your brother David has said, you have quite a sizeable extended family.'

Lucy looked down at her hands. The fear she would say something out of order was palpable. Worry over what he thought of her had occupied her mind since the moment she returned home from the dinner party. She shouldn't care what he thought of her, but she did.

'Yes, apart from Eve, who is my aunt's eldest daughter, and her siblings there are quite a number of other first cousins within the Radley family. It makes for a loud and rambunctious Christmas at Strathmore Castle.'

Avery sat forward on the couch.

'I must thank you for the dinner party, Lady Lucy. Your guidance was invaluable. Without your assistance I am certain I would have made a complete hash of things.'

Lucy smiled. His good opinion of her suddenly mattered intensely. Her hand drifted to the warm spot under her hairline at the top of her neck. She felt her mouth go dry, surprised at her own outward display of coyness.

Is this what it feels like? Is this how the spark of love begins? What happened to your wanting to be friends? Oh, my heart, tread carefully.

Whatever this feeling was, she had to admit she liked it. The lure of discovering how deep into her skin it could seep beckoned. The first tentative step forward had been taken.

Avery cleared his throat.

'Do you have a passion for reading, Lady Lucy?'

The way he made such a special effort to pronounce her name and title revealed the gulf which existed between them. She noted he clipped the accent off the end of his words in an effort to sound more like a gentleman. She hoped it was not just for her sake. If ever she was to gain his friendship, they had to move past such formalities.

'Lucy. Please call me Lucy. All my friends and family do,' she replied.

He looked away and she could have sworn she heard him whisper her name. Almost like a prayer. When he met her gaze again, she could see the vulnerable side of him was once more securely locked away.

'Lucy. But only if you call me Avery when you consider it socially acceptable,' he replied.

Lucy felt her mouth forming into a grin and had to muster all her resolve to force it back down to a small smile. She had to play this with a detached air. If she appeared too keen, she feared he would suspect she had some sort of secret agenda and retreat back into his shell.

'Avery.'

He chuckled softly. 'I forgot you and I were just beginning to discuss books the other night when we were called in to dinner. You must think me rather foolish for forgetting.'

As she watched him laugh, the soft lines in the corners of his eyes wrinkled. A second wave of heat coursed through her body, catching her breath. She shuddered.

'I could never think you foolish, Avery,' she murmured.

The moment had come for her to make a move. Any second now Eve was likely to return and the opportunity would be lost.

'In fact, I was thinking only the other evening how astute you are. You saw how others behaved during the dinner and made every effort to copy them.'

She shifted forward in her seat; the time had come.

'I realize we don't know one another that well, but if you like I would be more than happy to offer my services in assisting you to learn more of the ways of society. With my dear sister Clarice indisposed, it makes sense that someone else from within the family steps forward and helps. What do you think, Avery?'

She allowed his name to slide slowly off her tongue, thrilled to be able to use it to his face. When he hesitated to respond she silently chided herself for being too forward.

'That is a very generous offer, Lucy,' he replied.

She forced herself to blink slowly, displaying a calm demeanor. He had to think this arrangement was a mere trifle to her, that it meant nothing. Meanwhile, her heart was thumping loudly in her chest. She was desperate for him to say yes.

'I am not certain how I should reply. Is it socially acceptable?'

'Of course. Then we have an accord. Excellent,' she quickly replied.

Her hand shot out and she watched with overwhelming relief as he took it. The deal was sealed.

'I shall consult my social diary and see when it is suitable to meet with you. Outside of parties and balls we can meet here. I am sure Lord Langham will not mind,' she added.

The door opened and Eve entered the room, followed closely by David. Lucy feigned a disinterested air. David was the sharpest man she knew. He would miss nothing. He came to her and placed a brotherly kiss on her cheek.

'Lucy, nice to see you this morning; what a lovely surprise,' he said.

His voice was calm and even. If he suspected anything was amiss he was giving nothing away. She gave him her best sisterly smile. David was one gentleman who knew the ways of attraction and seduction. Before his marriage, he had a well-deserved reputation with ladies of the social scene. She was certain he could tell she was up to something.

'Fox,' he said, nodding in Avery's direction.

Cool and calm as ever, David did not give Lucy a clue as to his mind.

Cad.

'How is Clarice?' Lucy asked.

'She has returned to bed,' David replied. He looked at Eve, who nodded sadly.

Lucy rose from the couch, sensing it was time to make a strategic withdrawal. As David helped her to her feet, he nodded his silent approval at this move. She should not have been alone with Mr. Fox.

'Give Clarice my love, will you?' she said.

'Of course.'

After making a polite farewell, Lucy and Eve graciously exited Langham House. As they got into the carriage, Lucy sat heavily back against the well-padded leather squabs and closed her eyes.

The business of being a close but detached friend to Avery Fox was becoming problematic. Self-doubt clouded her mind.

'So, did he agree to your proposal?' Eve asked.

'Yes,' Lucy replied, but added nothing further.

The way forward with Avery was now clear, but where it would eventually lead was entirely unknown. Her heart still raced. Looking down at her gloved hands she felt the slight tremor in her fingertips.

I'm not sure I can do this.

Chapter Six

'I love it! The two of you look just as my parents do when they are at a party after they have had a row. Talk about stiff and proper,' Eve said.

She was seated at the piano playing a lively waltz, to which Lucy and Avery were attempting to dance.

Lucy and Avery shared a pained look.

They had spent all afternoon in the drawing room at Langham House trying to polish Avery's dance skills, with little progress.

'You cannot expect to learn all of these and have it as second nature in a matter of days. It will take time,' Clarice offered.

She was laid up on a long daybed under the window, having refused to remain in bed nursing her morning sickness. The dowager countess Lady Alice sat in another chair, embroidering small blue birds on to a white linen baby smock.

'Thank you, Clarice, your encouragement is precious,' Avery replied.

Lucy took his hand once more and they began the intricate dance that was the waltz. For all of Eve's good-natured ribbing, he and Lucy had actually come a long way with their dance lessons.

His quadrille was passable, and he was able to get through a whole set while holding a conversation. His skill at the waltz, however, was less than acceptable.

'I would suggest if you are at a party and think you cannot manage a dance without stepping on the toes of your partner that you cry off. We wouldn't want you to get a reputation as a country clod,' Lady Alice offered.

Avery was about to correct the dowager and remind her that he was indeed a country clod, but something in her look stopped him. After their first misstep, Lady Alice had made every undertaking to make Avery feel welcome in his new home. In the dowager, he sensed a kindred spirit. She was warm, but there was a definite strength about her which he admired.

'Sound advice,' he replied.

Coming from a life of living rough and scrounging for the next meal, the change in his circumstances since Waterloo still left him scratching his head. Never in his wildest dreams would he have ever imagined living in a place like Langham House, nor dancing with such a beauty as Lucy Radley.

'Place your hand in the small of my back,' Lucy instructed once more.

Avery nodded.

At the first twirl, he stepped clumsily on the edge of Lucy's skirt. A curse was halfway to his lips when she shifted slightly to the left and he regained his foothold. The warm smile she wore did not falter.

You really are a skilled dancer.

'Keep going,' she whispered.

He saw her make a sideways glance in the direction of her cousin Eve as they passed the piano. He gripped Lucy's right hand and swung her into a strong, confident turn.

'Better!' Lady Alice cried.

Lucy's blue eyes sparkled with delight. Since their discussion in the library he had surmised that Lucy had been chosen to assist him in the ways of the *ton.* If it were true and she found him a burden, she hid it well. For his own part, being this close to her was a pleasurable torture.

If only you were not a duke's daughter and I were not a man without honour. What a pair we could make.

He pushed the impossible thought away. They were who they were and no number of dance lessons could change that fact.

'Excellent progress, Mr. Fox. But for our few remaining lessons, I suggest we stick to the quadrille. It's better to be a master of one dance than an apprentice of them all,' she said.

He frowned. Was she cutting him off from her assistance?

'Only a few more?' he replied.

'Yes, my family are leaving London for our estate in Scotland at the end of next week; the season is nearly over. My younger brother Stephen will be arriving from Eton tomorrow to accompany us. We won't be back in town for months.'

The peculiarities of upper-class society still escaped Avery. Why would people leave their perfectly comfortable homes in London to venture all the way to a chilly, windswept castle in Scotland? After winters spent in the mountains of Portugal and Spain, snow was the last thing he ever wished to see again.

Fortunately, Lord Langham's estate was in the mild climes of Norfolk. He was more than grateful for that blessing.

As the music stopped and Lucy took a seat next to Eve at the piano, Lady Alice held out her hand to him.

'Come, take me for a turnabout the room, Avery,' she commanded, snapping her fingers at him.

He assisted her from her chair and as she stood the dowager countess slipped her arm in his.

'In the event you don't want to dance with a lady, but still wish to speak with her, this is what you do,' she said.

Avery considered the whole idea to be utter nonsense. Walking slowly around the drawing room in endless loops was ridiculous, to say the least.

'Of course, at a ball you will have much more room to move, but you get the general idea. It allows you to be in a lady's company without the need for her chaperone to follow closely on your heels,' Lucy added.

Lady Alice laughed. 'Well, yes; there is that, but I've always found it's the best way to catch up on all the latest gossip. If you come home from a party or ball without at least two good titbits of scandalous news you should count your evening a failure.'

Avery chuckled. Lady Alice was a gem of the highest value. For a woman of her social rank, she spoke her mind unexpectedly plainly.

'And what am I to do with these pieces of gossip once I am in possession of them?' Avery asked.

A slow smile crept to Lady Alice's lips as she leaned in and whispered.

'Why, you come and share them with me, young man. Rumor is the currency of the *ton*; it can buy you all sorts of things.'

❧

Avery stood in his room and stared at the pocket watch he held in his hand. For two days, he had managed to resist the temptation to take it out and examine it. It was the longest he had gone without looking at the watch since it had come into his possession. As soon as Lucy and Eve had left Langham House, he retreated to his room.

He couldn't remember taking the watch out of his travel bag, but there it was once more in the palm of his hand.

This is why you could never marry someone like Lucy. What sort of a husband would you make for her? She certainly deserves better.

Now he was based in London, the prospect of selling the watch and being forever rid of it was a viable option. One he knew he should seriously consider.

He threw the pocket watch on the bed. Slipping his white cotton gloves off, he picked it back up with his damaged left hand. His ownership of the watch had cost him the full use of his hand.

And his honour.

As long as Lucy was prepared to tolerate him and teach him the ways of gentlemen he would continue with their lessons. He would simply have to overcome his growing attraction to her. Fair-haired Lucy Radley was a girl possessed of special delight.

The twinge of love had never pulled on his heartstrings, but

64

every time he looked at Lucy he felt his throat constrict. She had an effect on him that he didn't understand. The sparkle in her eye whenever she was close made him feel odd within himself.

At night as he drifted off to sleep, the image of her made his body harden with sexual need.

He puffed out his cheeks. With luck, there would be some Scottish lord just waiting for her to return to Strathmore Castle, where he would claim her heart. After that Lucy Radley would forever be out of the reach of Avery Fox.

Chapter Seven

L ucy's fears regarding Avery's fate at the hands of the unwed misses of the *haute ton* grew daily.

If Avery had remained in mourning for Thaxter, he would not be gadding about London each day. Nor for that matter would he be at Viscountess Owen's late-season ball. Unfortunately, he had abandoned all pretense of mourning his long-lost brother and was one of the first people Lucy saw when she arrived with her parents at the Owens' grand home in Duke Street.

'Curses,' she muttered under her breath. She regretted her decision to wear one of her simpler white gowns. She would blend easily into the milling crowd, and would be lucky if Avery even managed to spot her.

The problem wasn't so much that Avery was in attendance, it was the impact his presence was having on the other women which immediately put Lucy into a state of unexpected panic.

While he was home at Langham House he was all but exclusively hers. Eve had conveniently taken on the role of musician each time, negating the need for Avery to request her hand to dance.

Here, at a large social gathering, it was open season on one of the most eligible bachelors in all of London.

Matchmaking mothers had somehow overcome their prejudices regarding his origins and the quirk of his northern accent and were milling around him. Their charming daughters in tow.

Lucy gazed around the room and could see small clusters of mothers and daughters all eyeing Avery off from a distance. All waiting for the right opportunity to make his acquaintance. It was like one of those African wildlife scenes she had read about in books: lionesses ready to pounce on a poor unsuspecting gazelle.

She would be lucky if she got within ten feet of him this evening.

'I see Mr. Fox has established himself as the popular bachelor of the evening,' Lady Caroline noted.

Lucy moved slowly to one side of the ballroom, reluctantly following her mother. When she saw another young lady pull out her dance card and offer it to Avery she stopped. Her jaw dropped, leaving her mouth agape. Her plans were beginning to unravel and slip from her control.

'Lucy, darling, are you coming with me or not?' her mother asked.

She waved her mother away. 'I've seen a friend and I must say hello. I shall find you later.'

The duchess gave the merest nod of her head before continuing on her way.

Lucy slowly skirted around the edge of the ballroom, glancing in Avery's direction every now and then. By the time she reached the other side of the room, she was able to hear the lively conversation going on between the future Lord Langham and a gaggle of desperate young ladies.

'Oh please, Mr. Fox, I am sure you are only being modest,' a girl with a dance card pleaded. Avery, to his credit, held his ground.

'Miss Hawkins, I assure you I cannot dance the waltz. You would be lucky to make it from the dance floor with all your toes intact if I agreed to sign your card. Perhaps another time when I am able to do your request justice,' he replied.

A passing footman offered Lucy a glass of champagne, which she took. She sipped the soft, enticing bubbles while continuing to watch the cluster of girls all clamoring to catch Avery's attention.

'Pathetic,' she muttered into her glass.

At that moment one of the pressing mothers hit upon the clever idea of Mr. Fox taking her daughter for a slow walk around the room. He might not be willing to dance, but no gentleman would refuse a young lady a turnabout the ballroom.

Lucy gritted her teeth. It was going to be a long night.

As soon as Avery took hold of the arm of the rather eager Miss Hawkins, Lucy knew she had to act. The confident way he moved showed he had learned his lessons from Lady Alice well. She turned on her heel and made for a spot a little further across the room. If she had correctly anticipated the direction in which Avery and his lady friend were headed, they would most certainly pass right by where she stood.

She stopped on the edge of a group of guests, some of whom were known to her. She made hasty greetings before turning side-on to them.

Anyone headed toward the group would think she was with them, not standing on her own. As Avery and Miss Hawkins drew near, Lucy heard their stilted conversation.

'No, I don't know the viscount personally; Lord Langham secured me an invitation. No, I assure you I didn't go up to Eton the same year as your brother,' he said.

Lucy's mood lifted immediately. It was clear Miss Hawkins was trying to find areas of common interest with Avery and failing badly. She prayed that Miss Hawkins didn't suddenly display a previously undisclosed knowledge of the Portuguese language. Or worse still, a brother who had served somewhere in the war. That was one front in which she knew she could not do battle.

'Lady Lucy, what a pleasant surprise,' Avery said.

She looked up from her champagne glass with the perfect degree of surprise on her face, then counted for a long second before allowing her recognition of him to register on her face.

'Mr. Fox, how wonderful to see you this evening. I did not know you were here. Have you just arrived?' she replied.

The thousand-dagger look Miss Hawkins launched Lucy's way failed to reach its target. Lucy ignored her.

'Did you come with the rest of the Langham family? Are my brother and his wife here with you?' she added. It didn't hurt to mention her existing personal connection to him.

'No; David and Lady Clarice decided to spend the evening at home. Lord Langham and Lady Alice graciously allowed me to accompany them,' he replied.

She should by rights have let them continue on their promenade at this point, but Lucy was in no philanthropic mood. She was not going to give an inch to these shameless husband-hunters.

'Are you going to introduce us?' Miss Hawkins ground out.

Avery and Lucy shared a mischievous grin. Her eyes grew wide at the sudden realization that Avery knew he was being bad. He should have made the correct introductions, but had deliberately not done so.

She smiled serenely at Miss Hawkins.

'Lady Lucy Radley, daughter of the Duke of Strathmore. How do you do?' she said and thrust out her hand.

At any other time, she would have felt terrible at her own behavior; disgusted, in fact. Playing the ducal trump card was beneath her. If her mother found out what she had done, Lucy would be in for a very long lecture about her place in society and how one should behave. But at this moment she simply didn't care.

The stakes were rapidly rising.

Miss Hawkins blushed furiously and, letting go of Avery's arm, sank quickly into a deep curtsey. Over her head Avery and Lucy looked at one another. Lucy shook her head and silently mouthed 'Sorry.'

Avery nodded. They had both gone too far. Taking Miss Hawkins' arm once more, he bade Lucy farewell and continued circling the floor.

Lucy retreated to a less conspicuous place in the room and took a seat. From her vantage point, she spent the next hour watching as

Avery escorted young miss after hopeful young miss around the floor.

'Don't tell me you have given up the fight already? Shame on you if you have, young lady.'

She turned to see Lady Alice standing before her. The dowager countess raised her walking stick and pointed it at Lucy. 'Well?'

'I'm resting my feet,' she replied.

'Odd, because from where I was standing I could swear you were spying on our Mr. Fox,' she replied.

Lucy's mouth opened in a small 'o'. How foolish had she been to expect Lady Alice to swallow that feeble story?

Lady Alice took the seat next to Lucy.

'Are you afraid that someone else may steal your protégé? One piece of advice, my dear girl. Be careful. If you have been watching him as he has walked around the room with all those grasping hopefuls you would know he is decidedly uncomfortable with the whole business.'

She met Lady Alice's gaze, grateful for her implicit support.

'What do you suggest?' she asked.

Lady Alice turned and fixed her gaze once more on Avery. She nodded silently to herself.

'Continue to be his friend. With all these hungry women circling him, I expect Mr. Fox is feeling more like Mr. Mouse. Trust me, if he doesn't see you as a threat to his bachelorhood, you may stand the best chance of snapping him up. From what I have seen of the two of you, I think you would make a fine pair. He may just need to be convinced of that fact.'

Lucy considered the sage words of advice. Lady Alice had been the key to David and Clarice finally coming together and marrying. She had stood up to Lord Langham over his initial reluctance to allow Clarice to marry the illegitimate David.

'From what I have come to know of Avery, he is a good man. But don't forget he is an outsider in our world. Up to now you have been the perfect friend to help guide him through the dangerous shoals of the *ton*. You have been exactly what he needs. Now that he has learned to trust you, he may reveal more of himself to you.

Once you get to know him better, then perhaps you will know if he is truly what you seek in a husband.'

Lady Alice took Lucy by the hand.

'But whatever you do, my dear girl, *don't* throw yourself at him. Avery is still wary of us. You will lose him for sure if you do.'

Sitting and watching as Lady Alice made her way back through the crowd, stopping to greet friends, Lucy pondered the dowager's words.

'She's right,' she whispered.

Lucy was grateful for Lady Alice's advice. For the first time in her life she had felt unable to confide in her mother. Several times, she had come close to broaching the subject of Avery with Lady Caroline, but something had held her back. Perhaps it was the worry that her mother would try to help move the relationship along.

One thing she knew for certain, her plan to be nothing more than friends with Avery had been doomed from the outset. She couldn't look at him without her stomach becoming full of butterflies. Nor was she immune to the odd sensation which rippled through her body whenever he took her into his arms for a waltz.

The tentative friendship that they shared was at least a start. Something she could build upon. Where things led to from there, only time would tell. In this, the most important endeavor of her life, Lucy knew she had to follow her own path.

While the other girls would openly flaunt themselves in front of Avery, batting their pretty eyelashes at him and making come-hither faces, she would take a strategic step back. She would continue to be the female friend he could turn to for guidance. For safety in a stormy sea.

It all made sense.

Except.

What happened if he fell in love with one of the other girls? What if while Lucy was playing the role of the cool, almost disinterested, friend she lost him? What if while she was many miles away in Scotland, someone else snapped him up?

She puffed out her cheeks before letting the air whoosh out.

Why did it all have to be so difficult? Why couldn't she just sidle up to Avery, tell him she thought he was rather dashing and have him immediately sweep her off her feet to the nearest church?

Across the room, yet another of the unmarried misses was rounding on Avery, the girl's mother and married sister following closely behind. Lucy knew this young lady possessed both beauty and a substantial dowry. Unlike most of the other young ladies, she posed a real threat to Lucy's plans.

A twitch began to flicker in the corner of Lucy's right eye.

It took all of her self-control not to march across to her future intended and make her plans clear to all and sundry. If she had been in possession of a flag, she would have planted it in the floor right next to Avery and claimed him as her sovereign territory.

She winced. Jealousy was a strange emotion. She now understood the feisty look Millie gave to each and every woman not a member of Alex's family when they came within five feet of her husband. What she had previously thought were petty displays of temper, she now understood were firm demonstrations of ownership.

Lady Alice's words drifted back into her mind. 'Be his friend.'

She rose from the chair and gave the group of women chatting animatedly to Avery one last glance.

Enjoy your evening, ladies, because your cause is lost. He is mine.

Chapter Eight

'So, you do live here?'

A shiver coursed down Lucy's spine as she and Avery had their second encounter in under a week at Hatchards bookshop.

She looked up from where she knelt on the floor, next to the bottom shelf. The best shelf in the entire shop, as far as she was concerned. It was where they kept the gory, pirate-themed books, out of the direct view of delicate ladies.

'Why, Mr. Fox, don't tell me you have already finished reading the book you purchased on Monday?'

'Guilty as charged,' he replied.

As she stood, their gazes met and a second, more powerful thrill heated her body.

The signs of his having successfully avoided his valet this morning showed in his ruffled hair and hint of a beard. She congratulated herself on having given up on her plans to make him into a copy of her brothers.

I hope never to see you fully as a ton gentleman. You are far too inter-esting a man as you are.

Something about his manner of dress made him alluring. He

dressed more simply than most other men of the *ton*, but in doing so, he allowed his natural, charming self to shine.

She quickly closed the book she held in her free hand and put it absentmindedly back on the shelf.

Taking in his warm smile and sun-kissed complexion, she decided he would make an excellent pirate. She pictured him clad only in a white linen shirt, skin-tight fawn breeches and boots. Her imaginary hero would leap from his ship and spirit her away to sail the seven seas together. Forever.

'Lady Lucy?'

'What?'

He laughed.

'Whatever is in that book has certainly caught your imagination. I'm surprised you are not adding it to your purchases.'

She looked at the small pile of books which sat next to her lace-covered reticule on a nearby table. Her maid stood close by, doing her very best impression of being interested in a book on shipping tides.

'I think perhaps I have enough books. My allowance will only stretch so far,' she replied.

His face lit up and before she knew what was happening, he had reached down and retrieved the pirate book from the shelves. He examined the cover, flicked open the first page and began to read.

She exchanged a look of desperation with her maid Rose, who, having lost interest in her own book, was taking a keen interest in her mistress's gentleman friend. Her maid nodded her approval.

'Well! Not the sort of thing I would have thought suitable for a young lady,' he said.

Lucy noted the laughter at the edge of his voice. She grinned as she found herself powerless in the face of his infectious humor.

'You have caught me out, Mr. Fox. If my father knew I was considering buying it, he would forbid me from coming here again. I . . .'

She leaned in closer and whispered. 'Don't tell anyone, but I am ashamed to say that I *do* buy them, and have one of the footmen smuggle them in under his jacket.'

Avery closed the book and tucked it under his arm.

'Considering it is a book on pirates, smuggling seems a very apt way for it to find its way into your home.'

He picked up the rest of Lucy's purchases and skillfully balanced them in the palm of his hand. She motioned to take the other book he had tucked under his left arm, but he shook his head.

Reaching the shop counter, Lucy paid for her books. As the shopkeeper's assistant wrapped them in paper, Avery handed over the pirate book.

'Oh, and those as well. I plan to do a lot of reading,' he said, pointing to a pile of books stacked neatly to one side of the counter. Lucy's eyebrows lifted and a low whistle escaped her lips. Seven books was a good haul. When she peered over the counter at the topmost book, Avery's look turned grim.

'A double volume of recollections from the battlefield at Waterloo,' he said.

She frowned. How odd that he would want to read about an event at which he had been personally present.

As Avery signed for the books on Lord Langham's account, Lucy silently speculated about the terrible scars Avery hid from the world. What would happen if she did end up marrying him? Would he always hide them from her? How unsightly could they be?

He picked up the pirate book and handed it to her.

'A small gift of thanks for all that you have done for me, though if you do get caught with it, I shall have to deny all knowledge of its existence,' he said.

Lucy laughed.

Avery picked up his packages.

'Well, I suppose this is the last time either of us will be visiting the bookshop for a while. Pity. Though I am looking forward to the dinner at Strathmore House tonight. It was very generous of your father to invite me.'

Lucy screwed up her nose.

'I thought you said you planned to do a lot of reading. It wouldn't surprise me if you manage to get through all those books in the space of a week and then find yourself back here,' she replied.

'I am headed to Hampshire the day after tomorrow; I plan to take these with me,' Avery replied.

Hampshire?

'Why are you going to Hampshire?' she asked.

As she prayed Avery knew someone in Hampshire from his soldiering days, she felt the hairs on the back of her neck stand up.

'A week-long house party at Viscount Owen's estate. I wasn't that bothered about attending, but Lord Langham said it would do me good to get to know some people away from the restrictions of London's formal events. He wants me to make some new friends before he takes me up to Langham Hall. What sort of party lasts a week is beyond me, so I thought it prudent to stock up on some reading material.'

Lucy felt faint. She had not planned on others making such a bold move for Avery's time. Lord and Lady Owen had not one, but two unwed daughters. No doubt they had marked the future earl out as a possible husband. The Owens had made the decisive move to cut Avery from the herd.

While Lucy was off wandering the mountains and valleys of Scotland, the two young Owen sisters would be doing everything they possibly could to ensure one of them was the next Countess Langham. If Avery had any sense of the potential danger he faced, he hid it well.

'I see; how lovely. And who else will be in attendance?' she replied. The more she knew about her opponents, the better.

'I'm not certain. I don't actually know many people. Viscount Owen was rather vague about the details when he extended the invitation,' he replied.

I bet he was.

Lord and Lady Owen were playing a smart game. They were not going to show their hand too early. If Avery was typical of most *ton* gentlemen, marriage was something which suddenly happened to them. One day they were a bachelor, the next they woke up with a bride sleeping next to them.

A Strathmore House footman took Lucy's package and stepped back from the counter. She stared at the wrapped books. It was time to leave.

'I just hope my meagre social skills are up to the task of a whole week at a stranger's house, otherwise I could be coming back to London earlier than expected,' Avery said.

Lucy's mouth went dry. By assisting Avery with learning the correct manner of behavior, had she unwittingly polished him up and handed him to another?

All her careful plans for playing a long innings crumbled before her eyes. After tonight it would be many months before they saw one another again.

Fool.

'I am sure you will pass muster,' she replied.

'Well, until tonight, Lady Lucy,' Avery said and gave her a bow.

Oh, why did I have to teach you to be a gentleman? I should have left you as you were.

'Yes; until tonight.'

He escorted her to her carriage and they parted with a friendly smile. As the carriage pulled away and into the street, Lucy sat staring out the window, watching as Avery walked down Piccadilly with his books. And her heart.

Disappointment and anguish swirled through her mind. What on earth was she to do?

'We must get you home soon so you can be ready for this evening, Lady Lucy,' her maid ventured.

With her gaze still fixed on Avery's diminishing figure, a soft smile crept to Lucy's lips. She still had tonight. A whole evening in which she could show him how truly suited they were to one another.

She sat back in the seat and looked at her maid. Her new gold silk gown had been bought on the proviso she kept it for special occasions only. What better purpose could there be than securing the heart of her future husband?

'I think I'll wear my new gown tonight. But no tiara, just a simple hairstyle. What do you think?'

Rose straightened in her seat, and nodded sagely.

'The gown and your hair should be enough,' she replied.

§

'I thought you said this was going to be a small, private affair,' Avery noted as he stepped into the front entrance of Strathmore House.

It was a milling throng of well-dressed people.

David Radley chuckled. 'For our family, this is a small gathering. You saw the crush that was Clarice's and my wedding ball. I wouldn't be surprised if when Lucy eventually marries, my parents try to top that number.'

The elegance of Langham House paled into insignificance against the majestic size of the Radley family residence. To one side of the main entrance were not one, but two enormous ballrooms. Avery recalled the ornate ceiling of the summer ballroom, with its array of picture panels depicting Aesop's fables, from his previous visit for David and Clarice's wedding ball. With his natural eye for art, he appreciated the intricate paintings and their dazzling color palette.

'Amazing,' Avery said.

'It doesn't quite match Rubens' painting on the Banqueting House ceiling in Whitehall, but we like it,' David replied.

He took a glass of champagne from a tray held by a nearby footman and handed it to Avery.

'Try to enjoy yourself tonight. You are among family and friends; no-one will think poorly of you if you allow yourself to relax.'

Relax?

Avery's mouth was as dry as the morning after a heavy night of drinking. The palms of his hands, hidden by his evening gloves, were pooled in sweat.

After a pleasant hour or so spent with David, Clarice and some other members of the Radley family, Avery excused himself. He couldn't find fault with Lord Strathmore, his family or his guests. They were all very interesting people and they had welcomed him as if he were one of their own.

But as he made his way outside into the dim light of the garden, away from the terrace doors he knew he would never truly be one of them. He began to dread the forthcoming week at Lord Owen's Hampshire estate.

'I should have said no,' he muttered to himself.

His new clothes were cut from the finest cloth; his pure white cravat expertly tied by the valet Lord Langham had insisted he take into his service. Catching his reflection in the glass of the large terrace doors, he stopped.

The clean-shaven, well-groomed man who stared back at him was a stranger. Only his deep green eyes, half hidden in the poor light, reminded him of who he was. As well turned out as he was in his fine clothes, he still felt like a first-class fraud.

There were times he wanted to escape this new life. Unbeknown to the Langham family, he had indeed packed his old travel bag several times and made to leave the house in Mill Street. But every time something made him stop. Every time he thought of the pain Thaxter had caused the Langham family, the resulting guilt made him put the old bag back into the wardrobe and leave it there.

He snorted. How ironic was it that he was now trapped in this life of wealth and privilege because of his villain of a brother?

Adding to his discomfort this evening was the inexplicable absence of Lucy. She had not been at the pre-dinner drinks and by the end of the second course at dinner he had been forced to accept she was not coming.

No-one else in her immediate family made mention of her absence and he took this to mean the matter was not open to discussion. She had appeared well when they met earlier that day in the bookshop, but women were still largely a mystery to him.

The first two courses were an interesting proposition. No sooner had he congratulated himself for successfully navigating the soup than a new challenge arrived. Periwinkles.

He looked down at his plate and his heart sank. Being from a fishing village, he had spent many hours picking the little shells off the rocks and eating their delicious contents.

He gave a sideways glance to the other guests. They all had special forks in their hands and were easily extracting the meat from the shells.

'Not partial to periwinkles, Fox?' Alex Radley asked.

Avery hesitated. If he told the Marquess of Brooke the truth – that he had only ever used a pin and sucked the periwinkle from the shell – would that confirm his status as a fortunate upstart? An uncouth lad from Yorkshire?

'No; I had a bad experience with some when I was younger and have not been able to touch them since,' he lied.

Rather than sitting and staring at the untouched plate, he excused himself from the table, claiming the need for a spot of night air.

As he walked through the massive adjoining ballroom and headed out through the doors, he silently berated himself. Was it even polite for him to leave the table when there were ladies present?

How many social *faux pas* would he commit tonight and not even be aware of them? And where the devil was Lucy, his touch-stone? He felt the lack of her presence as a dull throb in the back of his head.

As soon as he got clear of the terrace, he wandered down to a small rose arbor and took a seat. Pulling out a cheroot, he lit it and sat back, drawing deeply on the tobacco, savoring the solitude. The high stone wall of the garden shut out any ambient noise from the street, creating an oasis of silent calm.

'I wish I could stay out here all night,' he said.

'But that wouldn't be very sociable,' a soft, feminine voice replied.

Lucy.

He rose quickly from the seat and threw down his cheroot, twisting it into the stone pavement with his boot. A huge sense of relief coursed unexpectedly through him. Now that she was here, the awareness of how keenly he had missed her earlier shocked him.

'Avery,' she said, breathing his name.

'Should you be out here alone?' he replied.

'But I'm not alone, I'm with you. Besides, this is my home; I couldn't be anywhere safer unless you locked me up in the Tower of London.'

She ran a hand down over her hips, straightening her already perfect skirts. The breath seized in his lungs.

Lucy was a vision of night garden beauty. Her long, pale golden hair was held in a soft style. A series of ringlets kissed her cheeks and ears. A single gold ribbon was tied in her hair. It trailed down her neck, stopping an inch or so above her naked décolletage. He had never seen her dressed in such a provocative way before. He swallowed.

Her gown of gold and silver was simple but elegant. He saw where it clung to the sensual curves of her figure. The effect it had on his mind and body was immediate.

He swallowed once more and tried to calm his breathing. Beneath his shirt his heart raced as blood pooled in his loins. It had been a long time since he had reacted in such a sexual manner toward a woman. He was powerless.

'I'm sorry I missed the earlier part of the evening; it took a little longer than expected to prepare myself,' she explained.

She nodded toward the garden chair.

'Mind if I sit with you?'

Avery stepped back. His head felt light and he knew it was nothing to do with the glasses of wine he had imbibed during the evening. Drinking in the vision of Lucy Radley was pure intoxication.

'Since this is your home and your garden, I shall leave you. If you like I shall summon a footman to come out here and watch over you.'

The huff of disappointment which escaped her lips did not go unnoticed.

Her lips.

How many times had he stood listening to her make small talk while he stared at her luscious lips? He wondered if she had ever been kissed. He doubted she had been kissed in the way he ached to kiss her. To possess her.

Lucy wet her bottom lip with her tongue and Avery knew he was fast losing the battle against his lust.

She came closer and their gazes met. Her eyes betrayed her inner thoughts. Whereas previously he had seen a friendly but guarded look on her face, she now wore something far more dangerous. Whatever she was thinking at that moment, he doubted it was innocent.

A cold chill of premonition ran down his spine.

She reached out and placed a hand on his arm. A silent plea for him to stay.

'Lady Lucy, I know little of social strictures, but I have learned that a young lady should not be alone in the garden with a gentleman not of her family. We are friends, but this is not appropriate,' he said.

In addressing her in such a formal manner, he hoped she would see the danger she was currently in. He made a move to step past her and go back inside, but she was quicker.

'Lucy,' she murmured.

She placed a tentative hand on the lapel of his evening jacket in the lightest of grips. Gentle, but firm enough that it would be awkward for him to pull away.

He reached out a hand and placed it on her shoulder, with the intention of gently pushing her away. Forever after, he would not be able to make sense of what happened next. One moment he was trying to be rid of Lucy, the next he had dragged her into his arms and was kissing her senseless.

§.

Held in Avery's embrace, Lucy exalted.

Finally, something she had planned was coming to fruition. The hours hidden away in her room, carefully planning the exact moment she would appear this evening, had all been worth it. Her mother's repeated messages to hurry up and join the gathering downstairs had been politely ignored. She would deal with her mother's displeasure later. Tonight, was the night she seized her own future.

Alone in the garden with the man she had set her heart upon, she was kissing him. And more telling, he was kissing her!

His soft warm lips captured hers. A gentle, uncertain kiss at first. Then she heard him groan and he pressed his lips harder against hers as his tongue swept into her mouth. She had always prayed that her first real kiss would be good, that her knees would be trembling. Avery was more than good, he was masterful. Her knees threatened to buckle under her.

Oh yes. Oh please.

She tasted the bitter tobacco in his mouth, surprised when instead of finding it displeasing she wanted more. Her lips yielded to his urgent passion, urging him on. Inviting him to lay claim to all that she offered.

Her hands now gripped tightly to the lapels of his jacket. She had heard enough in the ladies' retiring rooms at balls to know that if you wanted a man to keep kissing you, you held fast to him.

A warm, strong hand held the side of her hip. She wriggled just a little to show her appreciation. His grip tightened.

Avery's other hand slipped under the hair at the back of her neck and tilted her head. He leaned further over her, enveloping Lucy within his warmth.

With her heart racing, she felt a rush of adrenaline course through her body. Emboldened by his response to her entreaty, she slipped a hand under the bottom edge of his cravat. Her petite fingers searched for and found his naked skin. This was heaven.

He gasped.

She froze.

He released her from his embrace, his lips quickly leaving hers. Firm hands took hold of her wrists and pushed her hands away. He stepped back, gasping for air as a look of abject horror appeared on his face. He attempted to straighten his cravat.

'Oh god, what have I done?' he uttered.

For all her well-laid-out plans, Lucy had not counted on this response. Her mind went blank.

'We kissed,' she replied. Panic now threatened to overwhelm her.

'Why on earth did you do that?' he replied.

The expression on his face crushed all but the merest of her hopes.

'I thought that was what you wanted. I . . .' she stammered.

He thrust his hand, palm facing outward, toward her.

'It was the last thing I wanted. I knew I should have gone back inside as soon as you arrived. I sensed you were up to something.'

Hot tears sprang to Lucy's eyes. From the victorious thoughts of a moment ago, suddenly everything was going horribly wrong.

Avery's eyes narrowed.

'I must ask. Did you decide right from the outset that I was some kind of sport? A plaything for a rich, spoilt young miss to toy with? You must think me an utter fool.'

He raked his hand through his hair and chucked bitterly.

'And to think I believed you when you said you were my friend. That you only wanted to help. I'm surprised you were able to keep a straight face every time you gave me dance lessons.'

No. No.

'I did want. I mean I do want to be your friend. It's just that I want . . .' she cried.

He stepped back, anger evident in the sharp lines around his mouth.

'Want what? You want to put me on the end of a leash and parade me around London as your new colorful pet? Don't think for a moment I have been blind to the machinations of all the young misses fawning over me. Asking me in their soft, girlish voices how hard a life I must have led. How gallant and brave a soldier I must have been. I may be an outsider to London society, but I am not stupid.'

Lucy stepped forward, her hands reaching out in supplication, as she desperately tried to make him understand. As she attempted to take hold of his lapels once more, he angrily pushed her away.

'Let go of me, you cunning wench! Let me be!'

Wrong-footed, Lucy staggered back, falling hard against the sharp thorns of the nearby rose bush. She cried out in pain as the thorns tore through her gown and dug deep into her skin.

Avery's anger immediately disappeared.

'Oh no. Oh Lucy, I'm so sorry. I didn't mean to push you that hard,' Avery said, coming quickly to her side.

He tugged at the rose bush as Lucy screwed her eyes shut. All her dreams were in tatters.

'I'm sorry Avery. I'm sorry, I never meant to . . .'

'Ssh,' he murmured.

He leaned in close, tugging on the bodice of her gown as he attempted to free her. Lucy looked sadly away, overcome by the depth of her embarrassment and shame.

Avery struggled with the tangled gown for a minute or so before finally sighing and saying. 'I will have to undo some of the buttons at the back of your gown to get to the thorns. There is no other way I can free you.'

She silently nodded her head. Her humiliation was complete. Anything Avery did now simply didn't matter. All she wanted to do was escape from his hurtful words, go back inside and hide.

Avery unhooked four buttons, allowing the top of the gown to slip off Lucy's shoulders. The ivory skin of her right breast was bared to the chill night air. She shivered. With the fabric now closer to his reach, he slowly disentangled her from the rose bush.

'There, that should do it,' he said.

She turned around, and waited with resignation for him to button her gown back up.

'Please hurry,' she pleaded.

When he didn't reply she turned to him. Her gaze followed the direction in which his eyes were focused and her heart stopped.

At the edge of the garden path, only a matter of feet away, stood her father. Behind him on the bottom step of the terrace was Lord Langham.

'Lucy, go upstairs to your room and change. You will await your mother,' the duke said.

'Papa?' she whispered.

'Go,' he replied. The controlled rage in his voice brooked no misunderstanding.

She pulled the top of her gown back up and stepped away. As she put her foot on the bottom step of the terrace, she gave a backward glance to Avery.

His gaze was still fixed firmly on her father. It was if Avery had been turned to stone. As she reached the top step of the terrace, she heard her father say 'My study, Mr. Fox.'

In the privacy of her bedroom, she quickly changed out of the torn dress. After attending to the cuts on Lucy's back, Rose helped her into a simple white satin gown with matching ribbons. If she received her father's summons to join the dinner party downstairs, Lucy intended to be as near to invisible as she could for the rest of the evening. She sat quietly in front of her dressing mirror as her maid did her best to fix Lucy's hair.

A little while later, a knock on the door heralded her mother.

The duchess quickly dismissed Rose and closed the door behind her. Lady Caroline placed a large blue velvet jewel case on the dressing table and crossed to Lucy's wardrobe.

'Something a little more elegant might be in order,' Lady Caroline said. She opened the double doors of Lucy's wardrobe and searched for a moment.

'Where is your silver and gold gown?' she asked.

Lucy pointed to the torn gown, which lay on her bed.

Her mother sighed. 'Oh, Lucy; what have you done?'

'It was an accident, I slipped and accidently fell against the roses by the arbor,' Lucy replied.

She heard her mother's breathing falter on the edge of a sob. When the duchess turned back from the closet, her eyes were brimming with tears.

'My dear girl,' she muttered.

Lucy rose from her chair. Taking hold of her mother's hand, she gave it a gentle pat. Everything would be all right. She would apologize to all and everything would be forgiven.

'I'm sorry for making such a scene outside. It was foolish of me. I know Papa will be angry with me, but I promise to be on my best behavior for the rest of the evening. You will not hear a sound from my lips.'

She had learnt a salutary lesson this evening. She had underestimated Avery and in the process lost his good opinion and friendship. The pain she currently felt would eventually ease, as would the cuts on her back.

The duchess shook her head.

'If only it were that simple.'

A cold dread came over Lucy. What had her father and Lord Langham done to Avery?

'It wasn't Mr. Fox's fault; I sought him out in the garden,' she said.

'At first I don't expect it was; I had noticed you have taken a particular interest in Mr. Fox. But from what your father tells me, your Mr. Fox did not behave as a gentleman should have under the circumstances. He and Lord Langham saw the two of you kissing from the ballroom doorway and from what I understand, Mr. Fox was a willing participant in the exchange.'

Lucy hung her head in shame. Not only had she seriously damaged her relationship with Avery, but now he would be held in a very dim light by the rest of her family. And the Langhams. The evening was fast descending into disaster.

'I shall go and speak with Papa and explain the situation; I take full responsibility,' Lucy replied.

Her mother went back to the wardrobe and took out a deep pink velvet gown. It was one of Lucy's favorites.

'You will change into this and put on the gold and pearl tiara your maternal grandmother left you.'

She nodded toward the jewel box and handed the gown to Lucy.

'A tiara?' Lucy exclaimed.

'Yes; it is the same one I wore for the announcement of my

betrothal to your father. You will do the same for your engagement to Mr. Fox.'

The gown fell to the floor.

'No!' Lucy cried.

Her mother bent down and picked up the gown.

'Your indiscretion in the garden tonight left your father with little choice. You had the top of your gown open, and Mr. Fox's hands were on your naked person. The encounter was in full view of anyone who happened to be in the garden. Your father has demanded Mr. Fox make an offer for your hand in marriage, and Lord Langham concurs. Anything else will leave you irrevocably ruined.'

'And what did Mr. Fox say?' Lucy replied.

When the duchess sighed, any hope that Lucy might have held for Avery's forgiveness died.

'I am not sure of the conversation which is currently taking place in your father's study, but I expect the outcome will be as it should be. You and Mr. Fox will be getting married before we leave for Scotland.'

At that, Lucy knew her fate was sealed. Her plans to win Avery's heart and then his hand had completed failed. If, as she suspected, he hated her at this moment, she couldn't find fault with him.

'Now, let's get you changed and I shall come back and fetch you when your father is ready to make the announcement. You should take the time to compose yourself and find a happy smile.'

'Mama, I don't want to marry Avery Fox,' Lucy replied. The thought of being bound to a man who would resent her presence in his life filled her with dismay.

The duchess wrapped her arms around her eldest daughter and kissed her hair.

'I'm afraid you don't have any say in the matter anymore, Lucy. The moment you went into the garden to meet with Mr. Fox alone you set events in motion. I suspected you were up to something this evening, but even I hadn't thought you would go so far. Unfortunately, your uncle arrived not long ago and is now aware of what took place this evening. There is nothing else to be done. The Bishop of London holds the moral heart of this family under his command and he will make certain that no disgrace comes to it.'

When Rose returned to Lucy's room she found her mistress seated on the edge of her bed, the betrothal gown held limply in her hand. Lucy handed her the gown and stood silent while her maid worked on the long line of buttons up its back.

A short ten minutes later she descended the stairs. Carefully making sure she held her head up high and kept her steps even and sure, Lucy went to face her fate.

The first sign that something was amiss was the silence.

By rights there should have been a hum of activity on the ground floor. A buzz from the dining room. As she reached the bottom of the stairs, she saw Alex and David standing side by side. As she approached, her two brothers exchanged a pained look. David offered her his hand.

'Where is everyone?' she asked.

'The party is over; Clarice and Millie are sitting with Mama upstairs. Everyone else has gone home,' David replied.

Everyone.

Hope flared in her heart. Perhaps the senior men of her family had seen sense and were no longer pressing for her and Avery to marry. A gush of air escaped her lungs. Relief.

'Thank God,' she whispered.

Alex and David shared another grim look.

'It's not over, Lucy. Avery has refused to offer for you, but Papa will have his way,' Alex said.

At that moment, she wasn't certain which hurt more. The fact that she would eventually have to go through with the marriage, or that Avery had left without asking for her hand.

He must truly hate her.

'Ah, there you are,' her father said, coming out of his study. He beckoned to her.

Once she was inside his study, he closed the door behind him. Seated on a low leather couch by the fire was her uncle. The bishop rose from his chair and came to her.

'You may think me harsh in pressing for this union, but trust me, I have only your best interests at heart,' he said. His stern countenance reflected the seriousness of the situation.

Turning to the duke, he gave a nod of his head.

'I leave the rest of this up to you and Langham.'

The duke closed his eyes. 'Yes of course; good night, brother.'

As the door closed behind her uncle, Lucy fixed her gaze on her father. The steely look on his face said it all. There was no point in pleading with him; it was evident his mind was made up.

'Alex tells me Mr. Fox refused to offer for my hand and that he has already left.'

'Yes, on both counts, but Mr. Fox will return. It shouldn't take long for Langham to convince him of the need for the two of you to marry,' the duke replied.

She searched her father's face, hoping to find a crack in his grim facade.

'Papa, you cannot mean it. You must reconsider. I do not want this union, and neither does Avery. He has made his position clear.'

Her father dragged his fingers tightly through his hair. In the hour or so since she had seen him last, he had visibly aged. Worry lines etched his face.

'Unfortunately, I have not changed my mind, Lucy. You put us all in an impossible situation and there is only one logical course of action to solve the problem. As soon as Langham sends word that Mr. Fox has agreed to marry you, we will begin wedding preparations.'

Chapter Nine

A little over half a mile away, Avery sat outside on the balcony to his room and stared up at the cloudy London sky. Drawing back on his cheroot, he blew large puffs of smoke out into the air.

'Bloody hell,' he cursed.

The night had been a complete disaster. What he had assumed was going to be a relatively sedate affair had turned into his worst nightmare.

He lay his head back against the Portland stone wall of Langham House. The French doors leading back into his bedroom were closed firmly behind him. Since Lady Alice had made it clear he was not to smoke within the confines of the house, Avery had taken great pains to ensure no smoke drifted in from outside.

If he had his way, he would be sitting back in the pub at the Queen's Head in Lambeth, several drinks into a long night of getting seriously drunk. He had remained at Langham House only due to the overwhelming sense of obligation he felt toward Lord Langham.

'You must adhere to the rules of polite society, Avery, and offer for Lady Lucy's hand. You have no choice,' the earl pleaded upon their return to Mill Street.

He snorted. What did he care for polite society? And who the devil were they to tell him how to live his life? All the *ton* seemed to care about was ensuring people like him did exactly what they were told. To control his life even more than the army had done.

As for Lucy, he was convinced she had played him for a guileless fool. He slowly clenched the fingers and thumb of his damaged left hand, tightly winding them together. The pain of her deception burned deep.

Lord Langham had at least won part of the argument, with Avery reluctantly agreeing to stay on at Langham House. He hated himself for having allowed his newly found taste for the finer things in life to have played a part in his decision.

Outside of this house, he had few prospects for making his way in the world. His mangled left hand discounted him for manual labor, while his lack of formal education meant he would struggle to secure a coveted position as a clerk. London was full of former soldiers, all seeking to make a living. Many were able-bodied, but many others had lifelong injuries far worse than his own. He knew he had no right to self-pity. How many of those men would be clambering over him to marry the daughter of a duke?

'All of them,' he muttered.

During the heated row, he had endured with Lord Langham, he had been forced to concede that Lucy was not to blame for what had transpired in the garden. What on earth had possessed him to haul her into his arms and kiss her like that?

He shook his head, knowing full well why he had let his hands roam over the feminine curves of her body. Why he had succumbed to her enticing lips. It wasn't just the gown which had seized his imagination. From the very first time he set eyes on Lucy, everything about her had stirred his manly desires.

She was possessed of exactly the kind of feminine physique which Avery found sexually alluring. In any other circumstance, he would not have shown restraint with a young lady who offered her charms so willingly. He would have revealed the depth of his need.

It had been an eternity since his body reacted to a woman in the way it had with Lucy. A number of the girls at Lord Rokewood's estate had made their interest in him known once he was sufficiently recovered from his battle wounds. With his tussle of dark hair and bedroom smile, he was soon fighting off the amorous advances of several servant girls.

Not that he put up any form of struggle. Appreciating a woman's body and bringing her to the pinnacle of sexual pleasure was something he had learnt early in life. His virginity was lost not long after he joined the army. In the bedroom or the local barn, he was a master of the art of seduction. Nothing gave him more satisfaction than to hear a woman climax under the attention of his heated body.

An image of the soft cream skin of Lucy's breast entered his mind. It had only been a glimpse, but it left his body hard and hungry. Perhaps a marriage to her wouldn't be the worst thing which could happen to him. Lucy was a bright, intelligent girl. He sensed she would learn quickly about desire and passion. He could teach her a great deal more than just how to kiss.

He forced the lustful thoughts from his mind. Marriage to Lucy would be the gravest mistake of his life. Not only was he a man incapable of love, but if she ever discovered the truth of what he had done at Waterloo, Lucy would hate him. Knowing he could never truly love her would sentence them both to a lifetime of endless torture. Lucy at least deserved better than that in her life.

He took a brown glass bottle of ale from his jacket pocket and pulled the cork out with his teeth. The badly brewed beer went quickly down his throat. The spice of the hops cleansed his tired palate. No matter how fine a wine cellar Lord Langham maintained, nothing tasted better than the cheap beer Avery kept secretly stashed in his room. Along with his newly acquired fine tastes, he still held fast to some old ones.

Wiping his moist lips with the back of his gloved hand, he immediately regretted not having purchased more bottles on his early-morning shopping trip. He pulled out the few remaining coins from his pocket and examined them.

'Nothing will be achieved by getting yourself toad-faced,' he said.

He put the coins back in his pocket and flicked his cheroot over the side of the balcony and down into the street. Then, getting to his feet, he glanced over the side of the balcony, relieved to see there was no-one below whom he could have hit. One solitary carriage made its way along Mill Street, the clip clop of the horse's hooves echoing against the stone roadway.

'Not my night for making good choices,' he muttered.

He opened the door leading back to his bedroom and went inside. With Lucy's brother David resident under the same roof he knew tomorrow would be a full day of recriminations.

⚜

'So, he is still refusing to announce the betrothal?' Alex asked.

Lady Caroline nodded her head.

It was now three days since the ill-fated dinner party and Avery Fox had refused all entreaties for him to visit at Strathmore House.

'I don't know what sort of game he thinks he is playing at,' Alex added, slowly clenching his fist.

'I think that is very much the root of the problem. Mr. Fox does not see this as a game. He is being coerced into marrying your sister and he has obviously decided that no matter what anyone else says, his answer is no,' his mother replied.

'How is Lucy?' Alex asked.

'Who knows? She has spoken fewer than a dozen words to me and has spent most of the past few days holed up in her room. She refuses to see visitors and has not once left the house.'

'Poor Lucy, she must be going out of her mind,' Alex replied.

If anyone had actually asked Lucy what she thought of Avery's steadfast refusal to marry her, she would have informed them that she fully supported his position. But since she was not currently on speaking terms with pretty much anyone who had been at the dinner party, her opinion remained her own.

As long as Avery held out against those who continued to

demand their marriage, she clung to the hope of avoiding a loveless union.

'A cunning wench,' she whispered.

Her fingers instinctively went to her lips. Lips which Avery had kissed. His hot, passionate embrace had been magical. Memories of the warmth and strength of his arms around her still lingered. Whether he admitted it or not, she knew he had enjoyed their encounter. He had willingly kissed her.

In the garden, before he uttered those devastating words of rejection, and crushed her heart, he had wanted her. She knew it.

If only they had not been discovered. Given time she could have shown him she was far from a scheming young miss. That she was worthy of his love.

'Oh, don't be so ridiculous, Lucy! He hates you. He told you so himself. Just be grateful he doesn't care for the opinion of others. You have been spared,' she chided herself.

As is the case when two opposing forces of equal strength push against one another, nothing moved. Avery's stubbornness was matched only by Lucy's. Neither was prepared to capitulate and so things remained at a standstill.

On the morning of the fourth day of the stalemate, Avery answered the door of his bedroom. Ian Barrett stood on the threshold. Avery took one look at his former commanding officer and sighed. He didn't need to ask why Ian Barrett was paying him a visit. Someone had decided that the only way to break the impasse was to apply a stronger force.

'May I come in?' he asked.

Avery stepped aside and waved him in.

Ian turned to Avery and raised an eyebrow. 'Well, it certainly is a humble abode, if that was the look you were attempting to achieve,' he said. His gaze fell on the pile of dirty shirts and the half-eaten breakfast which remained on the sideboard. Strewn across the floor were books and scattered pieces of paper.

Avery let the remark go unanswered. He owed so much to Ian, including his life. He would never be able to bring himself to the point of showing him disrespect.

'It is what happens to a room when one decides to bunker down and wait out the siege,' he replied.

His answer was an honest one. He had refused all attentions from his valet and was now sporting a scruffy four-day-old beard.

'And how long do you intend to stay in your room? I can't see Langham allowing this sulk of yours to continue. Hiding away like this is childish to say the least,' Ian replied.

He dropped his hat and gloves on to the small table by the door and turned to face Avery.

'You are only doing yourself and your reputation irreparable damage by behaving toward Lady Lucy Radley in such a heartless and cavalier manner. The *haute ton* protects its own. Once this becomes public knowledge they will close ranks against you. I'm surprised that the Radley family have so far managed to keep it quiet. These things tend to get whispered among the servants and shared between the houses very quickly.'

What was it Lady Alice Langham had said? Gossip was the currency of the ton.

'But aren't I supposed to be one of them now? I mean, one of you,' Avery replied.

Ian shook his head.

'My family has held the title of Rokewood for nearly three hundred years. We have served as part of the royal Privy Council for most of that time. Only my brother's illness precludes him from being a close confidant to the Prince Regent. I am Albert's heir and know all the important families, yet even after all that, I am considered an outsider by many. Avery, my good man, to them . . . you are nothing.

'If you are not born into the upper echelon of London society, if you do not move within their circles and abide by their rules, they will not hesitate to destroy you.'

Avery scowled. What did he care about the *ton*? He didn't need or want to be in their good graces. He held fast to this opinion.

Almost.

'I couldn't care less what London society thinks of me. They can all go to the devil,' he replied.

Ian snorted and Avery knew he had disappointed him with his response.

'Don't be a fool, man! You might not give a tinker's cuss about them, but you will hurt others. In fact, you are already hurting innocent parties. Apart from the lady in question, other members of the Langham and Radley families will suffer. If you don't agree to marry Lady Lucy, she will be ruined. Her younger sister Emma will therefore be tainted with her sister's reputation. David and Clarice will likely lose the acceptance of their marriage they have fought so hard to win. Is that what you want? The Lieutenant Fox I knew is not that sort of man.'

A hundred foul curses streamed through Avery's mind. By calling his honour into question, the major was attacking him at his weakest point. At that moment, he was unsure as to whom he hated the most. Himself for allowing his stubborn nature to further corrupt his honour, or Ian for knowingly exploiting it to its fullest.

'And this is why you are here?' he replied.

It pained him to think that Ian would treat him thus. Worse still, he knew that he was right. He rubbed the palm of his hand across his beard and yawned. Sleep had not come easily to him over the past days as his conscience continually gnawed at him. Added to that were the constant nightmares which came with sleep. Nightmares which revolved around that fateful night in the garden with Lucy. Of the harsh words, he had said to her. Of her despair.

The current situation was not a tenable one. He could not spend the rest of his life holed up in his bedroom. Nor could he allow Lucy to be ruined as a result of his inability to control his lust. This was one tight spot out of which he could not fight. Escape was impossible.

'Shall I call your valet to come and clean you up?' Ian asked.

His disapproving gaze ran over Avery's not-so-clean shirt and generally unkempt appearance.

Avery sighed. If preserving Lucy's honour was all he could give her, then it would have to do.

'On one condition,' Avery replied.

He felt the invisible noose tighten around his neck.

'Yes?'

'That once I am presentable, you accompany me to Strathmore House. If I am going to my doom, I want you beside me.'

Ian Barrett headed for the door.

'I was always going to come with you. You struck a poor bargain, Lieutenant.'

Chapter Ten

The actual wedding ceremony was over rather quickly. A few words from the Bishop of London followed by a very chaste kiss on Lucy's cheek and it was done. As he drew back from the kiss, Avery in his nervousness attempted to lower Lucy's short lace veil once more. A blush of red appeared on her face as she put out a hand and stopped him.

Avery fixed a happy groom's grin to his face and accepted the congratulations of the assembled guests. His youngest sister-in-law, Lady Emma, gave him a big, tearful hug. Her fourteen-year-old brother Stephen beamed with delight. Lord Langham shook his hand and gave him a solid slap on the back.

'Well done, young man; Lady Lucy will make a perfect Countess of Langham. Solid bloodlines and impeccable family connections. I couldn't have chosen better if you'd asked me to find you a bride,' the earl said.

With his daughter Clarice married to Lucy's brother, the Langham and Radley family connections were further strengthened. No-one need mention the saved reputations of various family members. Avery and Lucy's wedding had smoothed over all the cracks.

Avery nodded. Everyone seemed particularly pleased. They constantly remarked how wonderful it was that the Langham and Radley families were bound to one another.

It didn't seem to matter in the slightest that Avery wasn't actually family. That he was in fact a distant relative who just happened to be next in line to the title.

He finished receiving the congratulations of the wedding guests and made his way to find his new bride. The Duke of Strathmore had agreed to Avery's terms for the wedding but with several strict provisos. The first being that appearances had to be maintained.

Lucy and Avery's marriage was a love match as far as the rest of London society was concerned, and the change from a church wedding to a private one at Strathmore House was due to the recent demise of the groom's brother. A perfectly acceptable reason. As a story, it worked; no-one else need know the truth.

'Shall we?' Lucy said as the gong sounded for the wedding breakfast.

Her long, white lace wedding gown fitted perfectly to her body. Somewhere a team of seamstresses had worked day and night to get it ready. The small posy of cream and red roses she carried matched perfectly to the stripes of Avery's wedding waistcoat. They looked the perfectly matched newlywed couple.

'Yes, let's do,' Avery replied and offered her his arm.

The wedding breakfast was a sedate affair; Avery partook of only two glasses of wine while Lucy didn't touch any of the food or drink. There were a few minor toasts and several short speeches. Seated side by side, Avery and Lucy barely exchanged a word.

Most guests had taken their leave by late afternoon.

When David and Clarice left just before seven o'clock, citing Clarice's need for rest, only the immediate Radley family members remained.

Millie came and gave Lucy a warm hug.

'Congratulations, sister; I hope everything goes as you hope for tonight,' she whispered.

She reserved a hopeful smile for Avery and brushed a kiss on his cheek.

'Be kind to her; she is a wonderful girl. You just need to allow yourself time to get to know the real Lucy. I beg of you, don't break her heart,' Millie murmured, *sotto voce*.

Avery nodded silently.

He glanced at his wife and saw her anxiety displayed in the hard way she continually spun her new wedding ring around her finger. It took all his strength not to reach out and stop her.

Finally, the time came for them to leave the wedding celebrations and go to spend their first night together as man and wife.

They slowly ascended the stairs together, forcing themselves to laugh as Alex offered a ribald wedding night jest. Millie dug an elbow into her husband's ribs in disapproval.

'It's this way,' Lucy said, as Avery stopped at the top of the grand staircase, uncertain as to where he was supposed to go.

'Our personal things have been moved to our apartment.'

The sad look on her face gave Lucy away. She was dreading being alone with him.

It had been less than two days since he'd visited the duke at Strathmore House and offered for Lucy's hand. Ian Barrett had sat silently beside him, offering moral support.

Once the duke reluctantly accepted Avery's conditions, matters had moved quickly. Firstly, it would be a private wedding. Avery was determined not to stand in front of London society and show them he had been brought to heel. He didn't need to be reminded that he had been put firmly in his place.

Secondly, there was to be no wedding ball. The duke had argued strongly against this, regarding it as a personal slight against his daughter.

'But Alex and David both had magnificent wedding balls. You attended David and Clarice's wedding celebrations; you know how much it means to the bride. You would deny my daughter her moment in the limelight?' the duke asked.

Lucy, having been summoned from her bedroom, had stood beside Avery, hands clasped in front. When Lord Strathmore further pressed his case, she simply held up her hand.

'It's all right Papa, if Avery doesn't want a ball then neither do I.'

If Avery felt as if he was being sentenced to his doom, his now wife had shown even less enthusiasm for their impending nuptials. He could not fail to notice her bloodshot eyes and tear-stained cheeks.

He had left Strathmore House that afternoon hating himself and the world.

Now, as they reached their private rooms, Lucy hurried to an adjoining dressing room. When Avery went to follow her, she stopped him at the doorway.

'Have a nightcap, I will be with you shortly,' she said.

She pointed to a large crystal whisky decanter which sat on a table in the main bedroom. After she closed the door behind her, Avery heard a key being turned in the lock.

Taking his cue, he poured himself a large glass of the golden liquid and after removing his jacket, took a seat by the well-stoked fire. The pay of a non-commissioned officer did not normally stretch to fine whisky. It was another taste he had quickly acquired upon his elevation to high society.

He took a sip of the whisky, screwed up his face and immediately set the glass down.

When Lucy finally appeared from the dressing room, he saw the look of disappointment on her face. She was still in her wedding gown.

He looked to the whisky decanter.

'What did you put in the whisky?' he asked.

A guilty look flashed in her eyes, but she shook her head vehemently in denial.

'Nothing; I don't know what you mean,' she stammered.

He gave a derisive snort. From the first moment, the whisky had slid down his throat, he knew it had been tainted.

'You wouldn't make a very good poisoner. I could verily taste the drug in the first mouthful. Were you planning to kill me on our wedding night?' he replied.

Lucy screwed her eyes shut as a desperate sob escaped her lips.

'I'm sorry, I sorry, I just didn't know what to do!' she cried.

He resisted the temptation to go to her and offer comfort. Thinking he'd narrowly avoided being poisoned by his new wife, Avery was not in a particularly forgiving mood.

'So, you thought murder would solve your problems?' Avery replied.

'No, of course not. I just thought that if you slept well tonight, you might be more amenable,' Lucy replied.

'Amenable to what?' he replied.

Wiping tears away with the back of her hand she straightened her spine. With her gaze fixed firmly on his, she recited what were obviously well-rehearsed words.

'I think I might have found a way out of this for us. If we are to end this marriage and be rid of one another it can be done. You will, of course, need to agree to my plan if we are to succeed.'

Rid of one another.

Avery was suddenly struck with the feeling he was about to make the worst mistake of his life. He pushed the emotion away, leaving it to linger in the background.

'Lucy. I promise I won't force you to the marriage bed. If you want your freedom, then I will do what I can to give it to you.'

'Thank you,' she said.

Having been set fast against this marriage himself only a matter of days ago, it shocked him to realize Lucy had actively sought a way out. From the moment, they had exchanged their wedding vows, he had resigned himself to the task of making the best of things.

Not so Lucy. She really didn't want to be his wife.

'Explain something to me. If you didn't want to marry me, then why in heaven's good name did you follow me into the garden that night? You had to know the risk of us being discovered. No girl of your social standing does that unless she has her sights set on marriage,' he said

Lucy's gaze fell to the floor.

'I came into the garden to warn you about your visit to Hampshire and the Owens' plans to match you up with one of their daughters. And yes, I thought to press my own case. I didn't understand until that moment that you can barely tolerate the likes of me. Now that I understand things more clearly, the thought of being married to you when you don't even like me is beyond my emotional capacity. If we had perhaps been able to remain friends, it might have been different. I would rather face ruin than live without love,' she replied.

He had to hand it to his new, reluctant bride, she certainly had a way with words. If she remained married to him in a loveless union, it would destroy her. Her bone-deep misery cut him to the quick.

He gritted his teeth. It had been many years since someone had made him feel such a worthless piece of humanity. He reminded himself quickly that Lucy was not Thaxter. That she too was suffering.

'You said you had a plan,' he replied.

When the time was right, before he finally let her go, he would attempt to apologize for the harsh way he had treated her. Perhaps they could manage to reach an understanding. Even form the fragile bones of a friendship once more.

'Yes, but not a very good one now that I have looked further into it. I had money coming from my mother's side of the family upon my marriage. I thought it would be sufficient funds for me to run away to France.'

'And now?'

She sighed. 'As of yesterday morning, I was informed that most of it goes to my new husband. Believe me, Avery, if I had enough money I would be in Calais right this minute. And you would be a free man.'

'So, I give some of the money to you,' Avery replied. A simple and agreeable solution to her problem.

Lucy growled with obvious frustration.

'It is part of the dowry contract, which states that the money only comes to you after a year of us cohabiting. You might have won on the minor matter of the wedding celebrations, Avery, but my father has trumped you when it comes to the issue of money.'

'You *did* say there was something we could do,' he replied.

'A divorce.'

Divorce. Even the sound of it had a chilling finality.

Avery's breath caught in his lungs. Lucy had caught him off-guard. He had anticipated tears or possibly a blistering row, but her open and honest response left him struggling.

Here on his wedding night, he and his beautiful young bride were calmly discussing getting a divorce.

For god's sake, man, take her in your arms and make love to her.

His mind understood one thing, but his sex-starved body screamed another. He was well within his rights to command her to come to their bed, to give him willing access to her body. To end this nonsense and accept the inevitable.

But here she was, offering him a way out.

'Considering the lengths that various people have gone to ensure our wedding took place, don't you think that is an impossibility? Even I know that a divorce could take years,' he replied.

She screwed up her face, her self-doubt evident.

'Yes, in England perhaps, but not in Scotland. I have a distant aunt who, I understand, managed to secure a divorce at the courts in Edinburgh. There is nothing to stop us trying that avenue.'

She stared hard at him and he sensed she was somehow sizing him up. Assessing and judging his true intentions. Wondering if he would support her in her quest for freedom.

'I can give you the name of a firm of reputable and reliable solic-itors in Edinburgh. One which my father does not utilize for his business dealings. They should be able to find suitable grounds for divorce.'

His heart went out to her as she choked on the last word. Any other girl in her position would likely have kept silent and endured whatever came of their marriage. Not Lucy. A divorce would mean the complete loss of her honour, but she was prepared to pay the price to give him his freedom.

'So, what will you do if we succeed?' he replied.

She sniffled back tears.

'I shall do as I had planned. I shall go abroad. Eve's brother

William is back in Paris, I am sure he would be happy for some company. My parents will no doubt give me travel funds once they know you have instituted divorce proceedings. They cannot run the risk of scandal tainting the rest of the family. In a few years, hopefully after Emma has married, I shall return quietly to England and try to pick up the threads of my life.'

Lucy's words were calmly delivered, but her still and fragile posture betrayed her pain. Emma was only twelve years old. Even if her sister married young, Lucy would spend at least the next six years in exile.

Tonight, should be a night for laughter and love; instead the bride and groom were conducting a cold discussion as to how they could end their brief union. The bride was facing years away from her country and family.

If he could feel any worse at this moment, Avery doubted it was possible. Even the painful injuries he had sustained at Waterloo hadn't burned to the depths of his soul as this did.

'Well, if we are agreed, I shall bid you good night. We can discuss this further in the morning. Thank you, Avery, it is nice that we have been able to agree on something,' Lucy suddenly announced.

He stood and watched in stunned silence as she turned on her heel and went back into the adjoining room, closing the door behind her.

Guilt welled up inside him. He knew it had taken every ounce of her strength not to break down in front of him. Once she was on the other side of the door he doubted she would be able to maintain her taciturn facade. Lucy was a woman incapable of hiding her true self from the world.

He had not heard the key turn in the lock. It would be simple enough for him to open the door and end all this nonsense right here and now. She was Lucy Fox now and he had his rights as a husband.

'No. I will not force her to be bound to me. If she wants me, then let her come to me of her own accord,' he muttered to the door.

He stared at the closed door for what felt like an eternity, but

Lucy remained on the other side. Finally, he retired to the big bed. Lying on his back in the dark, staring up at the ceiling, he listened for any sign that Lucy had returned. No sound came from the adjoining room. His wife wasn't coming back.

'Not how I thought my wedding night would be,' he sighed.

He fell asleep, a prayer on his lips that one day Lucy would find someone to love and share her life with. Whoever it was, it most certainly would not be him.

Chapter Eleven

W ith her eyes closed, Lucy leaned back against the door which separated her from Avery. Her confrontation with him had left her drained and empty.

'At least he has agreed to help end this farce,' she comforted herself.

In the days leading up to the wedding she had meticulously planned the wedding night. After having had *the talk* with her mother, Lucy had made up her mind. She was not going to bed with Avery and she most certainly was not going to consummate their marriage.

When the time came to give herself to a man it would be with her whole heart and soul, not just her body. From what she had gathered from Millie's occasional comments, she knew sex within marriage could be wonderful. It was something to share with someone you truly loved and who loved you in return. A mutual worshipping of one another's bodies.

From observing her parents as she grew into adulthood, Lucy knew they had a close, romantic relationship. Her father was often caught by his children holding and kissing his wife. The duchess did not shy away from the duke's attentions. Her mother's deep love for her husband was evident in the way she had explained the physical relationship that a man and his wife should share within their marriage.

Lucy had sat silent throughout the talk, hoping her mother would soon finish. She could only feign interest in her future married life for so long. Lady Caroline wrapped her arms around her eldest daughter, whispering words of comfort and love. Everything would turn out for the best.

Lucy puffed out her cheeks.

Her parents' love and happiness had given the Radley children a warm, loving home, so unlike those of many other children born into the upper echelons of London society. She was, as always, grateful for her life, but now, faced with a forced marriage, she found herself having to contend with complications for which her upbringing had not prepared her.

Neither her mother nor Millie understood the peril Lucy currently faced. If she allowed herself to become Avery's wife in the fullest sense, she would forever lose her heart to him. He, in turn, had made his position clear. He would never love her. To wake next to him each morning and look into those emerald eyes, knowing that he did not love her, would be a lifetime of torture.

His long black hair, which had been tied back in a simple hold at the base of his neck for their wedding day, would fall forward, framing his face. His morning beard would tempt her fingers to reach out and touch his face. To kiss his hot, tender lips.

Those lips.

'Stop it. Stop it,' she said, tightly clenching her fists.

Her resolute heart had set itself to love him and would not be denied.

'The sooner we part, the better.'

She pushed away from the door and surveyed the room. It was then that the folly of her plans for their wedding night began to dawn on her. She had not taken into account the likelihood that trying to drug Avery would fail. While he slept in the sumptuously appointed bed in the adjourning room, she now faced the prospect of spending the night on a short, uncomfortable couch.

She cursed herself for being too heavy-handed with the sleeping draught provided by Lady Alice at the wedding breakfast. Avery had not been fooled.

'Neither of you deserve this fate. In the morning, talk to him; tell him to let you go,' Lady Alice had counselled.

'That would just about sum up the sort of day I have had,' Lucy muttered in disgust as she looked at the small couch...

The only option apart from the couch available to her at this point was to go back into the master bedroom and take her place beside her new husband. The chance of meeting someone from either her family or the household staff while she attempted to sneak back to her old bedroom on one of the lower floors was too great a risk.

She went to the tall oak chest of drawers and rummaged around. Fortunately, a woolen blanket had been stored in the large bottom drawer. She draped the blanket over her shoulders. Quickly realizing the couch was not long enough for her to lie down, Lucy was forced to accept that she was going to spend the whole night sitting up.

'Not how I had imagined my wedding night would be,' she muttered.

She gave a glance to the door which separated her from Avery. She hoped he slept well. One of them at least should be well rested in order to tell whatever lies the morning required.

※

Avery woke early the following morning. Years of army life had ingrained in him the need to rise as soon as the first spark of sunlight graced the sky. Outside the window he heard the call of morning birds.

He sat up in the bed, momentarily wondering where he was. When his gaze took in the empty pillows beside him, he remembered.

Last night was supposed to have been the happiest night of his life. He was a married man, and with it should come all the benefits of a lust-filled wedding night. Lucy, his bride, should be lying sated and happy in the bed next to him. Instead she had left him to a long, lonely night.

Their conversation of the previous night began to roll around in his head. What the devil had he promised to her?

'A Scottish divorce, you dolt,' he chastised himself.

He had promised Lucy her freedom. With the morning now came the question as to whether he could deliver on that promise. He gave a quick look toward the door which separated him from his wife.

She wanted to be rid of him and was prepared to sacrifice her honour to do so. He in turn was honour-bound to try to give her what she wanted. He owed her at least that much. If he failed in his endeavor to end their union, then he would deal with the outcome. He looked at the clock by the bedside. It was nearly seven o'clock. The servants of the household would not disturb them any time soon. The newlyweds would be given time to sleep.

He rolled over and climbed out of bed, quickly throwing a dressing gown on to cover his naked body. Looking at the door which separated him from his new wife, he scowled.

With luck Lucy had slept well.

'Damn,' he muttered as soon as he opened the door and saw her slumped in the chair.

She stirred and opened her eyes.

'Avery,' she whispered, the gruff of poor sleep in her voice.

He lifted her from the couch and, holding her in his arms, carried her back into the main bedroom.

As soon as her head touched the pillow, Lucy's eyes closed. It was clear she had slept little, if at all, during the long night. He threw the blankets over her still fully dressed figure, before dropping to sit beside her on the bed.

He reached out and tentatively touched her hair. Lucy, deep in exhausted slumber, did not stir. Emboldened, he stroked his hand down her cheek, stopping when his thumb reached the corner of her mouth. For a moment, he was mesmerized. Watching as sleep finally took her deeply into its arms tugged at his heart.

His breath caught as he saw Lucy roll over and grab one of his pillows. She hugged it tightly to herself. She murmured in her sleep and buried her face deep into the pillow.

He gripped the bedclothes, knowing it would take only a moment for him to lose the modesty of his dressing gown and climb into bed alongside her. From there, events would take their natural course.

Avery pulled his hand away and stood.

Promises had been made, and he would make certain to keep to his side of the undertaking. His honour dictated he behave in such a way.

His honour.

He shrugged his shoulders. What did he, Avery Fox, know of such things? He had forsaken it all at Waterloo.

Lucy rolled over on to her side, facing away from him, still clutching the pillow to her face and breast. He took this as a sign to take his leave.

He quickly found a fresh set of clothes and dressed.

Halfway down the grand staircase, it hit him. What on earth was he doing? This was supposed to be the morning after his wedding. He should still be in bed with his new bride, not wandering the halls of Strathmore House alone. If he encountered another member of the duke's family, he would have something to explain. The sound of a door being opened and closed had him racing back to the bedroom.

❧

Lucy woke in the big bed.

For a moment, she lay enjoying the warm, comfortable blankets. There was nothing better than waking up in the morning feeling rested.

From outside she could hear the noises of the street. The jingle of horse bridles. The cries of the street sellers as they turned into Upper Grosvenor Street from Park Lane.

She looked toward the window. The sounds of London life were very loud for this early in the day. She glanced at the clock on the bedside table and gasped.

It was nearly one o'clock in the afternoon. She had slept the whole morning away.

She was most of the way to the dresser when she realized where she was. Last night she had spent many hours trying to fall asleep on the small gold and blue couch in the adjoining room, yet here she was waking up in the very same bed she knew Avery had slept in.

The warm smell of his cologne still clung to the pillow and the sheets. Her new husband was, however, nowhere to be seen. She put a hand to her face; Avery's scent now lingered on her skin. It was as if he had actually been in the bed with her, had touched her.

Wherever Avery was at this moment, she very much doubted he was thinking of her. She looked down at her rumpled clothes and frowned. She was still fully dressed. She quickly changed into a suitable nightgown and tossed the blankets about in the bed before ringing the bell to summon her maid.

After a long, silent period of dressing and making up her hair, she headed downstairs. She hoped her maid had taken her reticence to talk this morning as a sign of wedding night-induced fatigue.

No-one need know the truth of last night. At least, not yet. At some point, she knew the truth would out. But by then she and Avery would have secured a divorce and he would be long gone.

'Eight, nine, ten and turn,' she said quietly to herself as she slowly made her way down to the main ground floor.

The staircase at Strathmore House traversed four levels. The first was an even ten steps, followed by a landing. The second was thirteen steps, followed by a landing and a turn. Lucy had climbed and descended these stairs all her life. Why today of all days did she finally realize that the sequence of stairs was not in symmetry? She stopped at the third landing and looked back up the stairs.

'Nothing is as it would seem,' she said.

She had just recommenced her descent to the ground floor when she spied Avery coming out of a side door into the front entrance. He looked up and caught her eye.

He gave her a nod of the head, then stood waiting as she completed her journey to the ground floor.

'Did you put me in the bed?' she asked.

'A pleasure to see you, wife,' he replied.

A reminder of their conversation was on her lips when she saw her brother David was following close behind her husband, and understood Avery's answer.

'Good afternoon Lucy, hope you slept well,' David said.

Lucy ignored the comment. She was not going to give David anything he could report back to Clarice. There was little to be served in dragging other members of her family into this miserable mess. Lady Alice's attempt to be helpful had been a failure. During the long night where she had sat and contemplated her future, she had come to the firm decision that from now on she would keep her own counsel. When the time came to leave England, it would be with a clear conscience, knowing that she was not leaving anyone behind who would be held to account.

'David informs me that your father still intends to return to Scotland later this week. Now that our wedding has taken place and Parliament has risen, he sees no need to remain in London. He expects us to travel up with the rest of the family.'

David put a brotherly hand on Avery's shoulder. 'I was just telling my new brother-in-law how much Father said he was looking forward to showing him Strathmore Castle and the hills around. Being an army man, I expect Avery will be pleased to get out and do some hunting. Pity Clarice and I won't be able to join you until Christmas.'

Scotland.

Lucy and Avery shared an uncomfortable look. How on earth were they to arrange a divorce if they were holed up with the rest of the Radley family at Strathmore Castle?

'And as I was telling your brother, you and I intend to travel to Scotland as soon as possible. Ahead of your family,' Avery said.

Lucy heard the anger on the edge of his words. If there was one thing she had already learned about Avery, it was that he did not like having his life organized and arranged for him. Her father was going to have a fight on his hands.

'I'm so sorry, Avery, it had completely slipped my mind. This week has been rather busy,' she replied. No matter what she said at that moment, she knew it would be wrong.

David laughed, but his mirth quickly died when both Lucy and Avery fixed him with a dark look.

'Why are you here?' she challenged David.

Her brother was fortunately blessed with intelligence enough to know that something was wrong and not to push the matter further.

'I was here having my weekly meeting with Papa. I just happened to encounter Avery as I was leaving,' he replied.

Lucy nodded. Mired deep in thought regarding her personal predicament, she had forgotten that the usual business of running the duchy would continue. Life for others in the Radley family was no different this morning than any other day. It was only her life which had irrevocably changed.

David made his hasty farewells, leaving Lucy and Avery alone.

'I hope you got some sleep,' Avery said.

'Yes, thank you; it was kind of you to check on me and then move me to the bed,' Lucy replied.

He stepped closer and took hold of her hand. If anyone else from Strathmore House suddenly came upon them, they would see the newlywed couple deep in conversation and give them their privacy.

'Your family cannot possibly expect that we would be travelling with them to Scotland,' he murmured.

'We would have our own carriage, but I can see your point. We should be insisting that as newlyweds we be allowed to make the journey north alone,' she replied.

She saw his spine straighten and his shoulders push back.

'Then I suggest we leave for Edinburgh immediately. I don't particularly want to spend any more time accepting well- meaning congratulations from members of your family than is necessary.'

She closed her eyes, forcing herself to hold back the tears. She had been proud of herself for not crying after they had agreed to end their short-lived marriage. She had sat for hours in the chair trying to fall asleep, reassuring herself that it was all for the better.

A single tear escaped and ran down her face. She reached up to brush it away, only to find Avery had beaten her to it. The skin of his thumb felt rough against the soft, delicate skin of her face.

'Don't cry, Lucy. I promise to find a way for you to be happy,' he said. His reassuring words tore at her heart.

'Let me speak to Papa. I shall explain that we wish to spend some time alone. We could be in Edinburgh by the end of the week if we use the Great North Road and stay at the coaching inns.'

'I shall speak to your father,' Avery replied.

❧

Later that afternoon, Lucy was seated in the private sitting room of their apartment. She looked up from her sewing as Avery entered. A quick check of the room revealed her to be alone.

He took a step toward her before checking himself. They had agreed to maintain the newlywed façade in public, but when they were alone they could be themselves.

Taking a seat on the couch opposite Lucy, Avery noted how comfortable he felt in her presence. To all intents and purposes, he should feel this way with his wife. With the woman, he was now supposed to know intimately.

Lucy put her sewing down and sat, hands clasped softly in her lap. She was waiting for his news.

'So, how did things go?' she asked.

Avery paused. Depending on one's point of view, things had gone either very well or ominously badly. The duke had agreed to the suggestion of Lucy and Avery travelling up to Scotland on their own. Unbeknown to him, divorce proceedings would be underway before the Radley family departed London.

'Your father has arranged for one of the coaches to be ready to leave first thing tomorrow,' he replied.

'So that leaves us with only this evening with my family to get through.' Lucy said.

An inexplicable look appeared on Lucy's face. He couldn't tell whether she was relieved or disappointed at the forward motion in their plans. Looking down, he noticed she was winding her wedding ring slowly around her finger once more.

'And, of course, tonight with each other.'

Her head lifted and their gazes met. He reached out and took hold of her fingers.

'You cannot spend a second night on that couch. I suggest we find a way to share the bed without things becoming too awkward.'

When they finally turned in after a long evening with her family, the solution to their bed-sharing problem quickly presented itself. Lucy picked up the padded decorative bolster which lay across the end of the bed and, turning it on its end, pushed it into the middle of the bed.

With the large bale of fabric between them, they could both sleep in the bed without running the risk of actually touching one another. Avery nodded his approval.

'I shall be back soon,' Lucy said.

When she returned a short time later clad from neck to toe in an ultra-modest, full-length linen nightgown, Avery did his best to hide his disappointment.

Chapter Twelve

They left London early the following morning, both glad to be free of friends and family. Keeping up the outward appearance of newly wedded bliss had rapidly become an exhausting endeavor.

The first day they sat in companionable silence, each with a nose stuck firmly in a book. They stopped for lunch at a town en route and enjoyed a late summer picnic by a nearby river. The Strathmore House cook had packed a small basket containing a loaf of freshly baked bread, Stilton cheese and fresh fruit for the first day's journey.

'Try this, straight from the garden at Alex and Millie's house. Our sister-in-law missed figs so much after coming here from India, Alex had two fully grown trees transplanted from Kew Gardens,' Lucy said.

She cut up a fresh fig and handed it to Avery, who ate it with undisguised relish.

To the casual observer, they appeared to be like any other young married couple. Content and blissfully happy.

They stopped at a coaching inn late afternoon and after supping in a private room downstairs, Lucy and Avery retired to their well-appointed room.

'There is only one bed,' she whispered as soon as the innkeeper had closed the door behind him and left.

Avery frowned. Apart from the rather cramped bed, there was nowhere else to sleep in the room. The fireside chair would be impossible for anyone to get a decent night's sleep in.

'A makeshift bolster will have to do,' Avery replied.

Removing his greatcoat, he picked up two pillows and wrapped it around them. After placing them lengthwise down the middle of the bed, he stepped back and admired his handiwork.

'Not the most elegant piece of engineering, I grant you, but it will serve its purpose.'

They exchanged an awkward smile.

'I shall go downstairs and leave you to get ready for bed. I take it you want the window side again?' Avery said.

As soon as he closed the door behind him, Lucy threw herself on the bed and rolled over on to her back. Staring up at the low wooden ceiling she pondered her predicament.

A few days from now she would be rid of her husband. A husband she supposedly didn't want. She shielded her eyes from the light of the bedroom candle as the first of the tears fell. A sob escaped her lips.

'Stop it, stop it you foolish girl. You have no-one to blame but yourself. Just hold yourself together until you get to Edinburgh and then all will be well.'

She rolled over and buried her face in Avery's coat. With her nose close to the collar of his greatcoat, she caught the strong scent of his amber and cedarwood perfumed oil. A wedding gift from Alex and Millie, who had specially sourced it from a perfume maker in Bond Street, its scent reminded her of Avery. He had worn the scented oil every day since their wedding.

When all this terrible mess was over, and she was living in exile in France, she would always remember his enticing scent.

When Avery finally returned to their room an hour later, he found the room dark. As he climbed into his side of the bed he felt the soft bolster. He pushed it toward Lucy, but quickly came up against her back.

Any thought of asking her to move over and give him more room was quashed when he heard her sob softly. He pulled the blankets up and lay on his back in the dark.

If only he could comfort her. To take her in his arms and tell her everything would be all right.

He had slept this close to her for only two nights, but already it was pure torture. He could name a dozen other men who would have succumbed to temptation and consummated the marriage. Enforced their legal rights, as it were.

But not you, Avery Fox; you have to give her the freedom she demands.

As he slipped into a restless slumber, a small voice in the dark recesses of his mind whispered.

'If she wants you gone so badly, then why does she cry herself to sleep?'

❧

By the end of the third day on the road, they were less than fifty miles from Edinburgh. Soon their journey together would end and their lives would take different routes. Long hours of silence in the carriage sapped Avery's energy. Small talk was certainly not his forte and it made little sense to get to know one another better. As his head hit the pillow in their bed that night, he was quickly overtaken by sleep.

In the dark of Avery's dream came a now-familiar shape. For the past two nights, it had been the same dream. There were few images in this recurring dream, rather it was sound and sensation.

Someone unseen murmured low. Feminine fingers stroked his cheeks. Soft, pliant lips would press against his mouth.

One kiss.

Two kisses.

He now hungered for the third. Her warm tongue would part his lips. Seeking, probing his mouth. He groaned.

A delighted sigh would come from her. He reveled in the knowledge that she wanted him. The teasing fingertips traced a tantalizing line down his neck and settled in the soft curls of his chest hair. He swallowed, praying that she would continue her sensual exploration of his body.

Avery reached up and speared his fingers into her hair, pulling her close. But even as he deepened the kiss, he sensed her hesitation. His dream lover's bravery only extended so far. She pushed away from his chest and her lips left his face. Disappointment swelled in his heart.

'Don't go, my love; stay and be mine forever,' he begged.

'If only,' she murmured.

When he woke the following morning, Avery instinctively touched his fingers to his lips. Had his dream lover been a figment of his imagination? In the dark of the night, she had seemed so very real.

Glancing across to the other side of the bed, he saw Lucy's form. Her back was turned away from him, and the blankets she had stolen from him during the night covered most of her head. Between them the bolster remained firmly in place.

ↄ⸱

Lucy came down into the private dining room of the inn and took a seat in the corner booth Avery had reserved for them. The few other guests at the inn were busy tucking into hearty breakfasts and making their own travel plans for the day ahead.

Avery looked up and gave her a welcoming smile. She comforted herself with the thought that he wasn't a cad who would take delight at seeing her so miserable. He had accepted that they must part and was trying to make the best of the situation. She had to be grateful for that small blessing.

His years of deprivation and hardship in the army must stand him in good stead for whatever disappointments life threw his way. She envied him his self-restraint and resolve.

'Last day today,' she ventured.

He nodded.

'You should be in Edinburgh by late this afternoon.'

Avery frowned. 'Don't you mean *we* should be in Edinburgh?'

Lucy picked up a napkin and placed it in her lap. 'I see no need for me to make the journey east. When we make the last change of horses, I shall hire a carriage to take you the rest of the way,' she replied.

Avery put down his knife and straightened his back in the chair. She could tell, from his change of posture, that he was not happy with her plans.

I beg of you, Avery, don't make me come with you to see the solicitors in Edinburgh. That would be the end of me.

'So where are you going?' he replied.

She sucked in a deep breath and attempted her best display of nonchalance. Picking up a piece of cheese, she took her knife and slowly began to slice it thinly.

'Oh, didn't I mention that I was travelling on to Strathmore Castle? I'm certain I did. No matter. The rest of my family will arrive in a few days and I shall be waiting for them.'

The slight, almost imperceptible raising of one of Avery's eyebrows gave her hope. Hope which in the early hours of the morning she'd felt had deserted her. After Avery had long fallen asleep and was snoring softly, she had risen from their bed and taken a seat on the floor by the fireplace.

Concerned with the prospect of her uncertain future, she had not been able to sleep. Looking at Avery as he slept, she pulled her knees up to her chin and pondered her predicament.

No longer was she sure of her path in life.

Of one thing, she was certain. She didn't want this to be their last day together. A divorce no longer seemed the simple solution to her moment of madness in the garden at Strathmore House.

Millie had been right. Lucy would pay a heavy price for the folly of losing her heart to a man who didn't want it. But what was she to do? If she did nothing, by the end of this day Avery would be gone from her life forever.

She imagined how difficult it would be, many years from now

when she returned to England and met with her former husband. The stain of their scandalous union would remain with her always. Only her father's name and money would allow her to find a new husband. Avery of course would need to remarry to ensure the Langham line. Perhaps his future wife would be a kindly woman who politely ignored Lucy's existence. They could move within the same circles, always ensuring that their paths never crossed.

She brushed away a single tear. Crying had become so much a part of her daily life in the past week, she barely noticed it.

Avery stirred in his sleep and rolled over on to his side. From where she sat, Lucy could see his face. The day-old stubble of his beard brought a smile to her face. He really was a handsome specimen of a man.

And for another day at least you are still mine.

Would she go back to being Lucy Radley when all this was over? Pity. She liked the sound of Lucy Fox; it had an appealing ring to it.

She imagined her mother's reaction upon discovering Lucy alone at Strathmore Castle. Lady Caroline would do everything she could to support her daughter, but staying in England would be out of the question. Emma had a number of years until she came of marriageable age, hopefully by which time Lucy's shame would have been all but forgotten by the *ton*.

She refused to consider the reaction that her father and older brothers would have to the situation once they knew. Rows and recriminations were for the future. Here and now she knew she had a choice. Meekly accept the inevitable, or do something.

Now in the cold light of morning, seated across the table from Avery, she forced herself to think about her next move. She calculated her choice of words. From the long hours in which she had sat on the hard floor, she knew exactly how the scene between them had to play out.

Her words, casually delivered, had been rehearsed. The only natural part of herself she allowed free reign was her instinct. It reminded her of all that she risked. Of the heartbreaking price of failure.

'So, you are telling me you will travel alone, across the wilds of Scotland?' he replied.

She set the knife down and met his gaze.

'I shall be perfectly fine. I have personally known the staff who are travelling with us for a number of years. There is a pleasant coaching inn a little way out of Edinburgh where I can stay. I shall keep my wedding ring on for a day or so after we part to ensure that any gentleman who does cross my path realizes I am a married woman. Or at least I was once.'

Silence reigned for a minute.

'No,' he replied, raising his voice several notches.

She lifted her head, just enough to show surprise. She looked around to see if any of the other guests had noted the sudden change in Avery's voice, but fortunately they hadn't.

'No, you will not travel by yourself, Lucy. And please don't try to convince me otherwise. I shall accompany you to the castle. When I deem the time is right, I shall take my leave.'

To Lucy's relief, one of the inn's maids brought over a fresh pot of coffee. She and Avery fell silent while the girl topped up their cups.

'Are you sure?' she ventured once the maid had left.

'Adamant,' he replied.

❧

The mood in the carriage changed.

Avery could not put a finger on what it was, but he soon noticed that Lucy had become more animated. From the moment, they took the road which led toward Falkirk, she started talking. She had said little on the long journey up from London until this morning. From the moment, he declared his intention to come to Strathmore Castle, her whole demeanor altered.

She was like a prisoner who had suddenly received word of a stay of execution. Relief showed on her face and in her manner. The notion that she had been hoping he would come to Strathmore Castle crossed his mind more than once.

He sat back in the carriage and listened intently while Lucy explained the history of the area, highlighting the famous battles which had occurred at Stirling. She seemed especially taken with William Wallace and Robert the Bruce. An English rose she might appear to be, but within her chest beat a plaid-covered heart. He chuckled softly and closed his eyes.

Late that morning they stopped at Falkirk for lunch. 'They make delicious beef pies,' she said, pointing to a nearby bakery. He followed her inside and after escorting her to a nearby table, went to order the food. While he waited, he watched her out of the corner of his eye.

Lucy did not engage in conversation with anyone in the shop as he'd expected; instead she sat calmly with her hands in her lap, head cast downward. The morning's effort at joyful conversation had apparently exhausted her.

'So, you are off to Strathmore Castle?' the lady behind the counter said.

She nodded toward the front window, where the Strathmore travel coach was waiting.

'Yes. How far is it from here?' he replied.

'You should make it by nightfall tomorrow if you can avoid the late afternoon rain. The road between here and Stirling is quite good this time of year. Not so good when winter comes, mind you.'

She placed the pies on a small tray and Avery took it over to where Lucy waited.

'These look and smell good; I'm glad you recommended this place,' he said.

'I hope they meet with your approval. This is my father's favourite place to stop for food on the journey up from London. Not being able to share a meal with my family is one of my regrets of this trip. If only . . .' Lucy replied.

Avery felt a shadow cross his heart.

If only.

He schooled his expression in an effort not to show that her words had had an effect on him. She more than likely had not been aware of what she had just said. Not realized that by uttering those very words she had confirmed his suspicions. He now knew the identity of his dream lover.

He took a bite of his pie and hummed his approval. It really was a well-made pie. A thick crispy crust covering a delicious beef and gravy stew. Little wonder the duke made a point of stopping at this establishment.

She smiled at him, obviously pleased that he found the pie to his liking. A vulnerability he had never noticed before was now reflected in her every word and movement. The strong and sure Lucy who had offered him a divorce on their wedding night was gone. Something primal within him stirred. Only a fool could fail to notice that she was making every effort to keep his favor.

If Lucy was up to something, he couldn't discern what it was. As she sipped a cup of tea, eyes lowered to avoid his gaze, he guessed she had called his bluff by stating her intention to travel to Strathmore by herself. No woman of her class would ever do such a thing, married or not.

That being the case, she must have known what his reaction would be. Now, coupled with the knowledge that she had kissed him on the lips every night as he slept, he was intrigued to see what else his wife had planned.

'So, Strathmore Castle by the end of tomorrow. I must say I am looking forward to seeing your family seat,' he ventured.

Lucy gave a tentative smile.

'Yes; some say it is better than Edinburgh Castle,' she replied.

With the change to their plans, Avery began to wonder if he would indeed be seeing Edinburgh Castle any time soon. For the time being, he was content to see where things with Lucy led.

Chapter Thirteen

Finally, at the end of the journey to Scotland, broken by short stays at friend's houses en route, the Duke of Strathmore's travelling party arrived at Strathmore Castle.

Avery and Lucy had arrived a mere two days ahead of them. Time Lucy had spent showing Avery the castle environs and introducing him to the residents.

At night, they slept in separate rooms in the private family quarters, but with the arrival of the duke and duchess, they would be back to sharing a bed and a bolster.

They stood side by side on the stone steps of the keep, waving as the Strathmore convoy of coaches came to a halt inside the bailey.

Alex helped Millie down from their private coach. She gave a loud whoop of laughter as he swung her around by the waist once they were clear from the carriage.

'I can't believe I am finally here!' Millie exclaimed.

She raced up to Lucy and threw her arms around her. A warm and heartfelt hug soon followed.

'I hope you had as lovely a trip to Scotland as we did. Alex has told me so many interesting things about the Great North Road.'

Avery cleared his throat. 'Did you try the beef pies at Falkirk?'
Millie shook her head.

'I'm from Calcutta, where it's not the done thing to eat beef. I did however enjoy a very spicy eel pie – delicious,' she replied.

The rest of the family slowly alighted from the main Strathmore family coach and made their way over to the steps. Lucy gritted her teeth and forced a happy smile to her face.

When her mother stopped, she whispered in Lucy's ear. 'When you are ready to talk, I am here to listen.'

Like all good mothers, Lady Caroline could instinctively read Lucy's mood. It didn't take words for her to know that her daughter was desperately unhappy.

As she waited for the rest of her family to make their way inside, Lucy stopped and took Avery to one side.

'I just thought you had better know that from tonight we are sharing my old chamber in the castle. Unfortunately, for such a large place it is rather poorly set out for space. My chamber is small, to say the least, and so is the bed.'

'I see,' he replied.

❦

Later that evening, Avery stood outside watching the large bonfires which had been lit in several giant fire pits in the center of the castle bailey. The smell of the burning wood and sting of smoke in his eyes brought back memories of his years living rough. Around the various fires, the estate staff and Radley family members gathered and shared welcome greetings.

The chill of the night air did not appear to bother anyone, apart from him. Most of the men, including the duke, were wearing kilts. Avery shivered. Within minutes of arriving outside, he was freezing. Unwelcome memories of the mountains of Portugal flooded back into his mind.

As he buttoned his coat up and wrapped his scarf around his neck, he was glad he'd refused the offer to wear one of Alex's spare kilts. He hoped the duke would not take it as a personal slight.

'It's a tradition on our first night back at the castle for the staff to build this fire. It's a way of them welcoming home the Radley family. It's been a tradition at the castle for several hundred years. To be truthful, I think it is the one thing Papa looks forward to the most when we return home,' Lucy said coming to stand beside him.

He looked at her. The glow of the fire reflected in her face.

She looked over his shoulder and gave an approving nod. Avery turned to see a young man, not much past his early twenties, standing cap in hand several feet away.

'Come forward, James; Mr. Fox will be happy to speak with you,' Lucy said.

James stepped forward and stood in front of Avery. He gave a short, respectful bow which made Avery feel decidedly uncomfortable. He was no lord of the manor; people should not bow to him.

'Lieutenant Fox, sir. I just want to thank you for everything your men did for us on the day of the battle,' the young man said.

Avery swallowed. In young James' eyes he saw the haunted look of one who had seen war. Not just from afar, but the worst of the bloody skirmishes up close.

'And what regiment did you fight with?' Avery replied. He straightened his spine, surprised by his own eagerness to show that he was truly interested to hear the young man's words. The fact that he was more than likely only a few years older than James counted for little; it was the respect in which he was held that truly mattered.

'The Scots Greys, sir,' James replied, the pride of his regiment evident in his voice.

Avery nodded. The Scots Greys were a fearsome group, battle-hardened and reliable. It was their famous charge that had pushed the French columns back.

'You were in reserve for most of the day, from what I can recall. But came through when the ninety-third Highlanders were struggling to hold their ground.'

'Yes, Lieutenant Fox, but my unit got separated from the main charge. We were stuck in an awful position for most of the early afternoon. Bonnie's troops were a tough nut to crack. Every time we thought we had made headway, they pushed us back. We couldn't make it through to the main British cavalry. By late afternoon, just before the ninety-fifth arrived, we were giving ground with every minute. If it hadn't been for you and your men I surely would not be standing here today.'

Avery felt the lightest touch of Lucy's hand on his arm. He looked to one side of James and saw an older man, clearly James' father, standing next to his son. His eyes brimmed with tears.

'James is Mister McPherson's only son. As soon as they discovered who you were they asked that they be allowed to come and thank you properly,' she whispered softly.

The earnest looks in both men's eyes left Avery with little option but to gracefully accept their heartfelt gratitude. He reassured them that he would drop by the blacksmith's workshop at the first opportunity and share some more stories of Waterloo with them both.

As the blacksmith and his son walked away, Avery turned to Lucy.

'You should not go telling the castle staff that I am some kind of war hero.'

She frowned. 'I didn't. But why not? Major Barrett said you acquitted yourself with great valor.'

'Major Barrett was not with us for the last part of the battle, so he does not know what I did. Trust me, Lucy, I am no war hero. I just happened to be on the battlefield that day. That is all.'

She turned away, but Avery could see the tears which were running down her face. If there was one thing he could be certain of, it was his ability to make her cry. He reached out and took her gently by the arm.

'I'm sorry, I should not have been so harsh with you. I was just taken aback by the sudden declaration of gratitude from McPherson and his son. I didn't mean to make you cry.'

Lucy shook her head.

'It's all right; crying is something which seems to come naturally to me at present, much like breathing. James and his father have worked and lived at the castle for as long as I can remember.

The day that James returned from war unscathed, a huge celebration was held here in the bailey. Papa even allowed the villagers to hunt down two large wild boars on the mountain and have them roasted out here to celebrate.'

Avery listened to her words; they made uncomfortable sense to him. If Lucy had not made mention of his war record, then who had? He needed to know.

'You said it wasn't you who mentioned my war record to the staff. May I ask as to who did?'

She pointed toward her brother Stephen.

'He has taken quite a shine to you. He thinks you are a younger Wellington. As soon as my family arrived he was telling everyone what an amazing man he has as a new brother. You will have to excuse his hero worship, but you are the first man he has met who served directly during the war. Some of our other cousins worked in different capacities at the War Office, but to Stephen's mind it's not the same. He is young and impressionable.'

Avery's heart sank.

While Lucy and he had come to an understanding, Avery doubted Lord Stephen would be so forgiving when his hero suddenly disappeared from the Radley family circle.

'I shall talk to him. Put him straight. It would be wrong for him to form the wrong belief of the situation,' she added.

When the welcome gathering finally ended in the early hours of the morning, Lucy led Avery up the inner staircase of the keep to their new room. As soon as they stepped over the threshold, she hurriedly closed the door and locked it.

When Avery looked at the rest of the small chamber he saw why. The bed was positively medieval in its proportions. Sleeping in the same bed meant they would struggle to fit a bolster between them and sleep comfortably.

'I'm sorry; this is normally my room alone. Alex was adamant that he and Millie take the other private apartment. As heir to the title, it is his right. We shall have to make do with this one until the time comes that you leave.'

Avery shrugged off his coat. After a tiring evening, he was too exhausted to care. His mind ached for the relief of sleep. A dark mood had lowered down upon him as soon as the McPhersons offered him their heartfelt gratitude. He felt like a fraud in front of these people.

In his hometown, the McPhersons *were* his kind of people, not the likes of the privileged Radley family. Kind and friendly though Lucy's family were, he was not one of them.

He wasn't angry with Lucy, nor even with Lord Stephen. As always, when it came to the events of the day at Waterloo, he was angry with only one person. Himself.

In the two years, he had spent at Rokewood Park, the unspoken code was that no-one mentioned what had happened that day. Any mention of heroic deeds or valor was quickly quashed. Blood and death were too real to wrap up in the poetry of bravery and valor.

No-one wanted to talk about war. Least of all Avery Fox.

'Lucy,' he ventured.

'Yes.'

'I am sorry I upset you at the gathering tonight; it was not my intention. My only excuse, and it is a poor one, is that I am tired from the matter of our divorce, which constantly occupies my mind. Now that your family are here, we may be able to bring things to a timely conclusion.'

She gave him a small, forgiving smile, before seating herself in front of the dressing mirror. Avery sat down on the edge of the small bed, silently watching as Lucy began to pull the pins from her hair.

'I could help if you like,' he offered.

She looked at him from the reflection in the mirror and shook her head. Of course, she was right to refuse his assistance. They were married in name only; to allow any sort of intimacy would only cause further discomfort.

And yet as he slipped beneath the waves of sleep a short time later, he felt the all-too-familiar touch of gentle, feminine fingers on his face. Lucy's soft breath filled his lungs as her lips locked tenderly with his.

Now that he knew his phantom lover was real; that it was Lucy who gave him deep sensual kisses each night, he knew he should put a stop to it.

But as he speared his fingers through her hair and drew her down to deepen the kiss, nothing could stop him. He brushed his fingers over her breast. Touching her nipple, he gave it a gentle squeeze.

She stopped.

He slowed his breathing and kept his eyes gently closed, determined to maintain the illusion of being sound asleep.

'Avery,' she whispered.

He didn't stir.

Silence hung in the room for a moment. Sensing she was looking for any sign that he was awake, Avery made a point of mumbling in his sleep. He added a gruff snort for effect.

Her warm lips met his once more and their tongues tangled in a slow, enticing game of tease. For all that he was tempted to touch her breasts once more, Avery dared not risk it. He kept his hands firmly by his sides, while his brain screamed for her to continue.

When Lucy unbuttoned the top button of his nightshirt, Avery's breathing became ragged. She kissed the hairs at the top of his chest, gently humming with every kiss.

His body began to harden. If Lucy continued with her ministrations she would soon feel the extent of his burgeoning arousal. She would know he was awake.

With great reluctance, he brought proceedings to a halt. Yawning loudly, he stirred in his feigned slumber. Lucy pulled away and clambered back to her side of the bed. Avery turned over on to his side and faced away from her.

In the dark, he lay staring at the solid stone wall of the bedroom. The inner keep of the castle had few modern concessions, something which the inhabitants seemed to like. As he pulled the blankets up around his shoulders, Avery was left with one question as to Lucy's behavior.

Why?

Chapter Fourteen

I f Avery had intended to avoid the rest of the Radley family while he waited for an opportune moment to leave for Edinburgh, he was sadly mistaken.

While his own experience of family life had been a seemingly never-ending round of rows and beatings, the Radley family were an entirely different proposition. They were a sociable, amiable group of people who liked to spend time in one another's company. Coupled with the hero status which both Lord Stephen and now Lady Emma appeared to have bestowed upon him, Avery found himself constantly surrounded by family members.

The only person who seemed to make a concerted effort to avoid him was Lucy. At least during the day. When he woke most days, she would be dressed and gone from their room. At breakfast, she would sit quietly beside him and concentrate her attention fully on her toast and coffee. She made little effort at conversation. Avery felt it best to leave her alone and not press matters in front of her family.

What they would make of the situation when he suddenly up and left for Edinburgh filled him with dread. What sort of cad abandoned the beautiful daughter of a duke on their honeymoon?

One morning, as Lucy sat idly stirring a spoonful of sugar into her breakfast coffee, the quiet was broken by the arrival of the Duke of Strathmore, carrying a hunting rifle.

Out of the corner of his eye, Avery saw the Duchess of Strathmore give her husband a disapproving look. It was obvious Lady Caroline did not take kindly to guns at the breakfast table.

'Ah, Avery, glad to see you are up. I was thinking of heading up the valley this morning and seeing if we can bag a deer or two. Alex and Stephen are forming two legs of the hunt, we just need a fourth. Since David is not here, I thought you might like to tag along.'

Avery looked at the rifle slung over the duke's arm. It was a good solid piece, nice workmanship, but he doubted it was as accurate as his own trusty Baker rifle. He had brought all his possessions to Scotland with him, so the rifle currently resided in his partly unpacked travel trunk in the bedroom he shared with Lucy.

He was torn. He hadn't hunted since he was injured. With his damaged left hand, he wasn't sure he could handle a rifle properly.

'I'm not certain as to how much use I would be; I haven't fired a rifle since I got this,' he replied holding up his gloved left hand.

The duke gave a cursory nod of his head.

'Well, if you want to find out if you can still manage to fire off a decent shot, now is the time,' Lord Strathmore replied.

Avery looked around the table, and then finally at Lucy.

'Go on, it will do you good to get out of the castle for a few hours,' she said.

An hour later and Avery was standing, rifle in hand, in a wooded area of Strathmore Valley. The simple act of removing his rifle from his travel trunk and unwrapping it had been more difficult than he had anticipated.

Seated on the bed, he felt his heart pounding in his chest. The last time he had actually looked at his rifle was the afternoon of the battle. His mouth went dry. Nerves threatened to get the better of him.

'Pull yourself together, man, it's only a bloody deer,' he muttered angrily to himself.

As he followed the rest of the hunting party up the valley and into the woods, he kept repeating the same mantra over and over again.

You can do this. You were a soldier; soldiers don't fear death.

He stopped for a moment and tried to catch his breath. The year or so of recovery from his wounds and recent soft town living had left him short on stamina. The Avery Fox of old would be disgusted in the physical condition he now found himself in. In his army years, he would have run without pause to the top of the valley and sprinted back down just for fun. Now he stood gasping as he struggled to suck air into his lungs.

Forcing himself to a slow trot, he finally caught up with the rest of the hunters.

They were standing at the edge of a small clearing, the perfect spot to lie in wait for quarry. It wasn't long before the first deer showed. A young doe, only two or three years old, came into view.

Lord Stephen hissed 'Yes!' and raised his rifle. The duke put out an arm and gently lowered it.

'You know better than that, lad,' he rebuked the boy.

Stephen uncocked his rifle and pointed it to the ground.

'Yes, your grace, sorry your grace,' he replied.

Avery noted, not for the first time, the firm but fair way in which the duke dealt with his sons. The doe would soon be a breeding one; her fawns would carry on the future of the herd. If Lord Stephen went ahead and killed her, a valuable bloodline would be lost.

'I think you should stick to grouse today if we come across any,' the duke said.

A look of disappointment crossed Stephen's face, which was swiftly replaced with a huge smile when he saw Avery. He took one look at Avery's rifle and exclaimed. 'Oooh! Is that a real army rifle? Did you kill anyone with it?'

The duke and Avery exchanged a look of silent understanding. There would be no encouragement of Stephen's youthful fervor for battle glory. Avery had learnt over the years that it didn't pay to encourage young men to take a fancy to the weapons of death.

Stephen was not much older than Avery had been when he ran away from home and joined the army. Looking at the bright, hope-filled face of his fourteen-year-old brother-in-law, Avery wondered how on earth he had managed to lie his own way into the army at the tender age of thirteen.

Because with all that you had been through, you had long ago lost your look of innocence.

Reflected in the scars and lines on his face had been the signs of his childhood years of fighting, stealing and grafting merely to survive.

'Is that a Baker rifle?'

Avery nodded.

Stephen stepped closer and reached to touch the barrel. His fingers stroked the brass front sight with knowledgeable reverence.

'This really is an army-issued weapon, just like in the books. But it's been modified. The barrel has been heated and bent.' He frowned. 'Where is the bayonet?'

Caught off guard, Avery sucked in a deep breath. Stephen Radley was a well-read young man. But books and pictures were one thing. How could he possibly tell the impressionable boy that he had left the 24-inch bayonet of his rifle stuck in the chest of a young man on the battlefield in Belgium?

That his last, lingering memory of the bayonet was the blood which oozed along its blade as he heard the young French soldier breathe his last painful breath.

'They took them from us when we returned to England, for safe-keeping,' he lied.

The duke and Alex said nothing to challenge his story.

'Can you still fire a rifle?' Stephen pressed him further.

'Come now Stephen, leave Avery alone. You tire him with your childish notions. We are here to hunt deer, not discuss the war,' Alex said.

Stephen scowled at his brother's rebuke.

'I was only asking,' he replied.

Avery gave Alex a brief nod of thanks. Truth be told, he wasn't sure if he could handle the Baker. There was the palpable fear that his nerve would fail.

There is only one way to find out.

'I'm not sure Stephen, but I shall give it my best try,' he replied.

With the rifle on its leather strap slung over his shoulder, he followed the duke and his sons further up the steep hill. At the top was another small wooded area.

Alex stopped and held up a hand.

'There is a large old hart just the other side of the ridge. He must be a good ten seasons old.'

The duke came and stood beside him, studying the hart in question. Finally, when satisfied that it was an old beast, past its prime, he gave his consent for the hunt to begin.

'You take the right flank, Alex and Stephen; Avery and I will take the left. We are still downwind of him, so he shouldn't catch our scent.'

Avery stopped and fitted a shot to his rifle. In times past, he had been able to get a good three shots off in a minute. Now he doubted he would be able to reload in under two.

When his forefinger and thumb slipped, jamming against the trigger, he swore.

Lord Strathmore gave a low whistle, signaling his sons to stop their progress up the hill.

'Sorry, it's been a while since I used this,' Avery said. So much for the career marksman he had once been.

'Take your time; the hart is still grazing. Do you want some help?'

Avery shook his head, determined to do the job which had been second nature to him for nearly half his life. Finally, he got the rifle loaded and made his way up the hill.

The hart was old and grey. It had clearly seen many a winter. One antler was broken off, no doubt from fighting with other, stronger males.

'Your shot, Fox,' Alex said, lowering his rifle.

'What do you do with the carcass when you finish the kill?' Avery asked.

'Take it back to the castle. The meat will be roasted up for supper in a few days, once it has been allowed to hang. The rest of it will be given to the castle staff to divide up among the villagers. Someone usually takes the antlers and sells them. This is Scotland; nothing is ever left to go to waste,' Lord Strathmore replied.

As long as it wasn't a senseless kill, Avery could reconcile himself to the hunt. He had hunted enough deer in the mountains of Portugal, during the long campaign against Bonaparte's troops. At times, the only thing which had stood between the men of his company and starvation rations was bitter, fire-burnt venison.

He raised his rifle with his right hand and brought it to rest between the thumb and forefinger of his left hand.

The deer lifted its head and sniffed the air; something had roused its awareness. The members of the hunting party stood perfectly still.

As he had done many times before, he allowed his breathing to slow. Having been a sniper in his army days and therefore distant from the heat of battle, he was used to taking his time to compose his shot. Bullets were never wasted. He set his cheek against the rifle, smelling the oil for the first time in what felt like forever. Closing his right eye, he settled the gaze of his left into the gun sight. Gently lifting the rifle another quarter inch, he aimed straight at the deer's heart.

A shot rang out and the beast dropped to its knees. A quick and painless kill.

'Huzzah!' Lord Stephen cried, and raced up the hill to where the deer lay.

Avery stood rooted to the spot, staring at his lowered rifle. He had taken a life.

It shook him to his core.

His close brush with death had robbed him of his detached interest. Even at this distance, he could hear the slowing of the deer's heart as its life slowly ebbed away. He swayed, unsteady on his feet.

Lord Strathmore came to his side and lay a hand on his shoulder.

'The servants will bag and carry the carcass back to the castle. You don't have to go and check on the kill.'

Avery looked at Lucy's father as he felt the first wave of nausea wash over him. He sucked in a deep breath, steeling himself to go and look. It was only an animal, not a human he had just shot. What must the others think of him? So much for the battle-hardened warrior.

'I will be fine; let's go,' Avery replied. He steeled himself to face the inevitable sight of blood.

He made it halfway up the hill before he had to stop. Dropping to his knees as his stomach lurched, he could go no further.

He waved the others on, desiring privacy as he emptied the contents of his stomach on to a nearby green tussock.

When finally, he finished retching, Avery sat back on his haunches. He wiped the tears of humiliation away from his eyes.

'Some bloody war hero,' he muttered.

&

Back at the castle he sought refuge in his room. He was too embarrassed to remain out in the bailey with the rest of the hunting party. From the bedroom window, he could hear the loud whoops and cheers as the staff brought the trophy of the hunt back into the castle.

He went to the small wooden table which held his personal toiletries. Taking a cloth, he soaked it in the cool water of a washbowl and washed his face. Standing facing himself in the mirror, he took in the red of his bloodshot eyes.

The bedroom door opened and Lucy stepped inside, carrying a small cloth bundle. She locked the door behind her and put the bundle down on the bed.

She came to his side.

'How did the hunt go?' she enquired.

He shook his head. Word of his performance during the hunt must have reached her ears.

'I feel about as good as I look, if that is any indication. I cannot believe I embarrassed myself in such a way in front of your father and brothers. What must they think of me?' he replied.

She brushed a hand on his arm, something he had noticed she did more of lately. Just the occasional small touch, but he found it unsettling.

Lucy's tender exhibition of affection would make telling her of the decision he had made on the way back to the castle all the more difficult.

He hated himself.

'From what I hear you handled the rifle well and made the kill clean. That you didn't go up and look at the dead hart really doesn't matter,' she replied.

He scowled at his reflection in the mirror.

'What about my rather unmanly display; what did they say about that?'

She reached up and touched his cheek.

'I don't know what you mean. No-one made mention of anything else. To be truthful they were rather impressed with your one-shot kill. Even my father is not that accurate with a rifle, and his was made by the King's private rifle maker.

'Yours is an army standard-issue rifle, which has been wrapped up in a blanket at the bottom of your travel bag for a long time. Considering how much it has probably been bashed about over the past few years, I'm surprised the sights were still set true. Perhaps it's because your skills as a marksman outweigh any impediment your rifle may have,' she replied.

He looked at her, astounded once more by her knowledge of all manner of things unladylike. How did his wife know about gun sights and how much they got knocked about?

'I was physically ill on the mountainside. I couldn't face going to see the kill. I've become what I've always hated and feared. A coward,' he replied.

She shrugged her shoulders. 'I expect it was a sudden recollection of being wounded. Your mind may have played a cruel trick on you. Nothing more,' she said.

He stepped away from her. Being in such proximity made his heart race.

'I shall speak to your father later this afternoon and ask that he allow me the use of a carriage. I think it is time I left for Edinburgh.'

Lucy swayed on her feet, rocked by his words. If there was a way that Avery could have felt more of a blackguard at that moment he didn't know how. A kinder man, a better man, would have taken her in his arms and comforted her. Told her that in time she would be all right. But Avery knew that if he so much as touched his wife, his resolve to leave would turn to ashes.

'Oh,' she murmured weakly.

'I told you I would see you safely to your father's castle and then I would be on my way. We agreed to this, remember? It's what you want.'

Lucy closed her eyes and nodded.

'Yes of course; my apologies. It was just a bit of shock to hear you were leaving so soon.'

She crossed to the bed and picked up the small bundle of cloth, offering it to him.

'What is it?' he said.

'A shirt. I began making it for you yesterday. It's a little plain. I thought I would have time to put some fancy work on the cuffs, but it is still serviceable.'

She forced it gently into his hands and stepped back.

If Avery had felt bad on the mountain earlier that morning, he now felt like wretched death. While he had been contemplating leaving his wife, she was busy making him a shirt.

'You needn't have done this, Lucy. Considering the circumstances of our marriage, I would never ask such a thing of you.'

'Consider it payment for escorting me here,' she said. She lowered her gaze and once more began to fiddle with her wedding ring.

He wondered how much longer she would continue to wear it. Once her family discovered the truth of their arrangement, he had little doubt that her parents would demand she remove the offending item from her person.

He sighed. What did they say about taking foul-tasting medicine? It was better to get it down in one swallow.

'Considering the fact that I am leaving for Edinburgh at first light, I shall enquire as to other more suitable lodgings for myself for tonight. I don't think it fair to you that we should have to share a bed for our last night.'

Lucy didn't acknowledge Avery's words. She simply went to the door, opened it and closed it behind her as she left.

Avery looked at the beautifully hand-stitched shirt. He had never been given such a personal gift before and now that he was leaving his marriage, he doubted he would ever receive such a thing again.

'Bloody hell,' he muttered.

Long after Lucy had gone, Avery stood staring out the small window of the bedroom, watching as the grey clouds rolled in from over the top of Strathmore Mountain. By late afternoon the top of the mountain would once more be hidden by rain clouds.

An honorable man would pack a bag and walk to the nearby village, taking whatever punishment, the heavens meted out. A better man would know to avoid the inevitable goodbyes with the Radley family.

Avery wished he was that man.

༄

Rugged up against the bitter cold of night, Lucy sat in her favourite spot up in the castle ramparts. It was almost a family tradition: when one of them was struggling with a problem they would seek the chill winds at the top of the castle to clear their minds.

Tucked away from the full onslaught of the wind, she sat down on the hard stone and pulled her knees up to her chest. With a thick woolen scarf wrapped around her head and neck, she was as comfortable as the Scottish autumn would allow.

She pulled out the oat cake she had begged from the kitchen and took a bite. Food, the great comfort-giver. If only she had remembered to bring her whisky flask up here with her.

After leaving Avery earlier that afternoon, she had wandered the outer areas of the castle grounds, taking great care to avoid any members of her family. The few servants she encountered gave her a respectful nod of the head but otherwise left her alone.

When the rain began, she made her way up to her favourite hiding place and sought refuge.

The door to the ramparts opened and closed. She prayed whoever it was wouldn't linger too long. The sound of footsteps on the walkway signaled that she was about to have company. So much for a moment of privacy.

'Lucy?'

Her mother's voice loomed out of the dark.

'Over here, Mama,' Lucy replied.

As expected, her non- appearance at the family evening supper had not gone unnoticed. She looked up and saw Lady Caroline standing, brow furrowed, with a small lamp in her hand.

'You shouldn't come up here in the dark, my darling; the steps are too dangerous. Are you alone?'

Lucy nodded.

'May I join you?' her mother asked.

Lucy shifted along in the little weather-protected nook and made space for her mother. Lady Caroline sat down.

'When I saw that you and Avery were not at supper, I thought you might have been spending some time together. Your father has just informed me that Avery is leaving for Edinburgh tomorrow, which seems rather odd.'

'He is going to see about securing a divorce; he won't be coming back,' Lucy replied. She screwed her eyes shut and dropped her head.

Lady Caroline sighed and put an arm around Lucy's shoulder.

'My poor girl. I knew I should have pressed you further the day we arrived, but I had hoped things would improve.'

'On our wedding night, I offered him a Scottish divorce. It's why we came up to Scotland ahead of the family,' Lucy replied.

'Why on earth would you do such a thing?' her mother replied.

'Because he hates me. He blames me for this forced marriage.'

The duchess fell silent. She took hold of Lucy's hand and gave it a gentle squeeze.

'You cannot consider a divorce; they are nigh-on impossible to secure,' she replied.

'Aunt Maude secured one in Edinburgh, so I reasoned we could.'

In the pale light of the lamp, a look of pained realization appeared on Lady Caroline's face.

'Oh, my sweet child. I don't know who told you that pack of lies, but I can assure you that your aunt and uncle were still very much legally married when he died,' she replied.

Lucy scowled. All she had heard from her great Aunt Maude was how she had gone off to Scotland and been rid of her odious husband. How she was now free to play the field and find a young and handsome lover.

'But?'

'But nothing. Your aunt told a great many tales when she left your uncle, very few of them true. The reality of the situation is that a Scottish divorce is as difficult as an English one to secure. While you may be able to get some form of annulment here in Scotland there is always the question of legitimacy of any children from subsequent marriages. English law might not even recognize the divorce. And of course, an English divorce would take years if you were even able to get one.'

Even if Avery did leave for Edinburgh and try to be rid of her, he would likely fail. Lucy looked at her mother and for the briefest of moments hope flared in her heart.

And then it died.

When Avery discovered the truth, that he would never be fully rid of his wife, he would hate her even more. Without legitimate heirs, the Langham title would die out and return to the crown. Her sister-in-law Clarice would never forgive Lucy for destroying her family's heritage and bloodline.

'You must talk him out of such a foolish notion,' the duchess added.

Hot tears rolled down Lucy's cheeks. If she had thought she was done with crying her heart out over Avery, she was wrong.

'I don't know what to do. I know he doesn't want me. He hasn't even made me a proper wife. We sleep each night with our backs turned to one another,' she whispered. The pain and humiliation of still being an innocent after many days of marriage threatened to overwhelm her.

Lucy buried her face in her mother's cloak and let the tears flow freely.

'You fell in love with him, only to have to let him go,' Lady Caroline sighed.

The price of her stubborn heart would be to lose the one man she thought she could love. With Avery gone and the disgrace of a failed marriage, Lucy would be damaged irreparably in the eyes of London society.

'I've tried to reach out to him, but every time he retreats away from me. Truth is, I am powerless to stop him from leaving. I told him I wanted a divorce and he has promised to give me one,' she said.

She pulled away from her mother and wiped her tears on her sleeve. With every heartbeat, the moment that Avery would be gone from her life drew closer.

Lady Caroline put a finger under Lucy's chin and lifted her head until their gazes met.

'You have to tell me here and now what do you want. I can try and help you, but you have to be certain of the outcome you desire. This is not child's play; this is a very serious situation and the decision you make tonight will have lasting repercussions for everyone,' she said.

The pain of hearing Avery inform her he was leaving burned fiercely in Lucy's heart. While he remained at the castle some hope still existed for her to find a way out of this unholy mess. If she let him go tomorrow without a fight, she would never forgive herself.

'I want my husband to want me as his wife. I want the same happy ending that Alex and David have found with their marriages. I want to be loved,' Lucy replied.

'And are you prepared to fight for it?'

Lucy nodded, her resolution only tempered by the fact that Avery would be leaving the castle at first light.

'What can I do? He will be gone tomorrow.'

A hopeful smile appeared on her mother's face.

'There is only one travel coach at the castle at the moment in working order. Your father had the family coach stripped down for repainting as soon as we arrived. It is in pieces in the blacksmith's workshop. If you don't want Avery leaving tomorrow, I can make sure the other carriage is suddenly unavailable.'

'Then what?'

'Then you will have to do what you should have done as soon as you realized you were in love with him. You can't keep dashing yourself against him, hoping it will make him love you. It will only push him further away and you'll destroy yourself in the process,' her mother said.

'What can I do?'

'Well, to quote a good old Scottish saying, you don't catch fish by throwing rocks. You need to bait your hook and lure them. First things first: you need to make Avery want to stay.'

Lady Caroline got to her feet and offered her daughter a helping hand.

'Sitting up here lamenting your situation will not do you or anyone else any good. Now come downstairs; we have a lot of work to do before this night is over.'

147

Chapter Fifteen

'Good morning, Lady Emma,' Avery said as he spied his sister-in-law in the hallway the following day.

With his departure imminent, now seemed as good a time as any to begin to make his farewells. He wasn't proud of himself for having deliberately missed supper last night and the family breakfast, but he couldn't face the Radley family as a group.

'Good morning, Mr. Fox,' she replied.

He frowned.

'When did I stop being Avery and become Mr. Fox?' he replied, perplexed.

Emma shook her head.

'You make my Lucy cry. I thought you were part of our family, and in our family, we don't make each other cry. She's sad because of you. I don't think I like you any more, Mr. Fox; you are horrid just like your dead brother.'

She began to cry. 'Why can't you love Lucy? She is the most wonderful sister and it hurts my heart to see her so sad.'

Out of the mouths of babes.

Emma turned and began to walk away. Avery quickly caught up with her and took her gently by the arm.

'I'm sorry I made you and Lucy cry, but it will all be better very soon. I promise,' he said.

Even as he spoke the words, he knew they were a lie. His leaving would only cause upheaval in everyone's lives. As he'd lain awake in his bed the previous night, he had faced the truth of what he and Lucy had agreed.

As a single man, he could easily return to London and not have to deal with having a wife. He could go back to his old life.

His old, lonely life.

As he watched Emma walk away, he considered her words. They didn't make sense.

Lucy had been the one who offered him a way out of their marriage. She had been the one who tried to drug him on their wedding night. She had proposed they seek a divorce in Scotland. Why then was she the one in tears?

More importantly, where the devil had she gone? He hadn't seen Lucy since she left their room the previous day. He'd overheard the servants and knew she had not attended supper the previous night. Upon returning to their room earlier that morning, having spent the night on a couch in the castle library, he saw the pristine state of the bedclothes. Lucy had not slept in their bed.

It was as if his wife had simply vanished from the face of the earth.

He continued out into the castle bailey. Alex was often out in the yard at this time of day and perhaps by speaking to him, he would get a clearer picture as to Lucy's whereabouts.

Apart from a few castle staff, the bailey was empty. No horses and no carriages were to be found.

He sought out the head stableman.

'Where is the coach? I was supposed to be leaving for Edinburgh this morning,' he asked.

The stable master scratched his wiry grey beard.

'Aye, that was my understanding too last night, Mr. Fox, but Lord Brooke made other plans this morning. He and Lady Brooke have taken the only available carriage to see where the Battle of Stirling took place. They won't be back for at least a day or so. You may wish to speak with His Grace if you want to arrange alternative transport.'

Something sparked in Avery's brain. He wasn't certain what it was, but he didn't like it.

Last night he had made firm plans with the duke for him to use the carriage to go to Edinburgh. He had been as vague as possible as to the reason why he needed to visit a city to which he had no real link, making mention of an old army comrade he wished to see. Lord Strathmore had agreed, but Avery could tell he didn't believe his story.

Had Lucy told her parents the real reason for his departure? The notion that he had been put firmly in his place had him clenching his fists.

'Very good, I shall discuss my travel arrangements with Lord Strathmore,' he replied.

The man shook his head.

'His Grace rode out an hour or so ago to visit one of the other villages. He will be spending most of the day talking to tenants, which means he won't be back much before supper.'

Avery turned on his heel and marched angrily back into the castle keep.

'Bloody ridiculous, what on earth do they think they are playing at?' he muttered under his breath.

He stormed along the hallway, headed for his room. He still had his travel bag in his trunk. If need be, he would pack what he could into the bag and walk to the nearby village. He would send for the rest of his things at a later date.

As he passed the doorway to Lady Caroline's sitting room, he saw it was open. Seated at her writing desk, the duchess was penning a letter.

He stopped and gathered his temper before knocking on the door.

'Avery, do come in,' Lady Caroline said, as she lifted her head and saw him.

He closed the door behind him at her instruction.

'Take a seat,' she offered.

'Thank you, no; I would rather stand,' he replied.

She came and took hold of his hand.

'Sit, please,' she implored.

He sighed with frustration, but did as she asked.

'Forgive my decided lack of manners this morning, Your Grace, but I have just come from outside and I understand that I am not able to leave the castle today. I also understand that Lucy has disappeared.'

Lady Caroline nodded.

'I don't expect it was quite the morning you had planned,' she replied.

'No.'

'Then I must ask your forgiveness. The lack of carriage and the change in Lucy's whereabouts are down to me.'

He bristled with barely concealed rage. Years of war had bred in him a deep-seated mistrust of arbitrary decisions made by others. They tended to have a detrimental effect on the lives of simple soldiers. Too many friends had died because of orders given by those far from the dangers of the battlefront.

'Lucy has gone up to the hunting lodge at the Key to lick her wounds.'

'What?'

Lady Caroline shifted in her seat.

'Whatever story you told my husband for your sudden, pressing need to visit Edinburgh I know to be a lie. Lucy told me the whole truth last night. You have humiliated my daughter, torn her heart out, and now you expect to just up and leave when you see fit. As far as I am concerned, Mr. Fox you can walk to the village, take a room at the inn and wait for a cart to take you to Edinburgh. I won't lift a finger to help you abandon your wife.'

The emotional punch he felt at Lady Caroline's words pushed Avery back hard in his chair.

What had Lucy told her mother?

'I think you have the wrong of it, Your Grace; your daughter wants me gone,' he stammered.

Lady Caroline arched a brow. 'Really? Well, if that is the impression she has given you, then she is a good enough actress to be on the stage. From where I sit, the pair of you are stubbornly refusing to see the reality of your relationship. You are both fools; and unfortunately, you are likely to reap a fool's reward if you continue on this path.'

She stood up and fixed him with her gaze.

'I do hope that you will come to your senses before it is too late. Close the door after you.'

Avery returned to his room, and pulled his old travel bag out from his trunk. He roughly stuffed clothes and as many personal items as he could fit into it before tossing it on to the bed. A mixture of rage and shame coursed through his veins. The last time he had been so summarily dismissed by someone, he had been a wet-behind-the-ears private.

'Sod the lot of you,' he muttered angrily.

He snatched up the bag and marched out of the room. If the Radleys wanted him gone, then he would walk to the village. By god, he would walk to Edinburgh if it came to it!

He crossed the enormous wooden drawbridge of the castle and headed down the hill. There was no one left in the castle to whom he wished to say goodbye.

In his pocket jangled the few coins he owned. He would need to get employment in Edinburgh before he had enough money to get back to London.

Rounding a bend in the road, he saw a cart approaching up the hill. He fixed his gaze to one side of the cart, intent on ignoring the driver. He failed to take into account the inquisitive and friendly nature of the locals.

'Morning Mr. Fox, I meant to catch you at the castle,' the driver said, tipping his hat. He reigned in the horse, and the cart came to a gentle halt.

Avery looked at the man and his heart sank. Of all the people in the castle he wished to elude this morning, it was the grateful sire of James McPherson, but there was no avoiding the man.

'Are you climbing up?' McPherson said.

'No, I am headed the other way,' Avery replied and kept walking.

McPherson chuckled. 'Then you are going the wrong way. The Key is further up the mountain.'

Avery stopped.

The Key. Lucy was at the Key.

A small voice whispered in his mind. 'Don't be a fool, man. Turn around.'

'Come on,' McPherson said, holding out his hand as Avery reached the cart.

Avery looked at his bag. What would a few more days in Scotland matter? At least he would have a chance to understand why Lucy had been so upset. Hadn't he given her exactly what she wanted?

He tossed his bag up onto the back. Then with a quick jump he got a foothold on the step. He dropped down beside McPherson, finding himself inexplicably smiling as he did.

They passed the castle and headed up a steep road which trailed to one side of Strathmore Mountain. McPherson whistled a jolly tune to himself. Once they were clear of the castle, Avery's mood lightened. Looking over his shoulder, he saw several large baskets sitting in the back of the cart.

'What's in those?' he asked.

'Provisions; I had to collect them and your good self before Toby and I headed back up the mountain,' McPherson replied. He nodded at the horse.

Avery swung a leg over the back of the cart and sat down between the two largest baskets. He looked inside the nearest. It was full of bottles of French wine. Turning to the other basket, he saw cheese, fresh bread, apples and several large pieces of salted pork wrapped in paper.

'How many guests are up at the Key?'

McPherson chuckled knowingly.

'Once you arrive, there will be two. You and Lady Lucy. I took her and my wife up to the Key at first light to make preparations for your arrival.'

Avery climbed back over the side of the cart and took his seat once more beside the driver. From the sly grin on McPherson's face, it was obvious he thought he was delivering supplies to the newly-weds' love nest.

How wrong he was.

'So, what exactly is the Key?' Avery asked.

McPherson pointed toward a rocky outcrop on the side of the mountain.

'It's where His Grace has his hunting lodge. It's called the Key because you have to pass through a narrow gap in the rocks to reach it. I'm told if you could fly like a bird it would look just like the inside of a lock, hence the name it was given when they built the lodge over one hundred years ago.'

They continued in silence for a while, until the oddest of realizations struck Avery. How did Lucy know he was going to come to the Key? How did anyone know, for that matter?

He recalled his conversation with the duchess that morning and the sudden unavailability of the carriage. The pieces of the puzzle fell into place. Others had conspired to ensure he found his way to the Key.

By rights he should be angry at having been manipulated in such a high-handed manner, but his interest was piqued. He was intrigued as to what exactly he would find at the Key. What had Lucy and her mother planned?

The cart passed into a deep cutting. Tall walls of mud and rock rose up on either side of them. The ever-present wind died away and the only sound to be heard was the jingle of the bit in the horse's mouth.

McPherson smiled at him. 'Now you can see why it's called the Key. You have to go in through this part of the lock and come out on the other side. The hunting lodge and the lake are still a little way ahead, but you will be with Lady Lucy soon enough,' he said.

Finally, the walls of the pass parted and they came out into what appeared to be another world. The high walls of the pass now formed a ringed wall a quarter mile or so across. Over to one side of the Key was a deep lake. As the road passed around to the left, he saw an oddly shaped stone building.

At first glance it looked round, but toward the back on either side it straightened out. The very back of the lodge was built into the mountainside. He blinked, trying to focus on this most unusual construction.

The cart slowed to a halt out the front of the lodge and McPherson jumped down. He let out a strong whistle, at which a stout, middle-aged woman appeared in the doorway. She waved at him.

'About time, McPherson, I was beginning to think ye'd gone to the tavern and forgotten about me,' she said, wiping her hands on the apron tied around her rotund waist.

'Ah my lass, how could I ever forget one as bonnie as you?' McPherson replied.

He kissed the woman on the cheek, and she playfully batted his wandering fingers away.

'Away wi ye, ye saucy devil,' she laughed.

Avery climbed down from the cart. He gave a respectful nod to Mrs. McPherson before helping with the baskets. He placed them on the front step of the lodge.

'I shall bring these inside in a moment. I just want to have a look around before I go in and see my wife,' Avery said.

The long-married couple shared a knowing grin. Of course, once he was inside, they fully expected Mr. Fox not to be leaving the lodge again any time soon.

McPherson led Toby over to a low water trough and allowed the animal to slake its thirst.

He pursed his lips. If only they knew.

Avery stood for a few minutes, watching as McPherson talked to the horse. He finally, slowly began to lead Toby toward the stable. Not for the first time did Avery consider how much more slowly things moved in this part of the world. In the army, he would have been bellowing for the man to hurry up and finish the task.

He picked up a wicker basket and headed toward the front door of the hunting lodge. At least he could move the unpacking part along with a little more haste.

Then he would confront Lucy.

Inside was exactly how he had envisaged a hunting lodge would look like. Big wooden benches, a solid stone floor and furs. Lots and lots of furs.

They covered most of the floor and the low couches, which were built in a semi-circle around a huge fireplace. He imagined many people all lying on the furs in front of the warm fireplace, sharing hunting tales.

On the walls, several large stag heads were hung, their unseeing eyes gazing into nothingness.

He spied a door to his right, guessing correctly it was the kitchen. One by one he brought the supply baskets into the kitchen. When he had the final one next to the pantry shelf, he began to unpack. From the amount of food, it appeared Lucy intended to stay indefinitely at the Key.

His own plan consisted of talking to Lucy and confronting her as to what sort of game she thought she was playing. His patience for the machinations of others extended only so far.

If his growing suspicions were proven wrong, Avery would take a room in the nearby village tavern for the night and in the morning, find his own way to Edinburgh.

'Mrs. McPherson, I think I might need to put a few more blankets on the bed,' Lucy said as she entered the kitchen.

When she saw Avery, she stopped. A look of immense relief flooded her face.

She sucked in a deep, audible breath and he watched as she began to furiously wring her hands. He curled his toes up in his boots, desperate to maintain his cool, emotionless mask.

Good.

He was certain Lucy had done everything she could to lure him to the lodge, but from her manner of behavior it was obvious she had not been certain of her plan's success.

'Avery?' she murmured.

He considered his reply, fearing to say anything that would

sound harsh. The tremble in her voice had not escaped his notice. Things between them stood on a knife's edge.

He bent down and picked up a bottle of Cabernet Franc, nodding his approval. The Duke of Strathmore knew his wine.

'This will go well with the Stilton cheese we brought up in the cart,' he said, pointing to the small basket with a damp cloth covering the top. He looked around and did a quick count of the baskets.

'I must have left one outside; I won't be a moment.'

❧

Lucy heard the door of the lodge close behind Avery and stood staring at the baskets.

He had come. Her husband had actually followed her up the valley to the Key. When her mother promised to do all she could to help, Lucy had to admit she thought the idea of luring Avery to her father's hunting lodge was a reach too far.

Yet here he was, in the flesh, carrying the last of the baskets into the kitchen. Whistling.

'Wouldn't want to have left this one outside, it has the pickled pork in it. The wolves would be knocking each other over to get to it,' he said.

She took the basket, forcing herself to clamp her lips. Wolves hadn't been in this part of Scotland for over a hundred years but emotionally she was walking on eggshells, desperate not to say anything which would cause a row and give him cause to leave.

As she unpacked the last of the food, Lucy stole a glance at Avery, only now realizing how tense she had been all morning since leaving the castle at dawn. If he hadn't come, she would have been crushed. The final acceptance of her failure to capture his heart would have been too great a loss to bear.

And now that he is here, what am I to do?

Before leaving the castle, she had busied herself with the task of packing and repacking her bag. Once at the hunting lodge, she had stood staring at the pass through the Key. Listening for the sound of hooves. Waiting. Praying.

Avery clapped his hands together. The baskets were empty and stacked neatly inside one another under a nearby bench.

'Now what?' he asked.

'Would you like to see the cellar?' she replied.

Avery chuckled softly.

'Is that so you can keep me distracted while the McPhersons take Toby and the cart and leave us stranded here alone?'

She felt a hot fire race up her neck, settling to burn brightly on her face.

Damn.

'I had no choice,' she stammered.

'Desperate times call for desperate measures? I must congratulate you on the excellent execution of your plan, but again I must ask. What now?'

Lucy shifted uncomfortably on her feet. Most of her plan had consisted of getting Avery to the hunting lodge. She had not thought much beyond that crucial detail.

'I just thought it would be nice for you to see the Key before you left the mountain. Who knows if you will ever be back this way again,' she replied.

Avery blinked slowly, but said nothing. Stubborn man, he was going to make her yield something of herself before he budged an inch.

Lucy straightened her back and took a deep breath.

'All right. I thought perhaps if you and I had some time alone we could at least re-establish our friendship. See if we could once again find some common ground.'

He pursed his lips and began to turn away. She was losing him. Forcing her heavy feet to move forward, she came to Avery's side. As she neared him, the scent of his cologne drew her closer. A slight raise of his eyebrows nearly brought her undone.

He was implacable in his obvious resolve to make her bend to his will.

'I had to try,' she whispered.

'Very well, then. Let's see what we can salvage from this disaster,' he replied.

The whoosh of relief which escaped her lips took them both by surprise. Avery took hold of Lucy's hand.

'How many days until McPherson returns?'

'Three.'

'Three it is, then,' Avery replied.

❧

'Do you know how to cook?' Lucy asked.

From the moment, she had sent the McPhersons back down the valley, she had been wondering how on earth they were going to survive. She hadn't the foggiest of ideas for what to do in the kitchen. Her culinary skills consisted of opening the occasional stolen bottle of wine from her father's cellar and begging for oatcakes from the family cook.

Another part of my badly cobbled-together plan.

She wondered if her mother had thought of that not so insignificant detail when she sat Lucy down the previous evening. The duchess was normally a woman who left little to chance.

'Bonaparte, for all his faults, had a very pertinent saying. An army marches on its stomach. Believe me, one of the first things a young soldier learns when he joins up is to hunt and cook. We didn't exactly sit down to a four-course dinner served by chefs regularly in the army,' Avery replied.

Lucy frowned. Why did he feel the need to remind her that she was nothing more than a spoilt chit?

'I wasn't casting aspersions on you Lucy, forgive me if that's the impression I gave. I know my way around an oven and pan, so rest assured we won't starve. There is enough food here to feed the two of us for probably a week. A little more if that lake has any fish in it,' he replied.

Lucy silently thanked her mother. Lady Caroline had obviously seen the preparation of food as an opportunity to force Lucy and

Avery to work together. She prayed her mother's foresight would hold her in good stead over the next few days.

'The lake has plenty of fish. Papa had it stocked a few years ago with brown trout. I have caught several good-sized ones,' Lucy replied.

Avery brushed the back of his hand gently up Lucy's arm. An unexpected act of reassurance which made her shiver.

'Excellent, then we shall be fine. I see Mrs. McPherson had the presence of mind to leave a pot of coffee brewing,' he replied.

With coffee in hand, Lucy gave Avery the requisite tour of the lodge and surrounds. They spent a pleasant hour or so walking around the lake and discussing the rock formations which formed the high walls of the Key. They talked about fish and rocks and of course, the Scottish weather.

Anything but the possibility of what would come out of their time here.

'It's quite sheltered here,' Lucy remarked.

Avery nodded. 'Yes, I expect it could be a pleasant area in summer if you were to come up here and spend some time.'

She looked away, unwilling to meet his gaze. A sad foreboding continued to concentrate her mind. Was Avery here because he had no other option? She doubted he had the funds to make his way to Edinburgh, let alone London. If she offered him money would he take it and leave?

The ever-present mountain mist turned into a light rain. Not heavy enough to make one dash for cover, but still sufficient to ensure a chill if one was foolish enough to remain outside.

'We had better head back to the lodge; the weather in this part of the mountain can turn for the worse quickly,' Lucy said.

Back inside the lodge, Avery picked up his travel bag. There was only one other door which ran off the main room. He poked his head inside.

A huge four-poster bed took up most of the room. Dark green-and-grey plaid curtains were held back with gold tasseled ties at each quarter. The Strathmore family crest of a rearing horse over three stars and under a crown, was carved into both the bedhead and foot. The trappings of wealth and power left no doubt as to who slept in this particular bed.

'If you like I shall sleep above the stables. I think it best,' he said.

Lucy appeared at his shoulder.

'No, you take the bed, I shall sleep out here in front of the fireplace. It's where most of the family and guests usually sleep when we come to stay. The furs are soft and comfortable. Besides, I don't want to sleep in the lodge alone,' she replied.

'I couldn't take the bed.'

'I insist. I do tend to wake a little during the night and I don't want to disturb you. Besides, it's warmer out here. You will need to sleep with the door open if you want to keep the chill from the air.'

She feared sharing a bed with Avery again. The temptation to touch him as he slept was too much. The last time she had kissed him, he had stirred and nearly woken. He already mistrusted her motives for getting him to come to the Key; the last thing she needed was for him to think she was toying with him while he slept.

'If you'll agree to helping with the task of preparing meals, then we have a deal,' Avery replied.

'Done.'

Lucy took a seat at the long wooden table in the kitchen. There was no elegant dining room at the lodge; it had been built as a private, cozy family retreat. Everyone ate in the kitchen or in the main room in front of the fire.

Avery served up several plates with cheese, bread and Mrs. McPherson's precious pickled pork. Lucy brought up a jar from the nearby cellar and placed it in the middle of the table.

'You cannot eat Mrs. McPherson's pickled pork without her special spicy chutney, it just isn't done,' she said.

He laughed. The stiff, formal rules of the *ton* did not apply in this place.

While Avery cut some slices from the very generously sized piece of pork, Lucy opened one of the bottles of wine.

'A nice Chardonnay from Burgundy for the midday meal. I find I can't handle a strong red until later in the evening, and then only a sip or two. Truth be told, I am more of a whisky drinker,' she said, pouring them both a glass.

The smile Avery gave her as he took the glass had her blinking hard.

'To you, Lucy; may your life always be filled with the gods' nectar.'

He raised his glass.

She sipped the wine. It was cool and crisp, with just the right amount of sweetness. A sharp contrast to the bitterness she had tasted when Avery told her he was leaving for good.

'Sit, sit; eat,' he said.

They sat on opposite sides of the table, savoring the freshly baked bread and lightly waxed cheese. The companionable silence would be a pleasant memory for them both to keep. She watched him slice the cheese thinly, thanking him when he offered her several elegantly cut pieces.

Finally, when she was beginning to struggle with a nearly full stomach, Lucy decided it was time to take the first step. If they were to ever reach out to one another, they had to start sharing details of their lives.

Her own life was similar to that of most girls in London's upper society. She had done little of note. Her husband, meanwhile, had a world of experience on which to draw.

'Avery?'

'Hmmm.'

'Will you tell me about your time at Waterloo? I've heard others speak of it, but I have never actually met someone who was there on the battlefield.'

He put down his wine and stared at the wooden table. An uncomfortable silence filled the room.

Stupid girl, why did you have to go and ask him that?

A thousand other topics of interest could have been broached, but her curious nature had once more got the better of her.

Lucy watched as his lips silently moved. Over a short period, a variety of emotions crossed his face, one quickly replacing the other.

She downed the last of her wine and started to rise from the table, angry with herself.

'I'm sorry, I should never have been so thoughtless as to ask such a thing.'

Avery reached out and urged her to sit back down. He took a deep breath.

'It had rained the whole night before the battle, so we were sitting in mud by dawn. I remember that for a June morning it was unusually cold. The sound of coughing punctuated most conversations between the other men. An hour or so after daylight, we moved to a disused sand quarry across the road from the Germans. The ninety-fifth was ordered to protect Wellington's right flank.'

He thrust a hand into his jacket pocket and pulled out his pocket watch. As she had seen him do most mornings upon rising, he began to turn it slowly over in his fingers.

'The battle started late morning and raged for most of the day. We fired when we were ordered to and waited in between. And so, it went on. At one point, there was a lot of yelling and cursing from several of the more senior officers. The battle was beginning to turn against us.

'After that, Major Barrett decided we needed to move our position closer to the action. The Prussians arrived late that afternoon to reinforce us and that's finally when the allies under Wellington started to get the upper hand. From what I understand, by nine that night it was all over.'

Lucy reached out and tentatively took hold of Avery's left hand.

'Were you there when the French surrendered? Did you see Napoleon?'

He closed his eyes and shook his head. She felt the connection between them break.

David and Alex were right; I always push too far. I never know when to let things be.

'I'm sorry,' she murmured.

He looked up at her. 'Don't be. I wasn't at the surrender. By the time the retreat of the French had become a rout, the ninety-fifth was out on the battlefield, fighting at close range. Wellington no longer needed us to protect him and we were sent to mop up the last pockets of resistance.'

Lucy's fingers ran over the soft leather glove Avery wore to cover his disfigured hand. He took hold of her fingers.

'So, what happened?' she ventured.

Avery puffed out his cheeks and then let all the air out in a sudden gush.

'I got careless. I thought the battle was over. Most French soldiers I encountered were already wounded or looking for a way off the battlefield. What I didn't count on was the former owner of this deciding he needed one last English soldier to add to his kill.'

He held up the pocket watch before setting it down on the table a foot or so away from him.

'To this day I don't know why I picked it up. I saw it on the ground next to a fallen French soldier. I was tired and didn't check him too closely. I just assumed he was dead. The gold back plate of the watch caught the late afternoon sun and I saw it glinting in the grass. I picked it up and as I did, all hell broke loose.'

He stopped talking and his grip on her hand tightened. They gazes met and Lucy immediately understood Avery's silent plea. She nodded. She would take Avery's secret to the grave. After all she had put him through, she owed him that much at least.

'He lunged at me with his knife. We fell into a deadly struggle. I won't go into the full details; suffice to say I had the bayonet from my rifle in my hand. I did what I had to do to survive. It was him or me.'

Lucy closed her eyes as they filled with tears. She knew enough not to press him further. He had killed a man at close quarters, what else needed to be said?

Avery swallowed hard.

'The last thing I remember with any great clarity was a searing pain in my left hand and stomach. Then I remember falling. When I recovered consciousness, it was dark. All I could hear were the groans of other men as they lay dying around me. The stench of canon smoke still hung thick in the air.'

'Were you in a hospital?' she asked. A vision of Avery being borne on a stretcher from the battlefield planted itself in her mind.

'No, I was still on the battlefield. The guns had fallen silent, so I surmised that we had won. I passed out again and when I came around a second time it was some time after dawn the following morning. The smoke had cleared, but the air now reeked of death.'

'What! How could they have left you on the battlefield injured?' she exclaimed.

He looked at her. 'However, I attempt to explain this to you, you must not take offence. I am simply trying to give you a glimpse of what the end of a battle is like. The accounts of war tend to exclude the messy aftermath.'

'Go on,' she replied.

'When you have a grand party at home, you have lots of servants to come and clear away the food and the dishes. Everything is left neat and clean. An army doesn't have that luxury. The medical facilities and personnel are crude to say the least. In fact, more men die of infection after the battle than actually die in combat. It is often considered a blessing not to be found by the army medical butchers. It takes days for them to scour the battle site looking for wounded soldiers. The rudimentary treatment they give often hastens a man to his death.'

'So how long were you left out in the field?'

It had never occurred to her that wounded men would not receive immediate and vital medical assistance. Lucy knew the facts and figures of the battle. She knew when it had started and where the various major skirmishes had taken place, but she knew nothing more than those scant details.

Avery withdrew his hand from hers. 'Major Barrett's batman found me late on the second day. I had rolled on to my side during the night and looked for all the world as if I were dead. If he hadn't recognized the green of my uniform and given me a touch with his boot, I expect I would have remained there and died.'

'Oh, Avery,' Lucy whispered.

He picked up the bottle of wine and poured them both a second glass. Lucy wiped away her tears and sat waiting for him to continue.

'I spent a horrid few days at a makeshift hospital. I don't remember much of that time, only the screams of other men as they went under the knife to remove bullets.'

'And you came back on a troop ship? I remember hearing of the crowds at the docks as they unloaded the ships. I wanted to go and see, but my father refused,' she replied.

His eyebrows lifted. The duke had been right in refusing Lucy such an imprudent whim. The sight of badly wounded and dying men was not something a beautiful soul such as Lucy should ever behold.

'Actually, no, I didn't come back on one of the troop ships. They brought me back to England on one of His Majesty's private yachts, the *Sovereign*. Not that I had the opportunity to enjoy any of the comforts it had to offer. I was kept unconscious with laudanum until they got me to Rokewood Park. Fortunately, the wound in my hand had not turned septic and they were able to save the fingers. The knife wound to the stomach took a lot longer to heal.'

Lucy looked at the pocket watch, sensing Avery's gaze as it followed.

'Ah yes. The pocket watch. When I was finally reunited with my few personal possessions, that little beauty was with them. I didn't have the heart to tell anyone that it wasn't mine or that I had killed the man to whom it rightfully belonged. I just kept it. Most ironic thing of all is that it doesn't work.'

Avery got up from the table and wandered over to the fireplace. He picked up a small log from the fireside basket and stood with his back to her, holding the log just above the flames. When he finally threw the log on the fire, scattering sparks, his shoulders slumped.

Lucy sat silent at the table as Avery's pain and guilt washed over her. He lifted his head upward.

'You see, Lucy, my brother Thaxter and I are not so different. Both men without honour,' he said, turning back to face her.

Lucy pushed the glass of wine away, it had suddenly lost its appeal.

'Thaxter accepted that he was evil right from the start, I just fought it until the truth was too overwhelming to deny.'

Lucy shook her head. She would never believe that Avery was cut from the same cloth as his dead brother.

'You are not at all like Thaxter. You have a sense of self-awareness that I don't think he ever possessed. As for your lack of honour, I think you are wrong,' she replied.

The Thaxter Fox that she had known would have claimed the pocket watch to be a family heirloom. Something that was his by right. Avery knew the pocket watch belonged elsewhere. The difference between the two brothers was a chasm no admission of guilt could cross.

If Thaxter had been in Avery's place she knew he would have jumped at the opportunity to seize her dowry, force her to his bed and break her under his will. Avery had kept to their wedding night agreement. He had acted more honorably than many other men would have done under the same circumstances.

They stared at one another for a moment before Lucy decided it was better that she change the subject. She sensed Avery had revealed as much of himself this day as he was able. She would not press him further. Her mother's words of advice rang in her ears. *Don't push him, let him come to you. He has to trust you enough to be comfortable showing you his true self.* She was desperate not to repeat the mistake she had made in the garden at Strathmore House.

'I have some books if you would like something to read,' she said.

'That would be nice. I returned all the books I borrowed from the castle library. I didn't expect to be going back, and considering my family history of stealing from the homes of other people I made sure to only take what was rightfully mine. And of course, the watch.'

He picked up the pocket watch and put it back into his coat pocket. The way he spoke about it, it was as if he expected the previous owner to walk through the door at any moment and demand Avery hand it back. Even after two years of possessing it, it was clear he did not consider it his own.

They cleared the kitchen table, after which Lucy brought a small pile of books into the main room and set them down on a nearby table. Avery picked up the topmost book and read the title.

'*Adolphe*. Is this new?' he asked.

Lucy nodded. 'Yes, it came out late last year. I don't mind it. Mama says it is a little too melodramatic, but I find it an interesting change from Jane Austen. The only problem is that it is written in French, so you may have problems reading it if your French is not entirely up to scratch.'

He smiled. 'Yes, well, most of my French vocabulary is not something one puts into print. You may have to read it to me some time.'

She handed him a second book. '*Arthur Mervyn*; odd title, but hopefully you haven't read it. It's a gothic love story.'

She ignored his raised eyebrows. He took the book and settled into the chair opposite hers in front of the fire.

The rest of the long afternoon was spent in relative silence as they both had their noses firmly planted in their respective books. Once in a while Lucy would sneak a look over the top of her book and catch a glimpse of Avery. His brow was more often than not deeply furrowed as he concentrated on the tome.

The one time he caught her staring at him, she swore he winked at her. She forced herself to dampen down any hope. They had made progress that much was true. Now she needed to heed all caution, to hold back her reckless nature. She would only have herself to blame if she tried to force the pace and Avery once more retreated at the onset of her advance.

Afternoon wore into evening. The deep shadows from the tall rock face crept across the ground outside as the sun slowly set.

'Supper?' Avery said.

Lucy stretched her arms out wide, wriggling her fingers to get some feeling back into them.

'Lovely. What can I do?'

'It depends on what you would like,' he replied.

She rubbed her eyes and closed her book. The long afternoon had left her in a strange frame of mind. Tired, but more than that, it left her reflective of her current situation. Something had to change.

Earlier that day she had been sure of how things should be, of what she wanted. Having listened to Avery talk about his life, she was no longer certain that she was what he needed.

'A little of the remaining bread and perhaps some dried fruit and cheese. I am not that hungry,' she replied.

He smiled. 'I noticed a nice port in the cellar when we went to have a look earlier. Do you think your father would mind if we partook of it?'

'Well, I won't tell him if you don't,' Lucy replied.

❧

'What time is it?' Lucy asked several hours and glasses of port later.

Avery shrugged his shoulders. 'I haven't the foggiest, but I would say it was late,' he replied.

The fire still burned fiercely in the grate, but the candles they had lit earlier in the evening were burning down to a thumb of wax.

'Are you coming to bed?' he asked.

Lucy gave him an odd look.

'I shall sleep on the furs by the fire a little later. There are things I need to do before I turn in.'

Avery went into the kitchen and poured some warm water from the kettle into a wash bowl. He scrubbed his hands and face clean, then sat down on the low wooden bench.

'That was a really silly thing to have said,' he muttered, clasping his hands together.

He was annoyed with himself for having made such a light comment about his wife's sleeping habits. If she really was his wife in more than name, he would have every right to ask when she was going to bed. Instead, she had accepted that he would continue to treat her as an acquaintance and given him the response the situation deserved.

Something had changed tonight. They had spent hours talking as friends. Sharing stories. It reminded him of the last time they had been simply friends. The day in the bookshop. It seemed an eternity ago.

When he made a slight jest, Lucy had laughed. Not just a titter, but an open and hearty laugh. The reflection of the fire flames in her eyes had made them sparkle.

In all the time he had known her, he could not remember her laughing in his presence. At parties and balls before their marriage, he had seen her openly smile. But not since.

Something shifted within him, giving him pause. He was the reason for the dulling of Lucy's soul.

He rubbed his tired face and pushed away the foolish notion. It was the end of a long day; he really should get some sleep. He went back into the bedroom, but stopped. It was nonsensical for her to sleep on a pile of furs when there was a perfectly good bed for her to sleep in. And it was big enough that they would not require the use of a bolster to keep away from one another.

Out in the main room, Lucy was busy piling more wood on the fire when Avery returned. She picked up the empty basket next to the fireplace and balanced it on her hip.

'Where are you going?' he asked.

She nodded toward the door.

'More firewood. It helps to bring it in from outside to dry out by the fireside for a day or so before using it. A couple of trips and we should have enough wood to get us through the next day.'

He reached out and took the basket from her.

'You shouldn't have to lug wood, it doesn't fit your station.'

Lucy frowned.

'You clearly haven't seen my brothers and me out chopping and carrying wood at the castle. Papa makes us all do it, even Emma. He says it serves as a reminder of how fortunate a life we all have.'

'Really?'

'Yes. And it works. David chops wood at his estate at Sharnbrook. He says it keeps him strong. Clarice, for some reason, says she likes to sit and watch him.'

Avery chuckled. Knowing David Radley, he expected the wood-chopping display he gave his wife was the prelude to other activities. What girl wouldn't fall for a man showing off his muscular prowess? He also doubted that David would ask Lord Langham's daughter to carry wood.

'You go and attend to your toilette, I shall bring in the wood,' he said.

After bringing in several baskets of wood, Avery turned in for bed. He was pleased with himself. He had managed to carry the baskets without dropping them or giving himself a handful of splinters.

Lucy had placed several large logs on the fire and was now seated in the big leather armchair nearest to the warmth. With a book in her hand, it was obvious she intended to stay up for a good deal longer.

As his hand settled on the door handle to close the bedroom door, Avery stilled. He was always closing Lucy out of his life. So ingrained had it become, he hadn't realized until now the message it constantly sent.

He left the door ajar. Not entirely welcoming, but at least a little way open. He climbed into bed, and most unusually for him of late, quickly fell into a deep sleep.

🙚

Once Avery left the room and headed to his bed, Lucy opened the book and settled in for the long night ahead.

She sat staring at the pages of *Mansfield Park*, unconsciously listening to Avery's breathing as it slowed and became a soft snore. Much as she was enjoying it, she couldn't concentrate.

Finally, she closed the book and put it down.

The logs in the fireplace still burned brightly, enhancing the growing clarity in her mind. Tonight, she felt she had finally caught a glimpse of the real Avery Fox. The shame he expressed over his ownership of the pocket watch was real.

He certainly wasn't like his late brother. Thaxter, had in her opinion, been a shadow. A man always lurking on the edge of being seen. Darting out of sight when others caught a glimpse of the real Thaxter Fox.

She sighed. It was so very wrong to think, let alone speak ill of the dead. Even of someone like Thaxter.

Lucy rose from the chair, intent on making a fresh brew of coffee. The rain of the late afternoon had awakened her senses. She could hear it still raining heavily on the roof of the lodge. It left her restless and unwilling to seek the comfort of sleep.

As she passed into the kitchen, she noticed Avery had left his pocket watch on the table.

She picked it up, taking the time to admire the intricate engraving work on the back of the case. With a deft flick of her fingers, the case opened.

A gasp escaped her lips and she hurriedly looked to the doorway, half expecting that at any moment Avery would suddenly appear and demand she hand over his most prized possession.

It was odd to now know that it wasn't in truth his.

At first the inside of the watch looked much like others she had seen before, but an added feature soon caught her eye. It had three faces, not just one. At the top left was a white face, numbered from one to thirty-one. The face opposite it, to the right, had the months marked out.

'Aren't you a clever little piece of work: a watch that shows the date as well as the time,' she said.

She frowned when she saw the watch movements were stopped.

'I wonder if I can get you to work again,' she mused.

Carefully placing pressure on the back of the watch, she prised it open. Engraved elegantly across the bottom was the word Vacheron.

More importantly, inside the watch was engraved a name.

P Rochet.

She smiled.

'I always knew your provenance, little watch. You come from

Paris, if I am not mistaken. And now I know you once belonged to Monsieur Rochet.'

Her cousin William Saunders had sported a Vacheron watch very similar to this when he recently visited from France. It was an exquisite watch, something that no simple foot soldier would have been expected to own. Who was P Rochet, to have taken such an expensive timepiece into battle with him?

A thrill of excitement tingled her fingers. One thing she knew for certain, Vacheron watches were made specifically for individual clients. If Avery wanted to know for whom the watch had been made, he could easily write to the watchmaker.

And then what?

With one last look at the frozen time on the watch faces, she closed the case and set the pocket watch back down on the table. This was Avery's watch, and if he chose to discover the identity of the man he had been compelled to kill that was entirely his choice.

Surely, he must have taken the opportunity at some point to remove the back of the watch and see who had made it. Or had he? Men were odd creatures at times, when it came to their possessions. Perhaps knowing the name of the former owner would mean nothing to him.

When finally, the water on the stove was hot enough to make coffee, she poured herself a cup. Taking her place once more by the fireside, she sat savoring the mellow brew while contemplating the conversation of earlier that evening.

It was sad to think that holding his gloved hand in hers might be the closest they would ever get to one another.

'You are a silly girl, Lucy. You promised you wouldn't fall in love with him, and look what you have gone and done,' she chided herself.

If only falling out of love was so easy.

The pain she felt every time he looked at her wasn't simply from longing to be a real wife. She wanted him to like her. If love was an impossible dream, perhaps this was the best she could hope for in a husband.

She had never thought love would be so hard. Her brothers were both settled into happy, love-filled marriages. Why then was she left to scramble in the dust for what little favor the gods had shown her?

Perhaps Avery was right: they should separate. She closed her eyes as her mind whirled in a turmoil of self-doubt. She doubted Avery cared much for the Langham title. If it passed on to another distant relative or the crown after he was dead it would matter naught to him. Even if they did remain married in name, he most certainly would not seek her out to provide him with an heir.

'Perhaps I could become one of those scandalous wives who takes lovers every day,' she muttered to the flames in the fireplace.

'Or I could just die an old maid.'

She walked back into the kitchen and after slipping the simple band of gold from her finger, she placed it next to Avery's pocket watch. Perhaps it was time to let him go.

She stood staring at the ring for a moment before turning and heading toward the kitchen door. She was almost through the doorway when she stopped.

'No.'

She raced quickly back to the table and snatched up the ring, putting it firmly back on her finger.

If their time at the Key ended in failure, it would not be through her lack of trying.

Chapter Sixteen

'Our second day at the Key and the weather looks fine. We should try and get out and take in the lake. I plan to catch a fish for our supper. Perhaps you could bring your sketchbook with you, and draw,' Lucy said.

Avery nodded, but inwardly he cursed. They were locked in this interminable conversation of agreeing with each other over the most minor of matters, all the while watching the slow destruction of their union. Neither one seemed able to break free and be honest with themselves or the other.

If it were due to them being stubborn, which he knew they both were, somehow, they would find a way. But the fact that they both seemed unable to change their minds about ending their marriage kept them on the same never-ending road.

Over the course of the previous day, he had thought of nothing else but Lucy. How selfish he had been toward her. The barren existence she would be condemned to live long after their divorce. He should be kissing her senseless rather than discussing drawing pictures of the rocks and mountain scenery.

He stifled a wry grin. After all that had happened, how odd it was that he should be the one trying to think of ways to salvage their marriage. Frustrated that they could not break through to each other.

A little while later Avery followed Lucy along the rough path which led down to the side of the lake. She pointed out a small stone bench.

'Stephen often sits there and reads when he comes up here with Papa. I think you will find it a perfect place to sit and sketch. You will be able to get a good outline of the tor as the midday sun crosses over the top.'

She pointed toward the sharp, ragged outcrop which towered over the Key.

'And what about you; won't I disturb your fishing?' he replied.

'No, I shall be on over the other side of the lake, there are a couple of good shady spots where the fish like to hide. I never fail to land at least one good catch.'

As Lucy headed off further around the lake Avery stood and watched her go, trying to etch her shapely figure permanently into his mind. The opportunities to enjoy her finely turned out female form were becoming fewer by the hour. If they kept on this same path, in a day or so they would be gone from the Key. Lucy to France and him to Edinburgh. Never the twain to meet.

'Just say something to her, for god's sake; stop her from leaving. You know that this is not what she wants,' he muttered angrily to himself.

Avery sat down heavily on the bench, surprised at this turn of events. Finally admitting that he didn't want to lose Lucy was the latest in a journey of self-discovery which had started the moment he arrived at the castle.

Across the lake, Lucy waved to him. She pointed toward the high rock face behind him. Avery looked up at the huge, sheer rock wall. The colors were incredible. Whoever said Scotland was a barren and harsh place, had not beheld the magnificence of its wild color palette.

He returned Lucy's wave, while muttering to himself. 'I should have accepted those paints from Clarice. Black and white sketches do nothing to show the beauty of this place.'

A low rumble in the distance signaled that another storm would be upon them some time later in the afternoon. Avery took out his graphite pencil and began to sketch the scene.

He squinted, trying to get an accurate picture. After a few minutes, he closed his eyes and tried to rest his mind. Years of practice had taught him the need to relax before his creative side could take over. When he opened his eyes, he looked down at the paper.

What had started out as a rough outline of the tor had unmistakably become the shapely leg of a naked woman. He smiled. Whether by conscious design or not, his muse had decided it much preferred to draw Lucy than the wilds of the Scottish countryside.

He was not fool enough to challenge his creative desires, even if he suspected it was a certain part of his anatomy which was effectively in control. Putting pencil to paper once more, he added in the outline of a well-formed buttock. Soon he was lost in lust-induced concentration, creating a detailed likeness of his wife.

A fat, heavy raindrop landed firmly on the page, stirring him.

He lifted his head. The palette of the mountain had transformed from reds and light browns into dark charcoal grey. The sky was near-black. Over the top of the tor, heavy clouds now threatened.

He stood up. Across the lake, Lucy was at the water's edge, struggling to land a fish. She had her net in one hand and her rod tucked up under her arm. She was completely oblivious to the oncoming storm.

'Lucy!' he bellowed, but his words were lost on the quickly rising wind.

The odd raindrop now became a steady shower. Bigger storm clouds loomed behind those which were bringing the first of the rain. Within minutes the whole lakeside would be under a heavy rainfall.

Lucy had still not noticed the rain or if she had, she was intent on landing her catch before she sought shelter. Avery quickly closed his sketchbook and tucked it into his coat pocket.

'Bloody woman,' he swore, as he hurried around the lake toward her.

It was a lot further than he had anticipated. By the time he reached Lucy's side, the storm was upon them. Vicious winds now raced across the lake, chopping its surface as they came.

'Come out of there! Leave the fish!' he commanded. He reached out and tried to take the net from her hand. She pulled away, her gaze fixed firmly on the net and the fish.

She elbowed Avery's arm away. 'Let go, I've nearly got him! Here you take the rod.'

The rain now soaked through Avery's hat. Lucy's hair was plastered to her head. Within minutes they would both be soaked to the skin. The quicker they landed the fish the sooner they could head back to the safety of the lodge.

Avery took the rod, knowing that Lucy was not going to let go of her catch.

She hitched up her skirts and put a foot into the water. At that moment, he was sorely tempted to put an arm around her waist and hoist her out of the water and over his shoulder. No fish was worth catching your death of cold.

He then caught his first glimpse of the fish on the end of the line and quickly changed his mind. It was a huge brown trout. He pulled a little harder on the line, drawing the fish closer to the water's edge.

She grabbed a handful of her soaking wet hair and pulled it behind her neck. Then with as much skill as he had seen in the best of army fishermen, she put the net under the fish and slowly lifted it out of the water. Her arms shook with the effort of landing such a large beast.

As he watched his wife struggle with the net, Avery saw Lucy in a new light. She was utterly drenched, but he could see she was determined to bring home her catch. She drew the net closer to the bank, patiently allowing the fish to use its weight to help her land it. When the net was within his reach, Avery tapped her on the shoulder and pointed to the net. She nodded. She had their catch under control.

Avery tossed aside the fishing rod and grabbed the wicker fishing basket. He flipped open the lid and came back to help her with the net. Working together, they lifted and dropped the fish inside the basket.

'Huzzah!' she cried, lifting her arms in exaltation as the fish landed with a loud plop.

Avery laughed. It had taken all of their combined stubborn, self-reliant strength to bring the fish in. Neither of them could have managed it on their own.

'Well done, Lucy! Now, can we go before we catch our death out here?' he cried, vainly trying to be heard above the wind.

She blinked hard at him and lifted her gaze to the sky.

A look of shock appeared on her face. She had not noticed the storm until now.

'We have to get out of here now!' she yelled.

Lucy snatched up the rod and net, while Avery grabbed hold of the basket. Together they ran back along the path.

The wind and driving rain hampered their retreat. The ground underfoot quickly turned into a dangerous slippery quagmire. Lucy fell at one point, crashing to her knees. As she struggled to get to her feet, Avery put his arm around her waist and pulled her upright.

'Come on,' he urged.

Hand in hand they made the perilous trip back to the lodge.

Chapter Seventeen

A very slammed the door shut behind him, closing out the storm. He threw the wooden latch into place.

He dropped the fishing basket on to the floor.

Lucy stood panting, struggling to catch her breath. She looked down at her clothes. Her boots and skirt were caked in mud. Her cloak clung like a drunk sailor to her skin. She was soaked to the bone.

Leaning against the door, slowly shaking his head, Avery had a thoroughly disapproving look on his face.

She recognized that same look from the night in the garden. Another statement of rebuke regarding her behavior threatened from his lips. She willed herself to believe that she didn't care.

'I can't understand how you could have been so oblivious to the storm,' he said.

'Me? You didn't bother to come and tell me until it was already upon us. If you recall, I was rather busy trying to land that fish,' she replied.

Frustration and anger coursed through her veins at this stubborn man. He wasn't going to admit that he had also been caught off-guard. So much for the soldier who had spent all those years living wild. A few months of good living in London and he had gone soft.

His hat was flattened to his head. The rain dripping from his coat formed a large puddle of water on the floor. From within his coat, he withdrew the sketchbook. The leather cover was wet. He opened it. A wry smile came to his lips and she heard him whisper, 'Good. The pages are not ruined.'

Avery removed his hat and coat, and hung them on a hook near the door. The rest of his clothes had not fared well in the rain. His shirt was plastered to his chest. The moment Lucy's gaze dropped lower she forgot all about his shirt. His trousers looked as if they had been painted on to his legs, the muscles perfectly outlined. When she saw the hard bulge between his legs she swallowed.

'You had better get out of those wet things,' he said.

'What?' she stammered, her mind elsewhere.

'Strip off your clothes,' he commanded.

A thousand denials filled her head, but her lips would not speak them.

When Avery pulled his shirt over his head, revealing his naked, hairy chest, Lucy thought she would faint. She had never seen his whole upper torso naked before. She had only ever touched him in the dark, reveling in the tactile sensation of his skin and hair. Daylight added a whole new perspective to the landscape of his body.

He came to her and quickly removed her cloak. He hung it on the peg next to his coat.

'Take the rest of your wet clothes off, while I get some towels to dry us both.'

He disappeared into the kitchen, leaving Lucy to stand in front of the fire, trying to warm her rapidly cooling body. She bent down and added some more logs to the fire.

When Avery returned with an armful of towels, she heard him growl with frustration.

'I thought I told you to get out of those clothes. Don't catch your death just because you feel uncomfortable disrobing in front of me. I am your husband.'

They turned their backs to one another and removed the rest of their clothes. Pneumonia was a real threat if they allowed themselves to catch a bone-deep chill.

When she got to the point of only having a chemise between her and nakedness, Lucy stopped. Closing her eyes, she turned.

'Would you please pass me one of the towels?' she asked.

She wrapped the towel around herself. It was enough to cover most of her torso, but her legs were left naked. She frowned at the prospect of Avery seeing this much of her body.

Behind her Avery chuckled.

'It's not the first time I have seen a partly clad woman,' he said.

Lucy steeled herself for more of his unhelpful comments and turned back to face him. Avery had a towel wrapped around his waist, covering his midsection, but like her, the rest of his body was naked. He had even removed both his gloves.

Avery picked up a second towel from a nearby chair.

'Come here, let me help you dry your hair,' he said.

She hesitated, before doing as he bade. Seated on a stool before the fire, she sat quietly as Avery ran the towel through her hair, sopping up the excess water. When her hair was dry enough to comb, he went into the bedroom and retrieved her hairbrush from her travel bag.

Seated behind her, he began to slowly, gently work out the knots and tangles. He hummed softly as he worked. It was a rhythmic cadence, rising and falling with the stroke of the hairbrush.

Lucy looked down at her bare legs. She should feel embarrassed at her lack of attire, but she didn't think to ask for more clothes. Truth be told, she found the idea of them both being semi-naked rather alluring. If Avery could take the step of removing his glove, she in turn could sit still and let him play lady's maid.

When Avery tenderly pulled a strand of her hair away from her face, she felt her breath catch. He was close. Her every breath took in the warm scent of his cologne. Slowly but inexorably she found herself falling under his spell.

'Did you get to draw the rock face?' she asked, struggling to put her emotions back on an even keel.

'No,' he murmured. He brought another towel to her hair, drying off some of the water which had been released from his brushing.

'Why not?' she replied.

From where she had sat on the other side of the lake, occasionally observing him, Avery had seemed most industrious in his efforts with the sketch book.

'Would you like to see what I drew?' he said.

'Yes please.'

He handed her the sketchbook. She carefully turned the pages, honored that Avery had finally shared another piece of himself with her.

Pictures of Strathmore Castle and its inhabitants filled the first dozen or so pages. She recognized a very close likeness of her sister Emma.

'I did that while she was sitting on the steps of the keep,' he said, looking over her shoulder.

'It's very good. You really do have an eye for a portrait. You should show Clarice some of your work. She has the artist's eye of appreciation for these things.'

'I don't normally share my drawings with anyone else,' he replied.

When she got to the last page, Lucy sighed. Avery hadn't drawn the tor; instead he had created a detailed likeness of her. Very real and completely naked.

'Oh, Avery,' she whispered.

A soft, warm kiss was placed in the nape of her neck. A second kiss was soon followed by another. Avery blazed a trail of hot kisses down Lucy's neck and over her shoulders. He lowered the towel and she heard the brush drop on to the floor.

He blew a sultry breath into her ear as he traced a single fingertip down her spine.

She shivered.

'Come to bed, Lucy. Come to bed, wife.'

'What about Edinburgh?' she whispered.

Her heart beat loudly in her breast.

He shook his head. 'I'm not going anywhere without you.'

She spun round on the small wooden stool and faced him. He took her face in his hands and his lips touched hers. A soft, enquiring kiss followed. She sensed he was waiting. Needing for her to yield to his silent entreaty. The little that she did know of Avery, she understood he would not move matters forward until he had her complete surrender.

'Yes,' she said.

She prayed he had not heard the undertone of pleading in her voice. She reached down and took a tender hold of his damaged hand. He began to pull away, but as their gazes met he stopped.

'Sorry, force of habit,' he said.

'No more secrets between us,' she said. In this she would tolerate no argument.

He nodded.

She raised his hand to her lips, placing loving kisses on the fingertips and the scars. He brushed her hair back behind her ear and leaned in once more.

'Come,' he murmured.

As he rose, he drew Lucy to her feet. In his eyes, she saw the passion and hunger she had yearned to know. He cupped her face in his hands and their lips met once more.

As his tongue swept inside her mouth, her thoughts fled back to that moment in the garden at Strathmore House. The echo of passion and need in Avery's kiss betrayed him. He *had* wanted her that night; she no longer doubted it.

Seized by this magnificent revelation, she offered him her mouth unreservedly.

He held her close; only the thin fabric of the towels separated their naked bodies. Their tongues danced a heated, carnal waltz, more in time with one another than ever before. Over and over Avery worked his sensual magic on Lucy's lips. Time stood still.

She was locked deep in his embrace, exalting in his unrestrained desire for her when she felt Avery's hand slip between them and pull the towel away.

The cool night air kissed her naked skin.

Avery released her from the kiss and took a step back. She watched as his gaze roamed over her body. An appreciative groan rose in his throat. Lucy closed her eyes as a heated blush burned on her cheeks and neck.

Avery chortled.

'Open your eyes, Lucy.'

When she did, she saw his towel had also been stripped away. He stood before her in all his male glory. Her gaze immediately settled on that part of his anatomy which was large, hard and very erect.

Oh, my dear lord.

Her trembling fingers found their way to her lips. What was it her mother had said about the marital act? All the images she had seen in Millie's erotic Indian books filled her mind.

He smiled, sensing her shyness. A single tear snaked its way down her cheek. He wanted her. Her husband finally wanted her.

Avery traced a finger down her cleavage. He cupped one plump breast in his hand and gently rolled its nipple between his thumb and forefinger.

Lucy felt a bolt of pleasure dart through her body. She shivered.

'I should ever be grateful that I was left with at least some use in these fingers. As you can feel they come to good use,' he said. She caught the wicked edge of his words.

At another time, perhaps she would be possessed of the wit to reply to his jest, but here and now the words escaped her. With every second, they drew closer to the moment of truth. To that which she thought she would never know with him. She stood on the edge of one existence, poised to take the step into another world.

Outside the wind rattled at the windows. The rain lashed against the glass. Lucy involuntarily shivered at the thought of the freezing gale which was just outside the door. The light through the nearby window was now dimmed as black clouds covered the sun.

It was barely past noon, but outside it was as dark as night. No-one would be coming or going to the Key this day.

'We cannot allow you to get cold,' Avery murmured. He placed his hands on either side of Lucy's waist and made an attempt to lift her up. When his damaged hand failed to make a strong purchase, she slipped.

He swore under his breath, but she quickly whispered, 'Let me help you.'

When he tried to lift her a second time, she jumped. With her legs wrapped around his lower back, he easily lifted her into a carrying position.

'That's the second time today we have managed to do something by working together. Let's see if we can succeed with a third,' he said.

Inside the bedroom, Avery tumbled Lucy on to the enormous bed. He trapped her beneath him and proceeded to kiss her senseless once more. She forced herself to concentrate on the kiss and not on Avery's erection, which was pressed hard up against her thigh.

She reached up and touched the soft, black hairs on his chest. She had managed to capture a glimpse of them a few times before, when he didn't think she was looking.

'They are beautifully soft,' she murmured, knowingly.

He chuckled. 'Yes, I have noted your appreciation of my chest when you kiss me each night. I'm glad you like it.'

A sly grin appeared on his face.

'How many times were you awake?' she replied.

A raised eyebrow was all the answer she needed. Her nightly attentions had not gone unnoticed; he had been awake the whole time.

His reluctance to leave her at the last stop before Edinburgh now made a little more sense, but why then had he pressed to go forward with the divorce?

'I don't understand,' she said.

Nothing seemed certain to her mind.

'To tell the truth, I don't think I fully understand the situation myself. Which, for someone who claims to know his own mind as often as I do, leaves me facing a bit of a conundrum. What I will say for certain is that we are *not* getting a divorce. You are my wife and I am prepared to try and make the best of things with you.'

Lying cradled beneath his heated body, Lucy considered Avery's words. They were not the most romantic she could imagine, but they were honest. If she and Avery were to make something of a future together, it was at least a beginning. And yet the sting of disappointment was ever-present.

She frowned. Lifting her arms, she tried to push him aside and sit up. Avery slid to one side, but as he did, he trapped her legs within his. Lucy was going nowhere.

'You are doing it again,' he said.

'Doing what?' she asked.

'Thinking too much. Just let things be and see where they take us. I want you to trust me, Lucy.'

Taking her face in his hands, he covered her lips once more with a scorching kiss. He kissed her softly at first, but it quickly grew into a heated encounter which had Lucy curling her toes. His hand trailed over the curve of her hip and he pulled her hard against him. She kissed him back as the tempo of their engagement edged a notch higher.

Oh!

Her inner voice began to throw words of doubt into her mind.

This is all wrong. You don't want him this way. Where is the grand declaration of love?

She teetered on the edge of self-destruction. One false step and she would surely topple into the abyss.

Lucy began to pull away, withdrawing from the kiss. Retreating to save her heart. With their lips now barely touching, she heard Avery's growl. Like that of a wounded lion.

She looked into his eyes, as Lady Alice's words rang in her ears.

'Anything of value has to be fought for and won. Do not give in.'

Reaching up, she ran her thumb tentatively along the day-old stubble on his chin. He really was a handsome devil and all she had to do was claim him as her own. Tomorrow and all its problems could wait. Avery would not.

'I do trust you; it's me that I doubt,' she said.

He breathed hot and heavy into her ear, while his fingers resumed their soft dance up and down on her hip. He stopped at her knee, gently pushing her legs open.

She bit her lip, willing herself to remain calm. When Avery's hand settled on the soft hair at the entrance to her womanhood, he stopped.

The moment of truth had come. He would not proceed without her express permission. No matter how the dance had begun, the next steps were those as old as time.

'Yes,' she said. Her decisive words dampened down her fears.

Avery slipped a long finger inside her heat and began to stroke. Her body immediately tensed at such an overwhelming intrusion. Never before had someone touched her in this way.

'We need to relax you more,' he murmured.

She nodded. 'How?'

What Avery had in mind became quickly apparent as he nudged her breast into his mouth and began to suckle hard on her nipple. Lucy felt her world shift on it axis.

Oh, my sweet . . .

He brushed her nipple against his teeth and she groaned. Her breath grew ragged with every stab of this delightful pain. Never had she thought such pleasure possible. Avery's finger now moved freely in her moistened heat. Long, luxurious strokes. A second finger joined the first, giving her the added sensation of being stretched. Her hips rocked back and forth with every stroke.

'Is that good?' he said.

Lucy, lying back in Avery's arms, found herself beyond speech. She touched his arm and squeezed. *Don't stop, whatever you do, don't stop*, her fingers implored.

His thumb found the nub at the top of her entrance and slowly circled. With each rotation, her heartbeat increased. How on earth was she going to survive such sweet torture?

Of one thing, she was certain: if he stopped she would go mad.

'Open your eyes, Lucy,' Avery said.

When she did, she saw his face was a picture of rapture. Giving her pleasure was increasing his own ardor.

'Touch me,' he said.

She reached out and touched his chest once more. When he let out a snort of frustration, Lucy quickly realized he was asking for *quid pro quo*. Virgin that she still was, now was not the time to play innocent with his needs.

He groaned as she took him firmly in hand. She stroked the length of his manhood, putting her study of the *Kama Sutra* to good use. When he closed his eyes on a second groan, she knew she had the rhythm just right.

He slowed his strokes and gently removed his fingers from her body. He untangled his legs from hers and rose over her.

'Look at me. I want to see your face when I truly make you my wife,' he commanded.

His hard erection parted the lips of her entrance and pressed in. She tensed, waiting for the oft-reported spear of pain, but it never came. Only a slight stretch and Avery was fully seated within her body. They were finally one.

His lips met hers in a deep kiss. Tongues thrust together in time, soon joined in rhythm by their hips. Avery rode her with deep penetrating thrusts. Lucy exalted in the sensation of feeling the length of him caressing her. Pleasure coursed through her veins.

'Give me your hands,' he ordered.

Taking both her hands, he forced her arms above her head, leaving her completely open to him. With the rocking motion of their joined bodies, her breasts bobbed about.

Avery chuckled. 'I think these need to be brought under my command.'

He sat back on his haunches and draped Lucy's legs over his hips. Thrusting once more deep into her, he took both breasts under his hands and gave each nipple a hard squeeze.

When Lucy cried out, he did it a second time. Leaning forward he took her right nipple in his mouth and gave it a gentle nip. She whimpered as the pain heightened her sexual arousal.

The tempo of their union grew to a frenzy. Avery penetrated

Lucy harder and faster with every stroke. His ravishing of her breasts took her to the limit of her endurance. She sobbed under his masterful lovemaking.

When she finally climaxed, it was with a sudden explosion of light in her brain. Pleasure crashed through her core, leaving her gasping for air. Avery slowed his thrusts but kept his hips angled. His hard erection continued to rub against her throbbing nub as her heartbeat slowed and she returned to the now.

Avery released Lucy's breasts from their torture. Looking up, she saw a satisfied smile on his lips. His virgin wife had been successfully bedded. Since she was now completely his, she accepted that he could afford to gloat just a little.

He withdrew from her body, the glint of desire in his eyes telling her they were far from done.

'Roll on to your side,' he said.

She moved to her left side, and Avery swung her right leg over his hip. When he entered her for a second time, she immediately understood the advantage the position gave him. With her moist entrance more open at this angle, he was able to achieve a deeper penetration than before.

Skillful hands gripped her hips as he drove into her willing body. At first it was long and deep strokes which rocked the bed. Then the length and pace of his claiming of her changed. He roared and, gripping her hips tightly, frantically increased his thrusts.

'No other man will know you. No other man will . . .'

Avery's climax cut short his words. He screwed his eyes shut as his sweat-drenched head dropped toward his chest.

Lucy lay her hand over his where it still gripped her hip.

He lifted his head and looked into her eyes.

'Are you, all right?'

She nodded. Tomorrow morning might be a different story. More than likely there would be bruises and twinges in various private places. At this moment, she felt the bone-deep pleasure which came from her body having been well loved by her husband. Added to that was the knowledge that Avery had reached his own sexual climax with her. Lucy was more than all right.

He withdrew from her body and rolled over. They lay in the bed and faced one another. 'Thank you,' she said. He brushed a stray lock of hair away from her face and kissed her lips. Wrapping his arms around her, he pulled her in close.

'You coped a lot better than I thought you might. I'm glad you trusted me. And yourself,' he replied.

They slept on and off for most of the afternoon, while the storm continued to rage unabated outside.

✌

When they eventually rose, they shared the task of gutting and cleaning the fish before baking it in the oven. Lucy stepped into the kitchen, carrying a bottle of her father's best wine from the cellar. She stood for a moment, admiring Avery's kitchen skills as he took the fish out of the oven and spooned some oil and herbs over it.

'You're a skilled hand at cooking fish. I take it you did a lot of fishing when you were a young boy,' she said.

He shook his head. 'Not as much as I would have liked. I learnt to properly land a fish when I served in the army. It was either that or starve.'

'But you must have received rations when you were out in the field?' she replied.

'If you call a dry piece of beef washed down with bitter, feeble coffee food fit for a soldier, then yes, we were occasionally fed by His Majesty's army. The rest of the time, we were left to fend for ourselves.' Avery took down some plates and assorted cutlery from a nearby shelf and set them out on the kitchen table. Lucy opened the bottle of wine and poured them both a glass. As she handed Avery a glass, they exchanged a grin.

When the fish was finally ready, Lucy took the sharp cook's knife and cut the fish into two portions. She served them up on to two plates and carried them to the table. She and Avery exchanged a shy smile as she took a seat. Later, when the time felt right, she would propose that they stay on at the Key for the rest of the week. Any supplies they needed could come up from the castle.

'So, which is mine?' he asked, nodding at the plates.

Lucy stabbed her fork into the biggest piece of fish and laughed.

'The smaller one,' she said as she stuffed a sizable chunk into her mouth.

The glittering ballrooms of London were many hundreds of miles away; no-one was going to critique her table manners in the wilds of Scotland. After the events of the afternoon, she was in a playful mood.

Avery sat back in the chair and studied her.

'You really are a conundrum, Lucy. When first I met you, I thought you were the epitome of an upper-class miss.'

'As well as a cunning wench?' she teased.

He frowned.

'I don't know. Just when I think I can put a label on you, you do something which makes me question everything I thought I knew. For instance, I would never have picked you for someone who went fishing in a Highland lake. '

She chuckled.

'And caught a magnificent wild brown trout.'

Their gazes met momentarily. Lucy felt the familiar flush of red burn on her cheeks and she quickly looked down at her plate. Would there ever be a day when she would feel completely comfortable in Avery's presence?

'I'm proud of you, Lucy.'

She nodded her head, keeping her eyes fixed on her meal. He reached over and gave her hand a gentle squeeze.

One step at a time.

Chapter Eighteen

Avery woke late the next morning. The pale light from the
Scottish autumn morning filtered through the rough glass of
the window and weakly lit the bedroom.

He rolled over and looked up at the ceiling. The stone roof had
been painted a pale cream color, one of the few concessions to
modern decoration in the rustic interior.

Out in the main room, he could hear Lucy moving quietly about
the room. He wondered how late it had been when she finally slept.

A second bout of lovemaking late the previous night had drawn
him into a deep and restful slumber. With Lucy curled up, her back
pressed against his chest, he had fallen asleep to the sound of his
wife's soft breathing.

His wife. She really was that now. Lucy Fox was wedded and
had most certainly been bedded.

He sat up in bed and stared at the slightly ajar bedroom door,
listening. Lucy had got under his skin last night and awoken something within. Making love to her had felt the most natural thing he
had ever done. She held nothing of herself back from him. A
generous and willing lover.

In that aspect of their relationship he hoped they would find perfection. As to the rest, he prayed Lucy had not set her sights too high. Love was something he couldn't see himself ever feeling for anyone. Having never known it in his life, there was every chance he would not recognize it even if it did happen.

He moved off the edge of the bed and crossed to the window. The storm had finally calmed to a steady, light drizzle in the early hours of the morning. Lying in the warmth of the blankets, his arm draped over Lucy's hip, he had thanked his luck that he was not out in such a terrible tempest.

'You've gone soft, Fox,' he chided himself.

Lucy began to sing. Avery immediately recognized it from the night of the bonfire at the castle. The staff had sung it over and over until late into the night. Lucy had explained it was a Robert Burns song, one which many considered the true Scottish national anthem.

'Scots who have with Wallace bled,
Scots, whom Bruce has often led,
Welcome to your gory bed.'

Avery shook his head. What a charming early-morning tune for his bride to be singing. He had spent a lifetime in the army listening to battle-hardened veterans singing sweet love ballads first thing most days. Soldiers in the field had little appetite for songs of battle.

The door of the lodge opened and a cold wind blew in, slamming the bedroom door shut. Lucy's cheerful tune disappeared outside.

Outside he could see Lucy, rugged up in her fur trimmed cloak and hat, slowly making her way toward the rocky pass which led out of the Key. In her hand, she held a small bag.

She was leaving.

'What the devil are you doing?' Avery bellowed at the glass.

In a panicked rush, he quickly rummaged around, searching for his trousers and shirt. He attempted to pull on his boots, swearing when he couldn't stuff his feet into them fast enough. Finally, he gave up and ran barefoot from the room.

He raced to the front door, stopping only for an instant to

quickly grab hold of his coat. He pulled the door of the hunting lodge open and ran outside.

'Lucy!' he roared, fear rising with every step. The sharp stones dug painfully into his feet, but he forced himself on.

At the sound of her name, she stopped and turned. The sheepish look on her face said it all. She had hoped to be long gone from the lodge before he woke.

'I thought you were still asleep,' she replied, as he reached her side.

He took hold of her arms and gripped them tightly while his gaze frantically searched her face. 'Where are you going? You can't leave! Not now. I won't let you!'

Realization dawned on her face and she shyly smiled. 'After what happened last night, do you really think I would leave?' she replied.

Relief flooded his mind. He loosened his grip on her arms. He pulled her roughly into his embrace, holding her tightly. 'Of course not, I'm sorry. I was still half-asleep when you left the lodge. What are you doing out here?' *You should be in our bed. In my arms.* He felt a sting of surprising emotion as he uttered the words. He had bedded plenty of other girls over the years; why should it feel any different with Lucy? *Because you know it should.*

'The storm last night was a particularly fierce one. This area is susceptible to landslides. I wanted to check the road.'

He looked at the bag. She opened it.

'Thought I should get rid of the fish remains before they begin to smell,' she said.

She turned, ready to continue her journey, but Avery reached out and took her by the arm. He had been feeling an ever-growing sense of protectiveness toward her from the time they left London.

'Not without me you won't,' he replied.

The smile she gave him when she nodded her agreement said it all. He had spoken to her as a concerned husband, and she, the dutiful wife, would obey. He wondered how often Lucy would let him instruct her without a word of disagreement. How much of her behavior was because of the events of the previous night?

When would willful, independent Lucy reappear?

A short while later, properly dressed, they set out from the lodge. A half mile or so into the pass, they began to see the damage the storm had wrought. Rocks had tumbled down the side of the pass and in places blocked the road.

'Looks like we might have to walk part of the way back to the castle when we leave,' Lucy noted.

They rounded a bend and stopped. Avery let out a long, low whistle. A whole section of the pass had collapsed during the storm. The road was completely impassable.

His mind switched immediately into military mode. How much food did they have at the lodge? How long would it take for a crew from the village to clear the road? How would Lucy cope if they were stranded for more than a few days?

'Well, that's a bit of an inconvenience,' Lucy said, with a shrug of her shoulders.

Inconvenience?

He gave his wife a quizzical stare. She didn't seem the least put out by the fact that they were now stuck in the Key.

He cleared his throat. There was obviously something she wasn't telling him.

'Lucy. Is there another way out of the Key?' Making a conscious decision to stay at the hunting lodge while knowing they could leave at any time was one thing; being stranded here with dwindling food supplies was an entirely different matter.

'Not really. Well, not a road, anyway; nothing that a cart could travel across. We will have to make our way back down the mountain through the fens. There is a small gap in the Key on the far side of the lake. Close to where I was fishing yesterday. We will go home that way, but not today. The storm has not completely blown itself out,' she replied.

'No?'

She pointed to the bank of dark clouds which still sat over the top of the mountain. The very last thing they needed was to find themselves caught out in the wild when the storm returned.

'These storms can last for several days. Everyone in the village and at the castle will be bunkered down indoors until it clears. No-one will venture out on the roads; it's too dangerous. We shall just have to find ways to occupy our time until we can get back down the mountain.'

Whether subconsciously or by design, Lucy licked her lips. Avery felt himself go hard. Suddenly the prospect of being stuck here wasn't so bad. The opportunity for them to spend time alone together, knowing that no-one would be arriving suddenly from the castle, had clearly crossed her mind.

'Minx,' he said, pulling her hard against him.

'Wife,' she gently teased.

Pulling her hat from her head, he speared his fingers through her hair. She wrapped her arms around his waist as their lips met in a heated caress. He groaned, exalting in the knowledge that she had accepted last night was the beginning of their life together.

It started to rain heavily once more. 'Damn,' she muttered as they drew apart.

Hand in hand, they quickly raced back to the dry comfort of the lodge. There was nothing romantic about being caught out in the driving rain for a second time.

❧

'By my reckoning we have another week's worth of food and drink.'

Avery was standing at the top of the cellar stairs, slowly lowering the hatch door.

'Some salted fish, ham, and pickled pork is the extent of our meat.'

Lucy painted a serious look on her face, placed her hands on her hips and marched over to his side. 'What about wine? I can go outside and catch some more fresh fish, but I refuse to stay a day in this place if there is no wine!'

When Avery snorted, she chuckled. He reached out and pulled her into his embrace, roughly kissing her on the mouth. Soft and sensual kisses she enjoyed, but when her husband handled her with vigor, Lucy felt her inner wickedness surface.

Thank god, I didn't let you go.

She playfully protested at his attentions, all the while resting her hand on his hip and pulling him ever closer. The kiss deepened, and in her newfound wantonness, prayed he would take her back to bed. She would never grow tired of the heady sensation of his body loving hers. Every time she had reached climax in the days since they had become lovers, Avery had claimed her mouth in a soul-searing kiss.

She thrilled to the sight of watching his passion-etched face as he thrust deep into her body, grinding his hips against hers as he came to completion. Joy filled her heart, knowing she pleased him in such an elemental way.

Most telling of all was the knowledge burning deep inside that their sexual encounters affected Avery as much as they did her. If she could at least bind him to her with her body, it would be more than she had hoped for on their wedding day. More than she had dared to dream during those long nights lying on the other side of the bolster from him. Watching as he slept. Yearning for his touch.

Slowly, he released his hold. The kiss ended.

She mewed with disappointment. The look of satisfaction on Avery's face gave her pause. He kissed her tenderly on the lips once more.

'Lucy. About the wine, my dear. Remember we agreed we were going to ration it? No-one is coming up from the valley to bring us more. You and I have been exceeding our rations for the past three nights. The only wine left is some red. There are several bottles of some Highland brew, but other than that we shall be drinking coffee from now on.'

He raised his eyebrows. The question was not so much about the lack of good wine, and they both knew it. It was more about making the journey back over the dangerous fens to Strathmore Castle and facing Lucy's family.

And their now-combined, but still uncertain future together.

Her mother would not be worried about her safety; landslides regularly happened in the mountains. And she was with Avery, a former soldier who the duchess knew would not knowingly allow Lucy to come to harm.

'Yes,' she sighed. The fens would have to be tackled.

Memories of the last time she crossed the boggy, cold, and dark marshes flashed into her mind. She puffed out her cheeks. Never had she thought she'd be leading anyone across that desolate and threatening landscape.

'You said you had crossed them before, so you know the way back to the castle?' Avery asked.

Lucy suspected he had not meant to question her ability to see them safely home, but the look of concern he failed to stifle still hurt. Trust a soldier to want to know that the way ahead was clear of danger.

'Of course,' she lied.

The last time she had made the perilous journey, her father had led the way. Alex and David had been carrying lanterns and several residents of the village had accompanied them. She had been little more than a walking passenger while the duke tested the ability of his two eldest sons to read directions from the summer night sky. If only she had paid better attention that day, rather than complaining about her sore feet.

Come on Lucy, you know you can do this. If you leave at first light, you just have to keep the mountain to the rear of your left shoulder and head for the travelers' hut. As long as you reach that by nightfall, making east for the road should be a simple enough endeavor.

'I have done the trek once before,' she added. In her head both Alex and David railed against her lying to Avery. His life as well as hers would be at risk. She had no right to let him believe it would be an easy journey. After everything which had transpired between them during the past days, she owed him the truth. After that they would have to work things out between them.

'It's not a gentle walk in the park. The fens can be a treacherous place. People have been known to set out across them and to never be heard from again.'

Avery nodded.

'I was wondering when you were going to tell me the truth of the matter. Your brother Stephen told me how terrible they were and Alex agreed,' he replied.

'Oh.'

'There is nothing to be ashamed of in admitting risk and danger, Lucy. The foolhardiest soldier is the one who does not accept that he may die in battle. The heroes of legend have become that because they understood that they were mere mortals. No-one is invincible,' he counselled.

'So, you know that I am relying on memory and gut instinct to preserve our lives? No-one is going to suddenly appear through the pass and come to rescue us. It could be blocked for many months, perhaps into next spring. We have to make our own way down the mountain,' she replied.

'Lucy. I have known that we faced an arduous task from the morning we saw the pass was blocked. In the years, I spent in the mountains of Portugal we faced many similar situations. Ice and snow often lay between us and survival.'

Avery raised Lucy's hand to his lips, tenderly kissing each fingertip. When he got to the finger on which her wedding band shone, he stopped. She recalled the moment she had put the ring back on her hand, determined to salvage her marriage. Not long after, she and Avery had made love for the first time. She vowed never to take the ring off again.

'We will not fail,' he said, the depth of his conviction taking hold of her heart.

Avery went outside to check on the weather. For someone who was only recently acquainted with the mountains of Scotland, he had quickly developed a deep insight into the behavior of the wind and clouds.

Lucy stood and considered her husband. When she moved away and went into the kitchen to add more logs to the fire, it was with the acceptance that anyone who took him on face value did so at their peril.

The rest of the day was spent in making preparations for the journey. Of greatest concern was the risk that they might not make it to the hut by nightfall and be forced to spend the night out in the open. While it was still early autumn, it was not uncommon for snow to fall on the mountain at this time of year. The danger of them freezing to death on Strathmore Mountain was very real.

While Avery went about the task of finding a suitable lantern and oil, Lucy took charge of the kitchen. As she stood stirring the pot for their evening meal, she found herself smiling. She took particular pride in cutting up the carrots, potatoes and turnips into neat little squares ready for the pot. She had made the stew exactly according to Avery's instructions.

'If only the other girls of the *ton* could see me now,' she muttered to the stove.

'Well, that should at least give us a few hours' light if we don't make the hut by nightfall,' Avery said as he stepped into the kitchen. He placed the lantern on the floor next to their other travel supplies.

He wandered over to the pot and after smelling the stew, gave an approving nod. Lucy ushered him to the bench at the table.

'Husband, please take a seat; let me serve you your supper,' she said.

She dished up the stew into two large bowls. As soon as they were placed on the table, Lucy put the lid back on the pot and removed it from the heat. Tomorrow they would carry the rest of the stew with them in a small tin pan, hopefully to reheat it at the hut later that day.

Taking her now-customary seat opposite Avery, she handed him a spoon. He took it with a smile. 'Thank you; this looks and smells delicious.'

She sat silently watching as he took his first mouthful of his meal. He quietly chewed. Then chewed some more. Finally, he swallowed. Lucy sat silently, spoon in hand.

The game lasted close to a minute until Avery suddenly sat back on the bench and laughed aloud.

'All right, all right; I've tasted worse, but that was a long time ago,' he said.

A wicked glint shone in his eyes. Lucy leaned forward, resting her elbows on the table, and studied him.

'And when exactly was that, Mr. Fox?'

She knew the nagging fear about their impending journey was uppermost in both their minds. Anything which added a touch of levity to the situation was welcome.

'Let me say this: the meal in question involved a mule and a small furry creature of unknown origin. I think an onion and several tomatoes were added to the mix, but they did little to make it remotely palatable.'

Lucy's spoon fell into her dish.

'You compare my concerted efforts at cooking to a soldier's potluck meal!'

She took hold of Avery's bowl and moved it out of his reach. Until he told her otherwise, he would not be tasting any more of the second-worst meal of his life.

To her surprise, he quickly rose from his chair and came around to her side. Standing over her, he reached out and lay his hand on her arm. 'I'm sorry, Lucy; I had no right to make light of your culinary efforts. You have done much more than could be expected of a woman of your high birth. I beg your forgiveness.'

She frowned, unsure if he was being earnest or not. The touch of his hand as it settled on her arm gave Lucy a start. Avery was serious.

All her life she had been subjected to the gentle teasing and laughter of her brothers; for a man react as Avery did left her perplexed. She looked up at him, giving him a shy smile.

Her husband was cut from a darker material than her brothers. That, of course, should be of little surprise considering their vastly dissimilar upbringings. She wondered how different a man Avery would have been if he had been given the same opportunities and privileges in his life as Alex and David.

His somber manner constantly hinted at a difficult childhood. Now that they had known each other in the physical sense, Lucy ached to understand Avery better as a man. She offered him her hand as she rose from the chair.

'There is nothing to forgive,' she said.

He placed a hot kiss on the side of her face. It rapidly made its way down her neck to the base. All thought of food quickly left Lucy's mind when Avery whispered.

'Come to bed. I hunger only for you.'

She closed her eyes, savoring the passion of his words. Relishing the expectation of his lips and tongue roaming over her naked body.

Lucy offered up her mouth. Avery hungrily took it, his lips ever-powerful in their claiming of her.

The journey from the kitchen to the bedroom was a swift one. Thoughts of the meal cooling on the table vanished as Avery stripped the clothing from her body. Her last coherent thought as he took her nipple into his mouth had nothing to do with food.

'Avery,' she murmured as she gave herself to him.

Chapter Nineteen

'If at any time you think we are lost, please tell me. I would rather we turn back and make it safely to the hunting lodge than be caught out in the fens in the middle of the night, 'Avery said.

They had left the Key at first light, carrying their supplies. Treasured personal belongings which they did not wish to leave behind were in Avery's beloved travel bag, which was slung lazily over his shoulder, along with his rifle. Lucy carried the all-important sack of food and a water flask, along with the leftovers from their previous night's supper. Avery also carried the lamp and jar of oil.

'How are we going to light the lamp, if we don't have a fire?' she asked.

He gave her a disapproving look.

'You think this is the first time I have had to face the prospect of crossing a mountain in the dark? Remind me some time to tell you about the fifteen years I spent in the army,' he replied.

As soon as the harsh words left his mouth, he regretted them. Lucy, as he was beginning to understand, was just being her usual practical self. She had not once complained about the task at hand nor the biting wind. A wind which cut through his coat like a knife.

The brutal winters of Portugal paled in comparison to the briskness of an autumn day in Scotland.

Lucy walked beside him, trudging along in her sensible leather boots. She did not even appear to notice the inclement weather. 'I didn't mean to sound as if I doubted you. Which I don't. I was just interested. I would love to hear some of your soldiering stories. I am intrigued by the life you led in the army. All those years before we met,' she replied.

He nodded his head. 'Of course, and I am sorry for being hard on you. I know you were only asking because you want to make sure we get back safely. Trust me, I would not have agreed to venture out here without having planned for as many contingencies as possible.'

He was loath to admit that allowing a woman to be in charge was something completely foreign to him. He wanted to trust Lucy's judgement, but it ran so much against the grain he found it a constant struggle.

They walked on for several hours with Lucy leading the way, the ground becoming more waterlogged as they made their way down the mountain.

'Do you know how far the travelers' cottage is from here?' Avery asked.

As he spoke, he stepped awkwardly on a clump of flat sedge. Trying to steady his step, he slipped and his boot landed in a deep pool of water. He dropped to one knee as his other leg sank down. The lantern he was carrying clattered to the ground, narrowly missing another water-filled hole.

'Blast!' he yelled, as icy water threatened to spill over the top of his boot. Lucy turned and grimaced. She offered him a helping hand as he struggled to his feet.

'Try to follow in my steps,' she said, picking up the lantern and handing it to Avery.

She pointed further down the mountain, toward a large piece of forested land.

'When we made the crossing, it took us all day to reach the cottage. Mind you, the weather was milder than at this time of year.

The cottage, if I recall correctly, is a mile or so on the other side of that wood.'

She looked up at the sky.

'We picked a good day to be out travelling; with luck, we should make it well before nightfall.'

Avery screwed up his nose. He had been in the oddest of moods all day, unable to point a finger to the reason why. In the end, he put it down to having to face the duke and duchess again.

'Papa wanted to wait until nightfall to see if Alex and David could navigate their way to the cottage by the stars. We had to wait out here in the open until the sun went behind the mountain. It was unbelievably cold.'

'And did they?' he replied. The Duke of Strathmore certainly had an interesting way of teaching his children life skills.

'Yes, they worked together and we made it safely to the cottage. Do you like Alex and David?' she replied.

He nodded. He was not judging her brothers. Assessing other men's strengths and weaknesses was something which had been instilled in him early during his army career.

'You have no idea how much I admire and respect the pair of them. For all the advantages that they have had in their lives, they are both very much aware and considerate of others less fortunate than them. They are the sort of men Thaxter should have aspired to become.'

Lucy walked back to where Avery stood. She gave him a reassuring slap on his upper arm.

'And which you already are.'

ॐ

They finally reached the travelers' cottage in the late afternoon. As it came into view, Lucy clapped with delight.

'I've found it!' she exclaimed. Pride rung in her voice.

Avery stopped beside her.

'Well done, Lucy. And you didn't need your father or brothers to help you.'

Once inside the tiny cottage, he felt the sharp edge of his anxiety dull a little. They had made it to safety for the night. They would not be left to stumble around in the dark on the dangerous mountain.

'Do they still have wolves in Scotland?' he asked.

'Not that I am aware of; well, not in these parts.'

She began to laugh. 'Is that what you have been scared of all day? I wondered why you kept looking over your shoulder. And why you had the rifle primed with shot. I think you were in greater danger from drowning in the fens than getting eaten by some hairy mountain beastie,' she chuckled.

He put the travel bag down on the rough wooden table which sat just inside the door. Truth be told, he had been concerned about wild animals. After the incident on the hunting trip, he wasn't certain he could handle the rifle well enough to protect them if they had come under attack.

'Mind you, the wild boars are a different story. We shall have to watch out for them as we reach the lower parts of the mountain. They are not the friendliest of creatures and are prone to attack without warning,' she added.

Avery quickly set about building a fire in the hearth, all the while trying to forget Lucy's warning about wild boars. He cursed himself for not having bought a replacement bayonet for the rifle.

The pot of stew had travelled well and they were soon seated at the small table in front of the fire, sharing a hot meal.

'So how does this hut, in the middle of nowhere, come to be stocked with dry wood and bedding?' Avery asked.

'Travelers cross the mountain quite regularly. The villagers make sure that anyone who happens to get caught on the mountain doesn't freeze to death. If anyone stays here, they let the steward at the castle know how much wood they have used and how much is left. Several times a year a working party comes up and makes sure the building is still weatherproofed and there is a good supply of cut firewood and straw.'

'I'm sorry,' he said.

'What for?' she replied.

He pursed his lips. 'I doubted your ability to get us here today. I spent most of the day waiting for you to give up and ask me to take the lead.'

She smiled and, leaning over, gave him a forgiving kiss on the lips.

'I know. And I also know it must have driven you half mad to follow some spoiled young miss all day, but you did it. I am proud of you. Many other men would have refused.'

'I think I may have said this more than once, but you are not a spoiled young miss. Some day you are going to have to accept that I was angry when I said that to you in the garden and forgive me.'

She slipped a hand inside his shirt, touching the soft hairs on his chest. 'I may be more amenable to forgiveness if you give me the right reasons.'

He glanced over at the small bed in the corner of the room and all worries of wild Scottish animals left his mind.

§.

'I forgot to bring the salt,' Lucy said.

Avery glanced at his pocket watch and put it down as Lucy placed a bowl of steaming hot porridge in front of him. Though it pained his Yorkshire-bred self to admit it, he had developed a liking for Scottish oats. Much as he understood the need for porridge to be made to the peculiar recipe favored by the Scots, the compulsion to add salt had thus far escaped him.

'Avery?' she said, taking a seat opposite him.

He lifted his head and smiled as his gaze took in the face he had grown fond of over the past few weeks.

Lovely.

It had been a long time since he had walked as far as they had the previous day. But with Lucy lying sated in his arms in the early hours of the morning, he had not felt the least fatigued. Her willingness to give herself so completely to him in their bed left him feeling a calm he had never known before.

'Yes?' he replied.

She pointed to the pocket watch.

'I know you don't like to talk about it, but I was thinking . . .'

He stilled. Even the mere mention of the watch left him wary. Until Lucy, he had kept the watch's existence secret from all but Major Barrett. Upon discovering the pocket watch among his possessions at Rokewood Park, he had been gripped by the overwhelming compulsion to hide it away.

It was his own shameful secret.

And yet he sensed Lucy was the one person who could truly understand how much the ill-gained timepiece troubled him.

When she held out her hand, he gave it to her. A sense of foreboding crept slowly into his mind. What was she planning?

Taking the watch, she sat it on the table midpoint between them.

'This,' she began and tapped the table, 'will always stand between us.'

He frowned. Was she jealous of a piece of metal? He forced the preposterous notion from his mind. 'I don't understand,' he replied.

'No, I don't expect you do. You see, I think you are blind to the effect it has on you. Of how much you diminish when you take hold of it.'

The words of denial burned on Avery's lips. What did Lucy know of such things? How could she know it made him feel less of a man every single time he looked at it? How much he resented it?

Damn.

For one who had lived her entire existence with wealth and privilege, Lucy possessed an uncanny ability to read others. He could say whatever he wished about the pocket watch, but her eyes told him she understood a great deal more of the truth than he had already revealed to her.

'So, what do you suggest?'

She had to have something in mind. This was Lucy. She always had something simmering away in that brain of hers. A brain whose sharpness he was increasingly beginning to appreciate.

She softly folded her fingers together.

'One night when I sat up alone at the Key, I took the watch and I opened the back of it. Did you know that there is a name engraved inside?'

A flush of surprise mixed with anger coursed through Avery's brain. Without asking and without his knowledge, Lucy had taken his treasured possession and pulled it apart.

'You shouldn't have done that; I haven't,' he growled.

She sat back in the chair for a moment. A strange expression, which he could not place, crossed her face before she suddenly leaned forward and slammed her clenched fists down on the table.

'No! I am not going to just sit here and silently accept what that thing does to you every time you hold it. Sit idly by as it consumes you.'

Avery closed his eyes.

Lucy knew exactly what the watch was, and what it did to him. Her perceptiveness hit him like a hard slap to the face. He opened his eyes to see Lucy wiping a tear from her cheek.

'If there is anything I can do to help free you from this burden, then as your wife it is my duty to do so,' she added.

She spoke of duty and concern, but his heart told him there was much more to Lucy's words. More than either of them were prepared to admit. They had come some way to a mutual understanding of one another. Yet Lucy, the open book, was able to read him better than he could read her.

She had him at a disadvantage. Having spent her whole life in a boisterous and loving family, she was equipped with strategic social skills he could only dream of possessing. While he was busy sizing people up for their weaknesses, Lucy was looking for ways to be their friend.

'I know this make of watch; my cousin William has a Vacheron. Avery, you need to get rid of it. We need to go to Paris.'

'Paris?'

'Yes. The name in the back is P Rochet. If we can discover the full name of the watch's previous owner from the watchmaker, we may be able to return it to his family,' Lucy replied.

Avery saw the light which shone in her eyes, a sharp contrast to the pain he felt in his tightly constricted chest.

He had never seriously considered the idea of trying to rid himself of the watch. There had been many long, guilt ridden nights during which he had prayed he had never set eyes on it. But to willingly relinquish possession of his ill-fortuned talisman filled him with dread.

How could he face the family of the French soldier, knowing he had killed their son? Worse still was the almost suffocating fear that once he was free of the watch, he might remain unchanged. His sense of honour would not be restored.

'William is resident in Paris. I'm certain he will be more than willing to assist us. He has many contacts in the city.'

Avery did not find that part of the plan at all to his liking. William had been the one Lucy was going to seek sanctuary with if their divorce had gone ahead. He didn't relish the kind of welcome he would likely receive from Lucy's cousin.

'It's all right, Avery. William is a good man; he won't pass judgement on what has happened between us. To be honest, I expect he will take to you with a glad heart, knowing he won't have to live with me under his roof for an intolerable number of years.'

Avery picked up his spoon and scooped up some of the cooling porridge. After taking a bite, he sat rolling the oats around on his tongue, unwilling to swallow them lest he choke. Lucy's words had him at a loss. He had only begun to get comfortable with the concept of having a wife. Now she wanted to travel with him to France and help him relinquish his ownership of the pocket watch.

Finally, he forced the porridge down his throat.

'I'm not sure that is such a good idea,' he replied.

Lucy huffed in frustration. 'Why? What are you not telling me?'

Avery rubbed his forehead. How could he put his fears into words? Lucy held a higher opinion of him than he did of himself, but it was he who had to live within his own skin. He looked at the pocket watch before finally forcing himself to meet her gaze.

'Because I'm a bloody coward, that's why. I cast up my accounts on the side of the mountain because I was too scared to go and look at a dead deer. How on earth do you think I will be able to face the family of the man I killed?'

'Because I will be standing beside you when you do. You just have to find your soldier's spirit again. Or is there something else you haven't told me?' Lucy replied.

Avery sighed. She was going to drag it out of him piece by piece.

'You of all people should know I'm not good at dealing with others. I was a soldier for many years, but until I had to fight for my life that day, I had never fought hand-to-hand combat. As a sniper, I was always away from the real heat of conflict. Even though I was killing the enemy, it was at a distance. I didn't see them up close as they died. At the end, I saw the Frenchman die and it haunts me every day.'

Lucy pursed her lips. He could see that she now understood the reason for his reluctance.

'All the more reason for us to go to France. You cannot spend the rest of your life avoiding the matter; I won't let you,' she replied.

Lucy would not be denied. Whether it was now or in ten years, she would see to it that they made the trip across the English Channel and sought out the Rochet family. She was adamant the watch had to go.

'All right; we should go to Paris,' he relented.

He was a military man, and military men were easy targets for logic and reason. Everything that Lucy proposed made crystal-clear sense. He needed to free himself of this burden. Apart from making travel arrangements and securing funds from Lord Strathmore, there was nothing to stop them leaving as soon as possible.

Much as it seemed a hastily planned errand, he knew they must not delay. If he remained in Scotland, the watch would prey on his mind, and he would likely lose his nerve.

Lucy reached out and took hold of Avery's damaged hand, raising it to her lips. It was only a matter of days ago that he would not have let her touch his hand without it being hidden in a glove. Now he no longer felt the need to hide from her.

'Good, then let's be on our way,' she replied.

She got up from the table and began to busy about their belongings. Within minutes she had packed all their clothing and only the breakfast dishes remained. There was a definite sense of victory in her demeanor.

'We can wash them in the brook which flows just the other side of the woods. There is a stone bridge not far from here,' she said.

Avery grabbed the bowls and piled them inside the small iron pot. He headed down to the water to scrub the pot clean. When he saw the so-called brook, he laughed. It was a roaring torrent. Trust the Scots to think a river such as this was only a small trickle.

As he dipped his hands in the icy water, he paused for a moment.

His life had changed so irrevocably since the last time he had sat by a stream and washed out his army meal kit. The years he had lived this way now seemed so foreign. Another life, another man.

Lucy's cheery Gaelic *halò* had him looking up. She walked with a spring in her step, oblivious to the light rain which fell. The water beaded on her woolen cloak and ran down in small veins. Small trailing ringlets of her hair escaped from under her Scottish blue bonnet.

My bonnie girl.

He turned away from her, stunned by the shock of thinking such words about his wife. Every day she got deeper under his skin. The emotions he felt were no longer just those which came from a sense of duty. Odd and unknown.

Was it possible he could be falling in love with her?

Lucy dropped Avery's travel bag on the river bank, and climbed down to meet him at the water's edge. She pulled out the water flask from the pack and plunged it into the water.

'A wee bit nippy for a swim I would say; what a pity,' she said.

He shook his head. Lucy was a constant source of amazement.

'Can you actually swim?' he replied.

She gave him a half-disgusted look.

'Yes. Though not in this water; I doubt it ever gets warm enough up here to venture in for a dip. We tend to swim in the loch lower down in the valley.'

They gathered up the rest of their belongings and after closing up the hut, continued on. By mid-morning they were clear of the mountain and could discern the outline of Strathmore Castle in the distance. They crossed over to the road and quickly began to make good time.

'What do you think your parents will say when we tell them about France?' Avery ventured.

Lucy stopped.

'Considering how things were between you and me before we went up the mountain, I would suggest my mother will be more than happy to know we are travelling to France together. Don't be surprised if she has us packed and on our way before the day is out.'

Chapter Twenty

L ucy wasn't far off the mark; within a matter of days she and Avery were on their way to France. They travelled first to London to arrange funds. Before leaving for Dover, they called in to see the Saunders family, who promptly loaded them up with letters and gifts to give to William. Eve pressed upon Lucy the need to convince her brother to return to England.

They sailed with the evening tide to Calais just over a week after they had arrived back at Strathmore Castle. As the ship sailed away from the dock, Lucy gave a huge sigh of relief. Avery had said little while they were in London, and she was in constant fear that he would get cold feet and attempt to cry off the trip. She dreaded the row that would follow if he did. They were going to France even if she had to haul him on board the ship.

Avery had taken to carrying the watch with him. Pulling it out of his jacket every so often, briefly examining it and then putting it away again. Standing beside him on the ship's deck, she could see the movement of Avery's Adam's apple as he swallowed what appeared to be a large lump in his throat.

'Would you like to go below deck?' she asked.

'No. I'm fine up here. The last time I sailed out of England, I left from Southampton. The view here is a little more interesting.'

He turned to her and took her by the hand.

'And it's nice to be travelling with someone. No matter what happens in Paris, I shall always be grateful that you convinced me to undertake this journey. And especially grateful that you came with me.'

They stood on the ship's deck watching as the crew hauled in the lines while the first mate bellowed his orders.

It was raining heavily the afternoon they finally reached Paris. Introductory visits to the duke's banker and connections would have to wait until at least the following morning when, with luck, the weather would clear.

Reaching the newly opened Hotel Meurice in rue Saint Honoré, they checked in. Lucy penned a quick note to William informing him of their arrival in Paris and left it with the concierge to deliver at the earliest opportunity. They then followed the porters up the long staircase to their well-appointed suite.

'Very nice; I've never stayed in a proper hotel before. The inns along the Great North Road do not exactly rival this place,' Lucy exclaimed as the hotel porter closed the door behind him.

'That makes two of us. I was busy trying to work out the logistics of getting our luggage upstairs when those boys picked up our cases. It's a nice touch that the staff can speak English,' Avery replied.

'Yes, Monsieur Meurice has seen the need for this sort of hotel with all the English tourists who are now flocking to Paris. He even owns the road coach in which we travelled over from Calais,' Lucy said.

The thirty-six-hour trip from Calais to Paris had been harder than the relatively calm sea crossing from England. The coach, though nicely built, left little room for comfortable sleep. A number of times during the long journey she had silently rued their decision to make the trip to Paris non-stop.

'I'm looking forward to sleeping in a proper bed. I would love a bath, but I'm too tired to wait for water,' Lucy said. She nodded her head in the direction of two large wash bowls set out on a wash-stand near the window. The pile of towels and washcloths did look particularly inviting.

She was halfway through a jaw-stretching yawn when something caught her eye. She immediately dropped her small travel bag on to the bed and raced to the balcony doors. She threw back the sheer lace curtains.

'Look, its Notre Dame! I can't believe we are so close!' she exclaimed.

Avery ambled over to her side and gave the cathedral a cursory look.

'It's big, I will give them that. But I still think York Minster is a better-looking church,' he said.

'Oh!' she huffed.

As he stepped closer, his cologne filled her senses. She felt strong hands on her shoulders and he leaned in.

'It's very old, isn't it?' he asked.

She nodded at what was a rather foolish question.

'And it is likely to still be there in the morning?'

'Yes.'

He began to undo the long row of buttons on the back of Lucy's gown. With the inclement weather, and the hot kiss Avery placed on the back of her neck, she sensed she would not be visiting Notre Dame this day.

'The manager said they will arrange to send you a lady's maid in the morning, but for tonight let me be your personal maid,' he murmured softly in her ear.

She groaned appreciatively. They'd been unable to share a bed for the past three days, so she was not surprised to find her appetite for his sexual attention suddenly flared hot. Unbridled lust begged to be slaked. How quickly she had developed the need for his strong, warm hands to roam over her body and bring her to fulfilment.

He stripped her naked and gently washed her body with warm water and rose-scented soap. Lucy tended to Avery's body in the same way. Both slowly washing the dust and fatigue of their long journey from one another's bodies.

When they were finished, Avery led Lucy to the big bed by the window. Under the cool, soft sheets they made love. A simple act of connection between them. A confirmation that they were united in their mission in France. Lucy reached her completion on a soft cry, which Avery drank up with his lips.

Gazing, mesmerized, into his eyes, Lucy watched as Avery reached his own fulfilment within her sated body. Every time he claimed her she felt renewed.

He eventually rolled off her and as they had become so accustomed to doing, Lucy lay with her back against Avery's chest. Spooned together, he wrapped his arms around her and they soon fell fast asleep.

Somewhere in the watches of the night, they both stirred and made love once more. As Avery stilled over her, the look of rapture on his face revealed by the moonlight, Lucy heard him whisper.

'Mine.'

Lying beside him later in the warmth of their bed, she stared out into the Paris night sky.

She pulled the blankets up around her neck, softly chiding herself for imagining that he could be feeling anything which approached love for her. Avery liked her, she was willing to concede that much. And he lusted after her body.

'He is a man; sexual union with his wife is as natural to him as breathing. It means nothing more to him than that. Don't go thinking that this marriage is anything but one of obligation for him,' she muttered.

Avery had faced up to the inevitable fact that a divorce was a near-impossibility and in doing so had decided to make the best of things. Lucy closed her eyes and told herself, she should count her blessings.

❧

The long, tiring journey from Scotland caught up with them the following morning, and it was two more days before they finally ventured out into the streets of Paris. Their first stop the morning they finally left their hotel suite was to the offices of Rothschild's bank. Avery handed over the letters of introduction and instructions from the Duke of Strathmore.

Little more than an hour later, they left the bank with money in their pockets and a line of credit established with the Hotel Meurice. Whatever future funds they required would be sent directly to their hotel.

'I cannot believe that I can simply walk into a bank hundreds of miles from London with a mere letter from your father and they just hand over a small fortune in francs,' he said.

He handed some coins to Lucy, who examined them closely.

'Nice to see that Napoleon is no longer on the currency,' she noted.

Avery smiled. Lucy always managed to find the right way to lighten the mood. Somehow, she sensed his apprehension now that they were actually in Paris and going to try to find the family of Monsieur Rochet. The face which had haunted his dreams now at least had a surname. Soon they would know more.

'So, what's next?' Avery asked as they climbed back into the carriage the hotel had hired for them.

'Vacheron, the watchmakers. You did bring the pocket watch with you?' Lucy replied.

Avery patted the right side of his coat. Even as he sought to relinquish ownership, the watch was never far from his reach. It took all his self-control not to take it out and look at it yet again.

'If we have good fortune with the watchmakers, then we shall put whatever resources we have at our disposal to find his family. That is, of course, if he has one,' she added.

Avery nodded his agreement. Lucy, as ever, was a level-headed, practical girl when the moment required. He expected she had thought their plans through over and over as they made the long, tiring journey from England.

The prospect that there would not be anyone in France who would be able to claim Rochet's watch had crossed his mind, but the need to assuage his guilt meant he would explore every possibility. Only after all avenues to locate the Rochet family had been exhausted would he consider returning to England with the pocket watch.

Lucy's enthusiasm in working to find the Rochets was compelling and Avery found himself caught up in it. For the first time in a long time he felt he had purpose in his life. Whatever the outcome of their mission, he prayed a small amount of his self-respect might be restored. To ask for anything more would be vanity.

Vacheron's Paris representative was located in a rather plain shop on Rue Saint Denis. As Lucy and Avery stepped inside the front door, they exchanged a look of surprise.

A small table surrounded by a handful of chairs sat in the middle of the small retail space. In the corner was a counter with a glass display case containing only two watches. The walls of the room were a dull brown oak, which on closer inspection revealed itself to be cheap paneling. The pale red carpet did little to lift the mood of the room. The room had a slightly damp smell about it, which Avery surmised to be a mixture of tobacco and a roof in need of repair.

'Not exactly the place I had envisaged such a fine piece of work originating from,' Lucy said, echoing Avery's own unspoken sentiments.

'Let's hope they put all their efforts into their watchmaking,' he replied.

Inside the shop they were greeted by a small elderly man, who quickly realized he would have to speak to Lucy if they were going to make any progress. After taking a seat at the center table, Avery handed over the watch. The Vacheron representative opened the back and read the name aloud.

Avery was able to make out a few odd words here and there as Lucy explained what they were attempting to do. He observed his wife with pride. Not only was her French perfect, but she spoke it like a true native.

The man nodded his head. He withdrew to a small room at the

back of the store and quickly returned with a large brown book which he set down on the table.

'He is going to see if he can locate the last known address of Monsieur Rochet,' Lucy explained.

They watched as the man ran his finger down the list of previous clients.

'Ah. Pascal Rochet,' the man said as his finger reached the right name.

A wave of nausea washed over Avery. Finally, the man on the battlefield had a name. The man he had killed.

Pascal.

Lucy pulled out her notebook from the satchel she had brought with her from London and began to take notes. She asked the man several more questions, humming softly as she wrote. While Avery tried to calm his breathing, Lucy remained businesslike and unaffected.

'Pascal Rochet was from Paris and now we have his last known address. The watch was purchased about six years ago, so we have to hope that his family has not moved in the interim,' she said.

It had not occurred to Avery until that very moment that the previous owner of the watch could have come from anywhere else in France. To him Paris was France.

'He wants to know if you want the watch repaired before you give it back to Pascal's family.'

Avery stared at the watch. He doubted that the workings of it would matter to the family. Nausea began to turn into cold dread. What had been thoughts and mere concepts was now becoming all too real.

'I don't know. I am finding it rather difficult to think at the moment. The only thing I am certain of is that I would like very much to leave,' he said.

He saw Lucy's gaze fall on his tightly fisted hands. She thanked the shopkeeper and taking the watch, handed it back to Avery. He stuffed it quickly into his jacket pocket and rose from the table.

They left the shop and got back into their carriage. Avery sat on the leather bench and stared silently out of the window. Forcing himself to take in the scenery was the only way he could deal with the tightness in his chest and the heavy pounding of his heart. As they made their way through the crowded streets of Paris, he was surprised to see that in many aspects it looked little different to London.

There were the crowds of well-dressed citizens and ragged poor jostling against one another as they made their way to and from their destinations. In doorways, he spotted the all-too-familiar beggars.

More often than not the male beggars were still in the rags of what had once been proud uniforms. The missing limbs or bandaged eyes revealing that both England and France had little time or care for wounded former heroes.

'It's just like home, only less crowded,' Lucy remarked.

He turned to see her staring out the same window at the passing parade. It was uncanny how at times she was so much in tune with his own thoughts. Almost as if she could read his mind.

He prayed she could not reach into his mind and see the depth of his cowardice. The hope he had felt before they left the hotel earlier that morning now lay consumed in the ashes of doubt. How on earth was he to face these people? And what of Lucy; would she still see him in the same favorable light if she knew the whole truth?

It had been a rash and foolish notion to decide to come to France. To seek out the family of the man he had killed at close quarters was madness. The sensible thing to do right this instant would be to call the whole thing off.

He would give Lucy a few pleasant days of sightseeing in Paris, call it a belated honeymoon and then go home. The pocket watch would be buried in the bottom of his kit bag somewhere out of sight and hopefully forgotten.

His mind began to race.

Perhaps if he threw himself into the business of learning to run his future estate, he could forever escape having to face the consequences of what he had done. A lifetime of thinking himself a coward was no more than he deserved. So long as no-one else knew.

He had convinced himself of this course of action when Lucy finally spoke.

'Have you thought what you might say to Pascal's family if we manage to arrange an audience with them?' she asked.

He shrugged his shoulders. What do you say to someone whose son or brother died at your hand?

Time and time again he had replayed those few frantic minutes in his mind. It had been so very brief, so horrifyingly real.

Fifteen years of hard soldiering had culminated in a bloody fight to the death. If he had not been able to overcome the Frenchman's desperate attempts, Avery knew he would have been the one lying dead on the battlefield in Belgium that fateful June day.

'Considering how little French I speak, whatever I say, it will be brief,' he replied.

Lucy frowned, disapproval evident on her face.

Avery sighed.

'Truth be told, I've been having second thoughts about the whole thing since the moment we arrived. Apart from offering them my deepest regrets, I don't have the foggiest idea what I could say.'

Lucy nodded.

'If we do manage to locate the Rochet family, perhaps I can help. As you can see, I speak fluent French. You just have to decide what you want to say, and I can translate it for you.'

I really don't deserve you. Lord knows you don't deserve to be saddled with me for the rest of your days.

Not for the first time did Avery chastise himself for taking Lucy to his bed. He had been selfish in allowing his uncontrollable lust for her to dictate the situation at the Key.

He offered her an apologetic smile. Having shared a bed and the pleasure of her body for several weeks now, there was no going back. His babe might already be growing within her body.

She leaned over and placed a comforting hand on his knee.

'I know this is difficult, but remember I am here with you. You won't be going through this alone,' she offered.

He bit his tongue, holding back the terse response which threatened at his lips. What the devil did Lucy know of such things? She had never stared a dead man in the face.

He pushed her hand away. Words of comfort and support were still so very alien to him he honestly didn't know how to deal with them.

'Shall we ask the driver to take us to your cousin's house rather than back to the hotel?' he asked.

With any luck William Saunders would have a decent bottle or two of whisky at his disposal. For a man who prided himself on his restraint with alcohol, Avery desperately needed to take the edge off his mood.

Lucy reached inside her leather satchel and pulled out a slightly crumpled letter.

'Will is going to call on us at the hotel just before supper. I received this note while you were in the barbershop having a shave this morning.'

She handed him the note.

It did little to lighten Avery's dark humor. The first thing which struck him as being odd was the fact the letter was addressed only to Lucy. Not to the both of them and especially not him. He felt the sting of being reminded of his humble origins.

The perfunctory note stated that William Saunders would be in attendance at Le Meurice at six o'clock to discuss matters with Lady Lucy Radley and her husband. He folded the paper in half once more and stiffly shoved it back at Lucy.

'Now what have I done wrong?' she asked.

'Nothing, you haven't done anything wrong. It's just sometimes I forget that I am not of your class. That to some of your acquaintances I do not warrant even the mere mention of my name. Forgive me if I am being overly sensitive about such matters. I should learn not to take personal slights to heart.'

Lucy growled. Avery could understand her frustration with him. He was finding it difficult to bear his own company.

'No.'

'No what?'

'No, I won't forgive you. Don't you dare ever take a step backwards if you think someone is being rude just because of your family background. You have served your country well and are now the future Earl Langham. No-one has the right to treat you poorly. Though in this case, I doubt Will intended to cause you offence. He more than likely just forgot your name,' Lucy replied.

'Will, is it? I take it you and he are close?' Avery snapped.

Lucy shot him a second disapproving look.

'For pity's sake, Avery, Will is family! You have nothing to get all riled up over. He is going out of his way to help you. A little gratitude might be in order when you meet him.'

Avery stared once more out of the window. He and Lucy sat in angry silence as the carriage continued on its way back to their hotel.

A tight constriction pinched his chest. He struggled to breathe.

'Stop the carriage,' he said and banged on the roof.

The carriage continued on. Avery rose up from his seat and began frantically banging on the carriage roof.

'Stop this bloody thing!' he bellowed.

Lucy reached up and flipped open the roof hatch. '*Arrêtez s'il vous plaît*,' she called out to the driver. The horses immediately began to slow their pace. The carriage pulled over to one side of the street. Lucy and the driver exchanged a few more words, none of which Avery understood.

'He says we are only a few hundred yards from the hotel. If we want to walk the rest of the way we only have to turn right at the next corner and we will be in rue Saint Honoré.'

'Good,' Avery replied.

He reached over and pushed the carriage door open. He stepped out on to the pavement, grateful as the fresh air filled his lungs. Lucy followed him to the door and offered Avery her hand.

For an instant, he toyed with the notion of waving her away and sending her back to the hotel. He wanted to be alone. But when he saw the hurt etched on her face, he knew he had no choice. Only a selfish heel would refuse her.

'Come on then,' he said, helping her down.

They stood and watched as the carriage pulled back into the street. Avery sucked in another deep breath and puffed out his cheeks. Fearing a repeat of the panic attack he had suffered on Strathmore Mountain, he prayed his stomach would remain calm.

Lucy silently took his arm and they began the short walk back to the hotel.

Chapter Twenty-One

L ucy avoided all but the barest of conversations with him for the rest of the morning. Avery continued to wrestle with his inner turmoil. Rather than try to explain the overwhelming sense of panic which had gripped him during the ride back to the hotel, he let Lucy continue to believe he was in a stinking foul mood.

At luncheon Lucy took a small platter filled with fresh fruit and cheese outside and ate alone on the balcony. As she left the room she closed the door behind her. The message was clear. Until Avery pulled himself from his dark mood, she was not interested in sharing his company. Another skill she had at her disposal, having grown up in a large family.

He partook of his meal at the small writing desk in their suite. It was only after he had pushed the piece of fish on his plate to the very edge that Avery realized he had been so preoccupied with his racing heart that he had not removed his gloves.

'Yet another failure,' he muttered.

He pulled his right hand from the fine leather glove, before gently releasing his wounded hand from the other. Looking down at the angry lines slashed across his skin, a rush of shame welled up inside of him.

'Bloody hell,' he cursed.

He had allowed the voice of self-doubt to speak loudly in his mind. To once more chip away at his self-belief and confidence in his endeavors. Poor Lucy, ever supportive of him, had borne the brunt.

She was sitting alone on the balcony of their suite, believing that he didn't want her help. That he didn't need her. Only he knew how far from the truth that was. There were times when he looked into her eyes and she made him feel he could conquer the world. But right now, he had allowed himself to be brought low, to once more feel the bitter sting of humiliation.

'Avery?' Lucy said.

He looked up. She was standing in the doorway, with a book tucked under her arm. In either hand, she held a glass of wine.

'It's warm outside, would you like to join me?'

It was so typical of Lucy. She wasn't demanding a grand statement of apology for his earlier behavior. She accepted him for his many shortcomings, and now she just wanted her husband to come and sit with her. To enjoy the Parisian sunshine.

'Yes, of course,' he said, abandoning his meal.

Outside, he took a seat beside her, and they spent the next hour drinking wine and reading.

* * *

'Tell me about William Saunders,' Avery asked.

The warm September afternoon had slipped away and their visitor was soon expected to arrive.

Lucy pursed her lips. She had seen Will for the first time in many years during his recent trip home to London.

'His mother is my aunt Adelaide on my father's side. Will has lived in France for many years. This year was the first time he has made the trip back to England since the end of the war. We are hoping that he might eventually move back to London. I know my aunt and uncle were disappointed when he didn't remain in London at the end of the season,' she replied.

She had known nothing of Will's role during the hostilities with France, but the night before she and Avery left Strathmore Castle her father had pulled her aside for a private conversation.

'I don't want Avery asking too many questions of William. While I cannot tell you too much of what he did for England's war effort, trust that there are still those in France who would seek to hurt him if they knew what he had done. And while I think Avery is a good man, we still don't know enough about him. His brother Thaxter was a rogue, so you have to understand why I must be cautious in this matter.'

To hear her father, speak of her husband in such a way hurt, but she did as he instructed. Even she had to admit that while matters had progressed significantly between them, Avery still kept much of himself hidden from her.

'It just seems odd to me that an Englishman could live in Paris during the war and not be arrested,' Avery said.

Lucy looked into his eyes.

'Do you trust me?'

'Yes,' he said with a sigh.

She relished the small victory.

'Will served England in its darkest hour and that is all I can tell you. A lot of what he did was necessarily covert, and real dangers still exist for him even now. If you are not prepared to trust him, then say so. I shall tell Will not to bother offering his assistance and we will have to make do on our own.'

A knock at the door ended the discussion.

'Just remember what I said,' Lucy added as Avery opened the door.

'Mr. Saunders?' he said.

William Saunders stepped inside the suite and immediately came to Lucy.

'Lucy, my love!' he cried.

She laughed, squealing with delight as William wrapped his arms around her and kissed her on the cheek.

'Cousin! So good to see you. I can't believe you are the first of the family to make the trip across the Channel to see me. Eve threatened to come when I saw her in London, but Father obviously wouldn't hear a word of it. He said she can come once she has found herself a husband.'

Will stepped back and offered his hand to Avery. An odd look crossed Will's face, but no sooner had it appeared than it was gone. Lucy blinked. If she had been asked to describe the look, she would have said it was one of recognition. But how?

'Welcome to the family, dear boy, you have certainly landed yourself the very best girl in London society. Have no doubt about that. Lucy truly is a treasure. Glad to see the two of you made it to Paris.'

A flood of relief washed over Lucy as Avery took hold of Will's hand and gave it a generous shake.

'I'm finding out every day that she has hidden talents,' he replied.

A second knock on the door heralded the arrival of a waiter with champagne and glasses on a tray. William directed the man to place the tray on a nearby table.

'Well, I did miss the wedding, so you'll have to indulge me in celebrating your recent nuptials,' he laughed.

Glasses were quickly handed around.

'A toast to you both. May you have a long and happy marriage and be blessed with many children,' William said, raising his glass.

Lucy shook her head. 'You may wish us a few children, but if we have as many as the King and Queen, I shall personally hunt you down with a large stick.'

'Any children we have will be a blessing, Mr. Saunders; thank you,' Avery added.

'Will. Please call me Will, all my friends do. And any man clever enough to secure Lucy's heart is my friend.'

Lucy turned her head away and forced a tight smile to her lips. When she looked back at Avery he was still calm.

Thank god.

Avery had at least determined to frame his mood better for William's visit. Tolerating his temper was a constant struggle. There were times she was sorely tempted to give him a clip over the ear and tell him to stop behaving like a child. And yet, the turmoil she often saw written on his face told her his demeanor was not simply as a result of being in a bad mood.

'So how are you finding Paris? Have you had a chance to see any of the city?' Will asked.

A thin line of worry creased Avery's brow.

'We only arrived a day or two ago, and I think we lost the better part of several days recovering from the journey. This morning we ventured to the bank and Vacheron's Paris representative,' Avery replied.

His voice was flat, all its strength gone.

'Did you have any success with the watchmaker? Lucy mentioned in her letter that you were seeking the owner of a pocket watch.'

'Yes,' Avery replied.

He reached into his pocket and took out the watch. Handing it to Will, he said, 'I took this from a dead man on the battlefield at Waterloo. My purpose in visiting Paris is to return it to his family.'

Will turned the watch over in his hand.

'It's a beautiful piece. Did you know Napoleon had one?' Will replied.

'Really?' Lucy exclaimed, finding her voice. It hurt that Avery had not mentioned the part she'd played in his mission.

'Yes. I also had one. I gave it to my father before I returned to Paris. He was not at all happy with my leaving England again and I needed to give him something to placate his disappointment. This is a very expensive watch, Avery. Your dead Frenchman was a man of means.'

Avery shrugged his shoulders.

'Yes, well, all the wealth in the world won't do you any good if you are dead. I'm certain Pascal Rochet would swap it and all that he owned to have seen another dawn.'

He took the watch back and put it in his pocket.

'I'm sorry for my poor humor. This day has been more difficult for me than I had expected it to be. There are times when I truly think I have lost my skills as a hardened soldier.'

Will put a friendly hand on Avery's shoulder.

'No need to apologize. The war took everything from many good men and gave nothing back. You served your country and now you seek to do a good deed.'

'I wish it was through philanthropic desire, but I'm ashamed to say much of this is from purely selfish need. I have come to France to try and regain my honour. Well, that was my hope until we got here; now I am not so certain that is possible,' Avery replied.

Will frowned at him. 'Why do you think you have no honour? From what I understand, you are a man who knows right from wrong and have acted accordingly. What better definition of honour can there be?'

'Are we going to dinner?' Lucy said, changing the subject. The tension in the room was palpable. She could almost hear the sound of Avery grinding his teeth.

Avery nodded. 'Yes, that would good. Can you recommend somewhere close by for us to eat? A spot of Parisian night air would be most welcome.'

'Yes, yes, of course. I have dinner reservations at Café de Foy, which is one of the oldest restaurants in Paris. An absolute must on your list of things to do while here.'

When William gave Lucy a tender hug, Avery said nothing. His cold hard stare however, spoke volumes.

'Good. Then if you gentlemen don't mind, I would like to prepare for dinner. Perhaps you could go and have a drink downstairs. I shall call for my maid and be with you shortly,' Lucy said.

As soon as William and Avery had left the suite, she threw herself onto the bed.

'Men! If it's not their temper, it's their need to save face,' she addressed the ceiling.

All day she had tried to be calm and understanding of Avery and his moods, but her patience was beginning to wear thin. Lack of sleep contributed to her frayed nerves.

In the nights since they had arrived in Paris, she had been kept awake by Avery's violent tossing and turning in bed. Broken words were torn from his lips as he wrestled some unknown devil in his dreams.

She had thought to ask him about his nightmares, but his increasingly foul moods had dissuaded her. She feared that the longer they stayed in Paris, the more withdrawn Avery would become. The sooner they were rid of the pocket watch the better. Only then could they return home to England and try to build a life together.

She looked at the gold wedding ring on her finger. Other recently married women within her social circle had large, ornate engagement rings which glistened on their fingers. At the moment, all Lucy had was a thin gold band of hope.

Chapter Twenty-Two

A very and William took a seat in a private corner of the hotel lobby, away from the other guests. A waiter brought them over a wine list and William quickly selected a bottle.

'I hope you appreciate a good drop of Burgundy, Avery. We are in luck: the hotel has my father's favourite year. He ships it to England by the case load, often via the Yorkshire coast. Lucy tells me your family hails from that region,' William said.

Avery nodded, but gave nothing away. His family connection to the smuggling trade which operated out of Robin Hood's Bay had ended with his father's and brother's deaths. Better that people thought his old home had been further up the coast at respectable Whitby. He intended to keep it that way.

When the bottle arrived, the waiter poured them both a sizable glass before taking his leave.

'No point in leaving it in the bottle,' Will remarked with a wry grin.

He sat back in the deep leather armchair opposite to Avery and took a long drink from his glass. Then, leaning forward, he put the glass down on a nearby table and looked at Avery.

He pointed at Avery's damaged left hand. 'I take it you wear the gloves to hide the scars. You were lucky to keep those fingers; from what I recall, they were a particularly bloody mess.'

A cold chill ran down Avery's spine.

William chuckled. 'You don't remember me, do you?'

'No.'

'I was there the night they took you from the coast at Ostend. In fact, if I recall, you were not expected to make it back to England alive. That was a nasty stomach wound you had. I am certain it was only the insistence of Major Ian Barrett that saw you survive.'

Avery looked around the room, suddenly realizing that Will had chosen a strategic place for them to sit. With his back to the wall, facing the doorway, Will had a perfect view of anyone who walked into the Hotel Meurice. In contrast, the large column to one side of the door hid him from view.

Everything about William Saunders was unremarkable. His brown hair was simply cut. His grey eyes revealed nothing of what was going on in his mind. Even his clothing was nondescript. It was as if his sole intention in life was to blend perfectly into the background.

'Who are you?' Avery replied.

Will examined his fingernails. 'Just a family member. Eldest son of a daughter of the House of Strathmore. Nothing more.'

'But how did you manage to spend the war living here in Paris? How were you not arrested by the French authorities as a spy?'

'My father is French. Saunders is the Anglicized version of our family name, Alexandre. My parents met and married in France a few years before the Revolution. Fortunately, they moved to England before the likes of Robespierre and his bloody thugs took power. That, of course, is not to say that my father's side of the family did not suffer. Both my French grandparents met their deaths during the Terror, along with numerous other close relatives.

'When my father saw how things were going under Napoleon, that France had exchanged one tyrant for another, I suggested I join the English army and fight. My father proposed another career. With my fluent grip of the language and a certain talent for getting out of sticky situations, he knew I was perfect for a particular kind of role.

'I came here the year after I left university at Cambridge and have been here ever since. There were many others in France also desperate to see Bonny gone. I worked with an underground network of English and French agents to help bring about his downfall.'

Tales had often circulated around the army camp about the role informants and spies played in the lead-up to battle, but Avery had never thought to actually meet one in person. The notion that William knew Avery from the days after Waterloo unsettled him greatly.

He remembered little of the days following the battle. His only coherent memories were of searing pain burning deep in his side and left hand.

'Sorry old man, it is wrong of me to play games with you. I was working for one of Wellington's secret units at Ostend when you were brought on board the royal yacht. In fact, I was the one who commandeered it from the Prince of Wales' household. They were going to send it back to England empty, but I saw a more pressing need to get some wounded officers out of Belgium.'

'But I wasn't an officer, only a lieutenant,' Avery replied.

Will picked up his wine glass. 'Well, you have Ian Barrett to thank for that. He insisted you be brought on board. He wasn't leaving without you. We had an argument with the captain of the yacht about the fact that the other wounded men were all officers and gentlemen. He thought you should travel with the other soldiers and be taken to hospital in London. Of course, both the Major and I knew you would never survive the journey and if you did, the butcher surgeons would finish you off. In the end, we hung the Major's jacket over your shoulders, had his batman address you as my lord and carried you on to the boat.'

During the past, few days Avery's thoughts had been wholly occupied with a dead man. It took Will's revelation to suddenly remind him how close he had come to joining Pascal in the list of the battle fallen. William had not lied when he said the decision to take Avery back to England on the royal yacht was one of life or death. It had taken the best surgeon the Earl of Rokewood could find to repair the knife wound which had twisted through Avery's gut. Almost a year of long and painful recovery had followed.

'I suppose I should say thank you; I clearly owe you my life,' Avery said.

Will waved him away. 'All in a day's work. It was just good to see a vile dictator brought down and both countries once more at peace. I take it your military career is now at an end?'

Avery closed his eyes and nodded. 'They didn't want to know me after Waterloo. I was fortunate to be taken in by the Barrett family as I had nowhere else to go. The army discharged me and cast me adrift.'

Fifteen years of faithful service and all he had to show for it was a mangled hand and some medals. A small pension, but not the sort of money he could survive on without finding gainful employment.

Before receiving word from London that Thaxter was missing, he had been at a loose end as to what to do with his life. The thought of returning to Robin Hood's Bay and taking up the family trade had at times been tempting. Each time he decided he would go back to Yorkshire, he was reminded of what he had left behind.

Finally, he had been forced to admit that the real reason he avoided going back to his childhood home was the chance of encountering his brother. Thaxter would no doubt have gone to great pains to show the world what little his long-lost brother had made of his life.

The thought of his brother mocking him, even after all these years, had kept him away. Hearing of his brother's elevation to earl-in-waiting had sealed the deal. The last thing he needed was to meet a well-heeled Thaxter when he was living on the charity of others.

'How can I ever repay such a huge debt to you?' Avery replied.

The smile disappeared from Will's face.

'You could start by taking better care of Lucy.'

The air escaped Avery's lips in a silent whoosh. He certainly hadn't been expecting that response from his savior.

'I know the two of you got off to a rocky start. Lucy wrote to me and told me the truth about your sudden and unexpected marriage. She also explained about her plans to leave you and asked if she might come and live with me here in Paris. I can see that the two of you have come to some sort of accord regarding your marriage, but it doesn't take an overly observant onlooker to see that Lucy is miserable. I just hope for both your sakes that she hasn't thrown her lot in with you only to now find herself bitterly regretting that decision.'

Avery was suddenly overcome with the uncomfortable sensation that his clothes no longer covered his body. As if all the rich finery he had become so accustomed to wearing had been stripped away, leaving him exposed.

'If you had had any sense you would have explained to her that you would never suit. She could then have come to me. I would have taken care of her. It crushes me to see her so unhappy.'

He sat forward in his chair and fixed Avery with a steely gaze.

'What I see in her eyes when she looks at you is a passionate love. I suspect you don't see it because you are too wrapped up in your own thoughts. I pray for your sake that it's not because you don't want to.'

'I don't know what to say,' Avery stammered.

'No, I don't expect you do. From where I sit, all I think you are concerned about is yourself and that bloody pocket watch,' Will bit off.

Lucy appeared at that moment and began to cross the lobby floor toward them.

'Just ask yourself what will become of your life with Lucy when you are finally rid of your burden? Think on that, Avery.'

'Oh, French wine in Paris. I do hope you have left some for me,' Lucy exclaimed as she reached the two men.

She was clad in an elegant blue-and-white striped silk evening gown, set off with a stunning white lace shawl. Avery's gaze ran appreciatively over her body. Whether she was in London or Paris, he knew Lucy could hold her own in fashionable society.

A stab of jealousy speared its way into his heart when William instantly stood and offered Lucy his chair. Avery cursed himself for having been too busy ogling his wife to observe the rules of polite society.

'Just a moment; I shall summon the waiter to bring us another bottle and a fresh glass,' William said.

'Thank you,' she replied.

She smiled only at William.

'You look lovely, cousin,' William added, giving Lucy a kiss on the cheek.

'And the sweet scent of lavender. Hmm . . . you truly are a delight.'

Avery flexed his fingers. The kiss was a tad too familiar for his liking. From where he stood, family or not, William had no right to be making such personal remarks to Lucy. Especially not in front him.

He had known William for little more than an hour and his opinion of the man was constantly evolving. Five minutes ago, he saw him as the hero who had saved his life. Now he was beginning to form an unshakeable dislike of the man. Who was William Saunders to tell him how to live his life?

Lucy pulled a piece of paper out of her reticule and handed it to Will.

'We managed to get a name and address for the previous owner of the pocket watch when we visited the watchmakers today. I thought you might be able to help,' she said.

Avery shifted uncomfortably in his chair. Much as his temper simmered in the presence of the self-assured Will, he knew Lucy's cousin was the best chance they had to make successful contact with Pascal's family.

'Oh dear,' Will whispered as he read the note.

'What?' Avery replied.

Will folded up the note and laid it flat on the table, his fingers resting gently on the top.

'I had hoped that since Rochet is a fairly common French name, your soldier could have come from anywhere in France. Unfortunately, we were not so lucky. I know this address. The Rochet family is well known in Paris, they are one of the major families who managed to survive the Terror relatively intact. While I never knew Pascal myself, I know his brother Jean-Charles.'

Lucy gave Avery a hopeful smile.

'But isn't that good news? We should be able to approach the family now and see about returning Pascal's property,' Lucy replied.

Will shook his head. 'Jean-Charles Rochet is not the sort of man to forgive you for taking this from his brother. He is more than likely to have you murdered.'

'So, what do you recommend we do?' Lucy said.

Will cleared his throat in a none-too-subtle gesture and looked at Avery.

'He would suggest we take the first boat back to England and forget about the whole thing,' Avery replied.

He looked to Lucy who, as he expected, was shocked. He cursed himself. He'd been a fool to let her become such an intrinsic part of his quest. Somewhere long ago it had stopped being his mission alone.

'There must be something we can do. I refuse to go home without trying to make contact with the Rochet family,' Lucy stated.

Something which felt a lot like pride swelled up within him. Lucy stubbornly refused to accept defeat. Possessed of a resolute heart, she would stand by her husband.

'Lucy's right in her thinking, Will. We have not come all this way just to give up because you are afraid of some Frenchman. I have done battle with one or two of them in my time,' Avery added.

Will shot him a look of disdain and Avery sat back in his chair, quietly savoring the moment.

How dare he sit there telling him what to do? He hadn't reached the rank of lieutenant by blindly following orders. After half a lifetime in the army, he knew something about dealing with difficult people. Avery Fox would decide what course of action he and *his* wife would be taking.

'Lucy and I will think of something. This Jean-Charles cannot be the only member of the Rochet family we could approach. What about Pascal's parents; are they still alive?'

Lucy sat forward in her chair.

'Yes, what about someone else?' she added. The appreciative look she gave Avery helped bolster his confidence.

Will looked from husband to wife and nodded his understanding. Avery and Lucy were not going to leave Paris until they had succeeded in returning the pocket watch to its rightful owner.

'Let me make some enquiries and come back to you. I'm not promising anything, but I know Madame Rochet still lives. If she is anything like most Parisians of wealth, she will have returned to Paris sometime earlier this month.'

Avery frowned. 'Why would she have left Paris?'

'Because August in Paris is unbearably hot. It was a relief to finally travel back to England to enjoy the mild English summer weather,' Will replied.

Lucy laughed.

'Mild? I wore a heavy coat for most of the past two summers.'

Chapter Twenty-Three

S o, it was agreed. Will would make a private, discreet approach to Madame Rochet and the Foxes would wait for her response.

However, what was not agreed upon were any future steps that might be taken if Pascal's mother refused to meet with Avery and Lucy.

They headed for the nearby Café de Foy, Will's favourite place to dine in the Palais-Royal. While they enjoyed the first of several glasses of champagne, they talked of the chilly evenings Lucy and Will had spent at Strathmore Castle during their younger years.

When Will quizzed Avery about his own childhood, Lucy sat and listened. The little that Avery did reveal only served to fill her heart with sadness. She couldn't comprehend why members of the same family would treat each other the way the Fox family had.

"Tis little wonder you ran away at such a tender age, Avery,' Will remarked, before changing the conversation to something a little lighter.

Lucy was grateful for her cousin's instinctive ability to know when to leave a subject alone.

'Ah, food,' Will said as the waiter placed a platter on their table with a great flourish.

'Belon oysters'? Lucy asked as she picked up the first of the natural oysters and popped it in her mouth. She sat back in her chair and hugged herself for joy.

Will chuckled and offered the platter to Avery. 'Packed in ice and brought in every day from Brittany.'

'These are good; even better than the ones we used to catch in Portugal. They certainly have plenty of meat,' Avery exclaimed.

The soft, sweet jewels of the ocean soon disappeared, leaving Will to order two dozen more.

Later in their hotel suite, Avery helped Lucy remove her shawl and gloves.

'Paris certainly gives London a run for its money when it comes to excellent food. I don't think I have tasted such flavorsome food in my entire life,' Lucy said.

'Yes, it was very good; the veal we had after the oysters was especially tender,' he replied.

She watched as he crossed the floor, opened the door to the balcony and stepped outside. Her mind drifted back to when she had first arrived downstairs earlier that evening. The tension between her husband and Will had been palpable, but whatever had caused them to disagree, Avery was keeping mum.

'Would you like a nightcap before we retire?' she called to him.

Avery didn't reply.

She picked up her shawl from the chair and slipped it back on before joining him outside. As she stepped out on to the balcony, he turned to her. The moonlight showed the lines of worry etched on his face. His emerald eyes lacked their usual spark of light.

'What's wrong?' she said.

He reached out and, taking hold of her hand, raised it to his lips.

'What William said tonight about Jean-Charles Rochet being a dangerous man should not be taken lightly. I want you to promise me that if things look as if they are becoming difficult, you will do as I say and immediately remove yourself to the English ambassador's house.'

'But . . .'

She would have continued to protest but something in his look stopped her.

'Much as you are entitled to your own opinion, there are times when I need you to do things without question. Paris may be crawling with allied troops, but it is still a dangerous place if you are English,' he added.

'Yes,' she replied.

Starting another quarrel with Avery would serve no gain. Today they had made progress with their endeavor. They had a name and Will was going to try and use his connections to make contact with Pascal's mother.

Besides, there were other ways to soothe her husband's temper. She rose up on her toes and placed a warm and inviting kiss on Avery's lips.

'Come to bed.'

'Madame Fox?'

Lucy turned and as soon as she set eyes on the woman, she knew who the woman was. Tears came fiercely to her eyes as she whispered. 'Madame Rochet?'

Madame Rochet stepped forward, her body supported by a heavy walking stick. She held out a trembling hand, which Lucy readily took.

Before she knew what was happening, a warm kiss had been placed on her cheek.

'Thank you my dear, thank you for coming to Paris.'

Lucy studied her. Immaculately dressed, perhaps not in the very latest of Parisian fashions, but her clothes were of a quality that only a well-funded woman could afford. A smile crept across Madame Rochet's face.

'You didn't expect me to be able to speak English?'

'No, no I didn't,' Lucy replied.

She most certainly hadn't expected to meet Madame Rochet that morning as she made her way downstairs to enquire about sight-seeing around Paris.

Avery had made his position clear with regard to her safety. She could venture down to the hotel lobby on her own, but other than that she was to stay by his side at all times. No risks were to be taken.

For all they knew, Madame Rochet might wish to do both the man who had killed her son and his wife great harm.

He had only agreed to a morning of visiting the local sites after Will assured him there was little chance of the Rochet family responding immediately to his communique.

And yet here before her stood Madame Rochet, embracing Lucy as if she were a long-lost daughter.

'My father was a Swiss diplomat, we lived in many places including London. I speak five languages apart from French,' she explained.

Lucy waived away the concierge who had been arranging a carriage for Avery and herself. With the arrival of Madame Rochet, their visit to the Louvre Museum would have to wait.

'My husband is finishing a late breakfast; would you like to come upstairs now and meet him?' Lucy asked.

Madame Rochet shook her head.

'A little later perhaps. I wish to speak with you in private first before I meet Mr. Fox.'

They settled in a quiet corner of the hotel's cafe and ordered coffee.

'I must say I was more than a little shocked when I opened the letter from Mr. Saunders earlier this morning. Fortunately, my eldest son Jean-Charles had already left the house before it arrived,' Madame Rochet explained.

Recalling Will's warning about Pascal's brother, Lucy smiled. It was a relief to know that Jean-Charles remained for the time being ignorant of Avery's presence in Paris and of his quest. An angry, vengeful brother would most likely cause Avery's well-intentioned plans to collapse and fail.

Lucy sipped her coffee, all the while desperately searching for the right words to say.

'So, Mrs. Fox, or is it still Lady Lucy? Mr. Saunders mentioned that you are the daughter of the Duke of Strathmore. For my own part, I could never quite get my head around the protocol of what to call a duke's daughter when she married.'

Lucy smiled. She found a private delight in being called Mrs. Fox.

'It's still Lady Lucy. My husband will eventually become the Earl Langham.'

'Yet he was only a lowly lieutenant in the army?' Madame Rochet replied.

'Yes, he has only very recently become heir to the title,' Lucy explained.

Madame Rochet gave a brief nod of her head, and Lucy silently gave thanks that she was not going to have to explain the unpleasant circumstances surrounding Thaxter Fox's demise.

Pascal's mother picked up a small piece of cake which the waiter had brought with the coffee. She took a bite and sat quietly chewing for a moment. Finally, she brushed the crumbs from her fingers and straightened her back.

'I think I am ready to see your husband now,' she announced.

Lucy hurried over and helped Madame Rochet to her feet.

As they made their way toward the staircase, Lucy thought to ask Madame Rochet what she had intended to discuss with her in the cafe. It was only when the older woman took a deep breath and lifted her chin up high, that realization dawned on her.

The coffee and cake had been all for show. Madame Rochet was doing everything she could to calm her own nerves before meeting Avery. Lucy took hold of her arm and they slowly ascended the staircase.

When they got to the door of their suite, Lucy stopped and faced her.

'He is a good man, my husband. He has risked a lot in travelling to France to seek out your family. I know you lost your son at

Waterloo and for that I am sorry beyond words. All I ask is that you give Avery the opportunity to set something to rights.'

Madame Rochet pursed her lips.

'Let your husband speak for himself and then we shall see.'

'Avery,' Lucy gently called as they entered the room, 'we have a visitor.'

Chapter Twenty-Four

As he stepped out from the bedroom and into the main living area of their suite, Avery saw Lucy standing and holding the arm of an elegantly dressed older woman.

He felt the ground shift under him when he saw the look on Lucy's face. Their message had been well and truly received by the Rochet family. And here, in the flesh, was the reply.

'Madame Rochet?' He gave her a deep, respectful bow.

'Mr. Fox,' came the tremulous response.

He quickly moved to take her arm, guiding her to a nearby armchair.

'You mustn't blame your wife for my sudden appearance at your door. I took a chance in coming to the hotel and it was pure luck that I saw her in the lobby. I knew she was English by the way she dressed and how she wore her hair. I can pick the cut of a London dressmaker's gown from across the other side of a ballroom. From the way Lucy's lovely fair hair is curled, I guessed who she was in an instant.'

Avery's discomfort at the situation he had so suddenly found himself in increased when Lucy softly chuckled. He scowled. Now was not the time for levity.

'Actually, my seamstress is French. I'm not so certain she would be happy to hear you say that, Madame Rochet,' she replied.

Madame Rochet clicked her tongue and winked at Lucy.

'Well, I shall never tell,' she said.

Avery sucked in a deep breath.

This was not how he had envisaged this meeting happening. He had dreamed of this moment for many days, but in his dreams the room was always much darker. The meagre light had cast shadows on the wall. While he sat on one side of the darkened room, the assembled family of Pascal Rochet were gathered across from him. Behind them stood Pascal's ghost, bearing silent witness to his untimely death.

Now Lucy stood in that very same spot.

It was all wrong.

'Come Mr. Fox, sit,' Madame Rochet commanded.

She pointed to the long couch opposite her. He raised an eyebrow in Lucy's direction. She silently nodded.

As soon as he took his seat, he felt the hot tears begin to well up. He closed his eyes and let his head fall forward.

How could he face her? To her he was no doubt a thief, one who had murdered her son to take what he desired.

'Thank you for coming today, Madame Rochet, I know this cannot be easy for you,' he said, his voice breaking.

'Avery? May I call you that?' she replied.

He gave a small nod of acquiescence. He could refuse her nothing.

'For you to journey all this way and seek me out must have taken some deep soul searching,' she said.

His head shot up. He blinked hard, forcing the tears to fall. Then he saw her clearly. Not the small, broken widow he had imagined. Instead an immaculately dressed woman, barely into her old age, stared back at him.

Her grey eyes pierced deep into his very essence, searching for the slightest sign of insincerity. Challenging him to reveal himself to her.

'Actually, Madame Rochet, it was the easiest decision I have made in a long time. Once my wife made me realize I needed to return the pocket watch to your family, I knew I had to come.'

He turned to Lucy.

'Would you please bring me the watch?'

Lucy retrieved it from his coat pocket and handed it to him. Avery placed it on the small table which sat between him and Pascal's mother.

Madame Rochet looked at the watch and gasped. She sat for what seemed an eternity, staring at the gold case. Finally, she leaned forward and with a trembling hand picked up the pocket watch.

'I had never thought to see this again,' she whispered.

She turned the watch over in her fingers several times before finally pressing the small button and opening the case.

'I'm sorry, but it is broken. I couldn't decide whether to get it fixed or not,' Avery said.

'Pascal was the same. Always in two minds about taking it back to the watchmakers and getting them to fix the broken spring,' she replied.

Avery watched as Madame Rochet sat tapping her fingertips on the glass of the watch face. So, the watch had been broken before Pascal took it to Belgium. For two years he had labored under the impression that it had been broken during their deadly struggle.

She closed the watch and placed it back on the table.

'Why?'

Avery ran his fingers through his sable hair. He had rehearsed his response to this question a thousand times, but now when it came time to speak the words, he was at a loss.

He looked at the watch, knowing it would be the last time he would see it.

'Because I lost my honour when I took it from your son.'

'You stole it,' Madame Rochet replied.

'No!' he cried and jumped to his feet.

His gaze searched wildly around the room, desperate to find something to focus upon. Finally, he saw Lucy. Tears were streaming down her face. He should go to her, try to offer her comfort. Instead he remained rooted to the spot.

'No,' he murmured.

'Please Avery, sit down,' Madame Rochet said.

He resumed his seat, eyes cast down.

'I didn't steal the watch,' he said.

'Then how did you come by it? You say you have come here to regain your honour; if so then you owe me the truth.'

She turned and looked at Lucy, who remained standing.

'Has he ever told you what happened that day, my dear?'

'Only a little,' she replied.

Madame Rochet picked up the watch once more and brandished it at Avery.

'I take back this watch, which rightly belongs to my family, but if you want me to give you back your honour then you must tell me the truth. Tell both of us the truth.'

Lucy walked over to the couch and took a seat next to Avery. He gave her a quick glance as she took hold of his hand and gave it a supportive squeeze.

'You must both understand that as a gentleman I cannot tell you everything that happened that day. It would serve no purpose for you to know the real horror of war. Those of us who have lived through it suffer enough without having to relive it,' Avery said.

'Tell me what happened to my son,' Madame Rochet demanded.

'Very well. It was late in the afternoon; the battle was over. I was looking for some of my men on the battlefield. Out of the corner of my eye I saw something shining in the grass. As I drew near I saw it was a gold watch case. Without thinking I picked it up.'

Avery's mind slipped back to that fateful day. His senses once more filled with the acrid smell of gun smoke and the stench of death.

He determined only to tell Madame Rochet and Lucy enough to satisfy their needs, nothing more.

When next he looked into his wife's eyes, he didn't want to see the haunted look of one who knew the reality of bloody battle. Lucy was the holder of the innocent peace he so desperately craved. He could not give back Madame Rochet her son, but he steadfastly refused to add further to her grief.

'As I picked up the watch I heard a groan nearby. A foot or so away lay a wounded French soldier.'

'Pascal,' Madame Rochet said. She closed her eyes and he watched as her lips moved in silent prayer.

Beside Avery, Lucy sat gently weeping. He dared not look at her. Every fiber of his being was concentrated on maintaining his composure.

'How badly wounded?'

He cast his mind back and immediately recalled the blood which had blackened Pascal's coat and turned one whole side of his shirt bright red. Not that it truly mattered now, but he felt a sudden compulsion to convince Madame Rochet that Pascal was doomed long before Avery had stumbled upon him.

'Madame, I am no physician, but I was a soldier for a long time. I have seen enough wounds to know that he would not have left the battlefield alive. I showed him the watch and asked if it was his, thinking to tuck it inside his pocket. I wanted him to know where it was when he died.'

'You thought not to keep it?' Madame Rochet replied.

Her grey eyes remained fixed on Avery, still seeking to find a falsehood in his story.

'No.'

He rose once more from the couch and walked to the nearby window. He needed to think, to explain himself fully. If Madame Rochet thought him a liar, he couldn't live with himself. He drew back the curtains and looked out the window at the faultlessly blue Parisian sky.

A small starling fluttered past the window and came to rest on the stone floor of the balcony. His attention was captured by the tiny black-plumed creature as it hopped around the small sunlit space.

'Avery?' Lucy murmured.

He stirred from his musing and risked a glance in her direction. Apart from the tears, she sat quietly with her hands calmly placed in her lap. Lucy was the strength he sorely needed. He knew she believed in him. Her calm demeanor revealed that she accepted he was telling the truth.

I must do this, I cannot fail.

He resumed his seat.

'Madame, may I tell you a little of my past?'

She nodded.

'The place I come from has a certain reputation for smuggling and thievery. While a lot of it is to do with avoiding government taxes . . .'

'Which every good citizen should do,' Madame Rochet interjected.

He nodded. In another life, he could imagine being good friends with the feisty French widow. She had the dry sense of humor he thought particular only to the north of England. She reminded him somewhat of Lady Alice Langham.

'Unfortunately, my father and brother took to the business with more gusto than most people would think appropriate. To be honest I come from a family of unashamed liars and thieves,' he said.

'Oh, Avery,' Lucy exclaimed.

'As you can understand it's not something I feel comfortable talking about in polite company,' he replied.

A bead of sweat formed at the nape of his neck and slowly trickled down between his shoulder blades. He had dressed warmly, expecting to be out in the cool of a September morning. Now, sitting in his and Lucy's warm, sunbathed hotel suite, he felt the discomfort of his shirt as it welded itself to his back.

'But I digress. Madame, I spent my whole childhood ashamed of my family's occupation. It and several other factors caused me to leave home at an early age and join the British army. The most important thing I learnt from my time in the army was that a man's honour was often the only thing he had of value. I consider myself no exception. Which means that when the battle was finally over, the last thing I had on my mind was to rob a poor dying soul.'

He rested his sweaty palms on his knees. Not having finished preparing for the day, he had not donned his gloves. His damaged hand was on show for all to see. Madame Rochet let out a small gasp of surprise when she saw it. She crossed herself and silently mouthed a prayer.

Avery, gaining more confidence in his ability to express himself, pressed on.

'Many of my fellow allied soldiers had no such qualms about stealing from the dying and the dead. One Prussian in particular I witnessed wrestling personal possessions from several felled combatants. Fortunately, another British officer had also seen him do it and took punitive action.'

Even now, two years after the event he still shuddered at the memory of Ian Barrett putting a bullet in the head of a man who had been fighting on their side only hours earlier. The Major had brooked no dishonor to the fallen, Allied or French. The Prussian had been stealing from the dead and running his sword through those who gave him any form of resistance.

He sucked in a deep breath and continued.

'As I bent down to put the watch in his pocket, Pascal must have thought I was going to rob him. He let out a roar and thrust a knife into my stomach. I remember us locked in a struggle for some time, and then darkness overcame me,' he said.

He paused for a moment.

'I don't remember much of what actually happened after that moment. I have broken memories of waking up cold on the ground at night, still on the battlefield. The next coherent recollection I have is waking up at Rokewood Park in the Northamptonshire country-side several weeks later.'

'Did you get those wounds at Waterloo?' Madame Rochet asked, pointing to Avery's damaged hand.

Avery met her gaze.

'Yes. I believe your son gave those to me, along with the deep and lasting scar on my left side.'

'I'm not the least surprised. This watch was Pascal's most prized possession. He would not have given it up without a fight,' she replied.

'Then he did himself and your family proud,' Avery replied.

He paused, silently praying Madame Rochet would take the watch and leave.

'Mr. Fox, thank you for the abridged version of events. But I want to know all that happened. Leave nothing out. I need to know exactly how my son died.'

Avery turned to Lucy, hoping to spare her and himself from the shared knowledge of what he had done that day. But true to form, she held her head up high and met his gaze.

'I am staying,' she said.

He rubbed the tip of his left thumb along the bottom of his chin, feeling the rough edge of his early-morning stubble. He had planned to have a shave before taking Lucy out for the morning. The sudden arrival of Madam Rochet had thrown their plans into disarray.

'When I say I don't remember much of what happened after that moment, I am not lying. You must bear in mind that I lost a lot of blood from my wounds. Coupled with a long period of unconsciousness, my brain did not retain all the information it had taken in.'

The room was silent. Madame Rochet was not going to give him an easy way out, and he couldn't blame her. If he had been in the same situation, he would want to know every minute detail.

'From what I have been able to piece together in my mind during the intervening years, I have come to the conclusion that in the ensuing struggle I killed your son.'

Lucy buried her face in her hands. Madame Rochet for her part, sat dry-eyed, staring hard at Avery. He met her gaze once again and knew she wanted to know more.

'I am certain the damage to my left hand happened as we wrestled over possession of his knife. I remember there being blinding pain and a lot of blood. That much is very clear in my mind. At some point, I must have known it had turned into a fight to the death. My vision was beginning to blur and my head was spinning. He swore at me in English, which I recall shocked me.'

'What did he say?'

'Words which only a soldier should use or hear. Do not ask me to repeat them. We were both becoming weaker by the second, but he still held on to his knife. He made one last lunge at me. I am certain it was to press home the advantage and finish me off.

'It was only at that final, pivotal moment that I felt a hard wedge under my leg. I had forgotten my bayonet was still hanging by my side. I fumbled for it and managed to release it from the scabbard. I raised it in front of me as he rolled over and threw himself on top of me. Everything went black at that moment.

'I do have fleeting recollections of waking at several points during the night, with him lying partially on top of me, but that is all I remember.'

Avery looked down at the floor, his hands shaking. He had never shared the whole story with anyone before, not even Ian Barrett. They had a gentlemen's agreement never to discuss matters of the battle.

'I have told you all I can about your son's death,' he said.

The memory of looking up into Pascal Rochet's dead eyes and then seeing the bayonet dug deep into his chest was Avery's alone. He would never share that horror with another living soul.

Madame Rochet pulled herself up from the chair. Avery rose to offer his assistance, but she refused him. From the way she looked at his hands, it was as if she could still see them drenched in the blood of her son.

'One final question, Mr. Fox. How did you finally come to be in possession of the watch? You say you were attempting to return it, and yet you still have it,' she replied.

Avery turned to Lucy and looked at her. How on earth was he going to deal with her once Pascal's mother was gone?

He crossed the floor and opened the wardrobe in which his clothes and possessions had been placed. Taking out his old travel bag, he returned to where Madame Rochet stood and placed it on the table.

'I lingered between life and death for several weeks after I was brought back to England. The fact that I was in the hands of a skilled surgeon most certainly saved my life. It was many weeks before I was recovered enough to rise from my bed and retrieve this bag from a nearby chair. They had placed it just out of reach, to spur me on to get well. In the bottom of the bag, wrapped up in a piece of bloodied cloth, was the pocket watch.'

Major Barrett's batman had found Avery late the day after the battle, assumed the watch belonged to Avery and taken it with them when they left Waterloo.

The stiffness in Madame Rochet's stance disappeared and her shoulders slumped. Avery stepped forward, afraid she was going to fall. Lucy quickly took hold of her arm. The brief shake of Lucy's head told him he should stay where he was.

He'd been so intent on making sure he explained things clearly, he had not seen Lucy rise from the couch and come to stand to one side of Madame Rochet. Once again, he'd been so wrapped up in his own concerns, he had been blind to his wife.

Now she stood before him, offering support and comfort to the woman whose son he had killed. A woman who aged and shrank before his eyes.

If only he could hold both of them and tell them how sorry he was for everything he had done.

'My world is wrong,' he whispered.

'Thank you, Avery,' Madame Rochet said, reverting back to calling him by his Christian name.

The battle of the minds was over.

'I'm so sorry for the loss of your son. If only it could have been anyone else,' he said.

The words sounded hollow.

'No. Then you would be having this conversation with someone who might not understand you so well. You are a good man, Avery. You were forced in the heat of the moment to defend yourself. While I cannot forgive you for what you did, I do not hold you to blame.'

She turned and took hold of Lucy's hand, holding it firmly in her grasp.

'Make sure he knows his honour is restored. I fear he might struggle to accept peace. Help him to understand.'

'I will,' Lucy replied.

'And now, if you don't mind, will you summon one of the hotel staff to assist me down the stairs and to my carriage.'

'Let me help you,' Lucy offered.

Madame Rochet patted Lucy's arm gently. 'You cannot go out in public with a tear-stained visage my dear; people will think you have had a row with your husband. I shall be fine with a servant to assist.'

'What will you tell your family?' Lucy asked.

Avery was grateful that Lucy had ventured the question which burned in his mind. Should they leave Paris immediately?

'Nothing . . . well not for a little while, anyway. I need time to grieve once more for my son. When the time comes, I shall have the watch repaired and give it to my eldest son, Jean-Charles. I shall tell him it came to me anonymously. The war is over, Avery, there is nothing to be gained by starting hostilities between our two families.'

She looked at Avery's damaged hand.

'I think we have all lost enough.'

Avery closed the door to their suite as soon as Madame Rochet left and leaned back against it.

He had done it. The pocket watch was now back in the hands of the Rochet family. He ventured a look toward Lucy. She was standing, arms wrapped around herself, staring out the window.

She had been his tower of strength throughout the interview with Madame Rochet. Without her presence, he doubted he could have got through it.

'Lucy?'

She turned to him and gave him a sad smile.

'Well, you did it. You got rid of the watch. It is now back with its rightful owner.'

He knew at this moment he should be feeling an immense sense of relief. But he felt numb. No outpouring of emotion.

Nothing.

Chapter Twenty-Five

L ucy played nervously with her wedding ring. Rolling it round and round her finger. The simple gold band, reminding her that she was committed to this marriage forever.

Supper in their room was a silent affair. They remained in their suite after Madame Rochet departed, Avery cancelling their earlier plans to go sightseeing. He barely ate, while Lucy stared at her plate of food as she forced back the threatening tears.

'I think I might go for an evening stroll,' he said. He pushed his untouched supper plate away. He stood, put on his coat and left the room.

⹋

'Just there, thank you very much.'

Avery looked up as a procession of three hotel staff bearing piles of boxes and parcels entered the room. Lucy followed closely behind. They put the boxes on the floor near to Lucy's travel chest. She gave the senior member of the group a handful of coins and bade them farewell.

'Well, that's most of it done,' she said proudly.

When she'd woken that morning, Lucy decided she needed to escape the stifling atmosphere of the hotel. She couldn't sit and endure the soul-crushing silence any longer.

In the two days since their meeting with Madame Rochet, Avery had barely spoken a word to her. The only time he had touched her was late at night. Even then their lovemaking lacked the fervor and passion of their earlier encounters.

Avery remained distant.

Initially Lucy put it down to the loss of the pocket watch, but now she was not so sure. Avery was not by nature a talkative man; she had learnt to accept that in her husband. This, however, was something else. He sat for hours quietly staring out the window or sleeping.

I will not cry, I will not cry. I must accept that this is my lot. I have to be strong.

Inwardly she berated herself. How foolish she had been to pin her hopes on Avery coming out of his shell and opening himself to her once the burden of the pocket watch was gone. Once a soldier, always a soldier. He remained a stranger.

When Will came to take her shopping, Avery didn't venture out of their bedroom to greet him. 'Is he ill or just being a complete ass?' Will said as he closed the door of the hotel room behind them.

'I don't know. He won't speak to me. I've tried to engage him in conversation, but he just says, 'Please Lucy, I need quiet,' she replied.

Will raised an eyebrow. 'So, he is just being an ass.'

Lucy gave him a pleading look. She had no idea how to cope with a silent, morose husband. All her life she had witnessed her parents' marriage. Never had she seen them go for more than hour or two before resolving their rare spats.

When the Duke and Duchess of Strathmore made up, the children knew they would not see their parents for the rest of the day. Now, as a married woman, Lucy understood what went on when her parents retired to their suite to 'discuss their disagreement'. The reason for her mother's smile when they finally reappeared was no longer a mystery.

Even Alex and Millie had managed to find a way to resolve their frequent arguments. Their marriage was based on heated passion and a deep knowledge of just how far they could push one another's temper. Most of all, they loved one another and were not afraid to let the rest of the world know it.

She didn't understand Avery. How could she when he refused to confide in her?

'Oh, let's not talk about anything tiresome or boring today, please, Will? I need to laugh and have some fun. Indulge me with a trip to every shop which sells fascinating knick-knacks. I have been in Paris for a week and not bought a thing.'

Will gave her a comforting hug.

'Your wish is my command. And I know exactly the right place for us to have a slap-up lunch. This is Paris, you need to stuff your face with macarons until you cannot breathe,' he replied.

Will was exactly the tonic Lucy needed. The day spent with him was filled with laughter, food and endless hours of shopping. By the end of it, Lucy had purchased special gifts for every member of her family.

Will offered to accompany her up to her hotel room, but Lucy declined. She feared he would take Avery to task for his behavior. This was a battle she was going to have to fight and win on her own.

As soon as she took off her coat and dropped down on to the soft comfort of the well- padded couch she knew she had made the right decision.

'Do we have any money left?' Avery asked tersely.

She frowned at him. To speak of money to a lady in her world was considered crass.

'Of course; Will shall settle any of the larger bills from the shops, father's steward will reimburse him. It's all taken care of; you need not worry.'

He walked over to the nearest pile of her purchases and stood over them. He opened one box and gave a sniff of disapproval.

Lucy's feet hurt. She was nursing a headache from eating too much sugar, and now her husband had shown an open disregard for her well-thought-out purchases.

Her good humor and patience with him finally snapped. She leapt from the couch, all thought of her aching feet fled from her mind.

'How dare you! How bloody dare you turn your nose up at my things! You horrible, horrible man. I hate you!' she shouted.

He clenched his fists. Anger etched the lines of his mouth.

'You have no idea how this trip has been for me, you treat it as if it's a holiday. Spending your day with your ladies' man cousin, when I am in the darkest of places,' he bellowed.

The familiar taste of tears flooded her mouth. In days past, she had stifled them, thinking not to show him how deeply affected she had been by the encounter with Madame Rochet. Today she didn't care.

Let them come.

'You are right, Avery, I have no idea. And do you know why I am clueless as to your current state of mind? It's because you have shut me completely out of your life. I thought we had become close after we crossed the fens; that we had a chance. Clearly, I was wrong. The moment something bad happens in your world, your whole existence becomes Avery Fox and no-one else. You make a point of not sharing anything with me,' she bit back.

She watched as a series of emotions played out across his face. An unwelcome sense of satisfaction pervaded her being as she saw he was struggling with her words.

'You want me to share with you the carnage of that day? Will you only be satisfied if you can smell the burning cannonballs and see death first-hand?'

Lucy slowly shook her head, bringing her temper back in check.

'You don't need to tell me about Waterloo, I know it is too painful for you. But you are more than that single day. I just want to share the rest of your life. I'm sorry if that is too much for a wife to ask.'

Any hope that she had finally gotten through to him was

quickly and most cruelly dashed. 'You will not see William Saunders again while we are in Paris, do you understand?' he replied.

Lucy snorted. 'You won't tell me what to do, Mr. Fox. If I choose to see my cousin every day while we are in Paris, I shall do so. Who the devil do you think you are?'

In three long strides, he came to where she stood and towered over her. If he had thought to intimidate her, he was sadly mistaken. With two older, imposing brothers, Lucy had fought this fight many times.

She looked deep into Avery's eyes. The same ones which she lost her soul within every time they made love were now fiercely trained upon her. Yet even as they struggled for supremacy over one another, she felt the surge of desire. How magnificent it would be for him to take her in an angry sexual encounter.

But only in that arena of combat would she yield. No man, brother or husband, would dictate to her how she lived her life. Especially not one who showed so little regard for her.

'You will stay in our suite until the time comes for us to leave Paris. Am I understood?' he ground out.

The sexual spell broke and Lucy gave him her best look of disdain before walking away. Intimidation failed as a tactic when the victim refused to meekly accept it.

'Let me know when you intend for us to depart and I shall be packed and ready to go. Until then I intend to continue spending time seeing the sights. I also have a second fitting with the *modiste* tomorrow afternoon. I ordered five new gowns from her this morning,' she replied.

From the sharp intake of his breath, she knew she had pushed just far enough to finally elicit an emotional response. She prayed it had not been too far.

'No! You won't be going anywhere. If I have to tie you to the bed, you will stay in this suite and do as I command. Do I need to remind you that I am your husband and you will do your duty as a wife and accept my orders?'

She picked up three of the boxes of her purchases and carried them over to a nearby table and took a seat. Avery was welcome to

continue the pointless argument, but she was not going to partici-
pate. She would not yield.

'Are we going to eat downstairs this evening?' she ventured.

A change of topic was always the best release when it came to
arguments with her brothers; she hoped it would be so with Avery.

When Avery didn't answer, she looked in his direction. Her
heart sank. He was standing, eyes closed, in the center of the room.

She rose from the chair and came to him.

'Why do you keep fighting me? What have I done to incur your
wrath?' she asked.

'Always questioning me, never doing just as I damn well tell
you what to do. If you were one of my troops I would have you
beaten for insubordination and dereliction of duty!' he fumed.

'But I'm not one of your reports, I am your wife and I love you,'
she calmly replied.

'I know that, Lucy.'

Avery walked to the closet, pulled out his hat and coat and
headed to the door.

'Where are you going?' she asked.

'Out,' he said, slamming the door loudly behind him.

Lucy stood and stared at the door.

'Avery,' she whispered.

Instead of insisting he go on to Edinburgh and seek a Scottish
divorce, she had lured him to the Key and tempted him into her
bed. A bed in which she now had to lie. If a cordial relationship
with her husband was the best outcome she could eventually
hope for, it was more than many women of her social standing
enjoyed.

She turned from the door. There was little point in waiting for
Avery to return. The only real choice left was to decide how long
she could allow her heart to remain open to him. Hardening her
heart and denying the love she felt for him was impossible.

While she wished her mother was on hand to offer sage words
of advice, she knew the truth lay in listening to her own heart. If
she was to succeed in reaching Avery she had to hold fast.

The rest of the afternoon Lucy spent going through her parcels and boxes, methodically making lists of who was to receive which gift.

For Emma, she had purchased a set of ribbons in blue, her sister's favourite color. She held the delicate ribbons up to the light and smiled.

'Perfect,' she murmured.

The afternoon slipped into evening. She ate supper alone and finished some letters to friends. Taking a seat outside on the balcony of their suite, she listened to the sounds of Parisian life as it went on in the street below. At a nearby cafe a band struck up a tune. It was soon accompanied by a group of singers who proceeded to render a tone-deaf version of 'Au clair de la lune'. Lucy smiled when the choir decided to add their own bawdy lyrics to the tune.

Paris is warm, she wrote. She and Avery had visited many places and the people were kind and friendly. She gave a detailed account of their happy day trip to Versailles, relying on her extensive knowledge of the Bourbon kings to make a convincing lie. When she finished the letters, Lucy checked them. Confident the facade of her wonderful honeymoon would hold, she arranged for them to be posted home to England.

The sun set and she finally turned in for bed. When she eventually succumbed to the power of sleep, Avery had still not returned.

He finally came back to their suite some time in the early hours of the morning. As he climbed into the bed beside her, Lucy could smell the strong odor of heavy liquor on his breath.

For the first time since they had come together at the Key, they did not make love. He rolled drunkenly over on to his side, his back turned away from her. The sound of his snoring soon hummed through the room.

Lucy sat up in the bed, clutching her pillow tightly to her chest.

Chapter Twenty-Six

The first time it happened, Avery put it down to Lucy being overtired. The strain of the long journey to Paris and their ongoing disagreement was beginning to take its toll on her.

The night following their fight, they made quick, perfunctory love. As soon as it was over, Lucy rolled over on to her side and faced away from him. Avery thought it odd, but accepted that she had been in a peculiar mood all day. His apology for their blistering row, followed by him coming back to their room drunk in the early hours, had been accepted with a curt nod of the head.

She had every reason to be angry with him. He had no right to take his frustrations out on her. Lucy had been nothing but supportive of him throughout their trip to France.

When it happened the second night, he lay in the dark listening to Lucy's breathing, seeking the tell-tale signs that she was asleep. Her breathing, however, remained steady; barely a whisper. She was awake.

And then it hit him.

Lucy had ceased to curl up against his back at night and whisper 'I love you' since the day they had met with Madame

Rochet. She had said little of what she thought of his revelations regarding Pascal Rochet. Under the withering gaze of Pascal's mother, he had revealed far more than he ever intended. Lucy now knew much of the vicious and desperate struggle which had taken place that fateful day. He prayed she did not judge him a monster.

Since giving up the watch he had retreated into his self-contained existence, the only place he felt safe in a world he sensed judged him daily.

'You are a Fox and everyone knows Foxes have no honour.'

The words of taunt thrown at him long ago by Thaxter still rung in his ears. Every day he wondered if he would ever feel like a true man of honour. How he could conceive of ever being a good husband when he felt like this was beyond his comprehension.

What was not beyond his understanding was the gnawing sensation that Lucy was slowly, irretrievably pulling away from him. Day by day, trapped in his private world of self- recrimination, he watched her retreat. Saw the pain in her pale blue eyes.

He was losing her.

Reaching out in their moonlit bed, he touched her hair. She shivered and pulled the blankets up around her neck, blocking him from any further physical contact.

The words were on the tip of his tongue. He knew he should tell her.

Lucy had given everything to him, and he had taken it. Greedily. Now as he stared at his wife's back, the fear that she had reached the end of her generosity filled him with dread.

His wife was from a family where love was central to all their lives. He could not recall having ever loved anyone. Whatever emotions he might have felt for his long-dead mother were shadows of memory. Until Lucy, no-one had ever loved him. Lucy had been brave enough to speak the words, but never once had he been man enough to offer up his own unbidden words of love. Never truly declared himself to her.

He was a fraud.

After lying on his back for a frustrating hour staring at the ceiling while sleep eluded him, Avery finally gave up and climbed out of bed. He dressed and left the hotel. He would seek the numbness of oblivion in the bottom of a whisky bottle.

❦

'Why are you here?'

William Saunders threw himself lazily on to the couch opposite. Avery looked down at the whisky glass in his hand and tried to ignore him.

'I don't think that is any of your business, Saunders. I do not answer to you,' he bit back.

Will sighed. 'Nor, apparently, to your wife. So, who do you answer to, Mr. Fox? Tell me; I am intrigued to know.'

Avery shook his head. He was three drinks into what he planned to be a long night. Why he was seated in the Cafe de Foy was anyone's guess. He had a perfectly good hotel in which to get drunk. The café was crowded and afforded him a greater sense of anonymity than the hotel where the staff all knew him by name.

He put the glass down. The cafe was only a quarter of a mile from the Hotel Meurice, but he knew Lucy would not venture out to find him.

He had admitted that much to himself, at least. He was hiding from his wife, because he didn't know how to face her. He was a coward.

'Have you come to lecture me once more on my marriage, because I don't think you, as an unmarried man, have any right to preach to me? When you too have a wife, then perhaps I might listen,' he replied angrily.

Who the devil was William Saunders to wade into his private matters?

'I had one; she died,' Will replied flatly.

Avery picked up the whisky glass and drained its contents down his throat.

'I'm sorry,' he replied.

'So am I.' Will got to his feet. 'Come with me.'

From the way he spoke, it was not a request. Avery knew an order when he heard one. He rose from the chair and after putting on his coat, followed Will to the door of the cafe.

'Merci, Monsieur Lacerte,' Will said, shaking the maître d'hôtel's hand. Monsieur Lacerte bowed and put his hand in his pocket. Avery looked away. Shamed to know that the very man who had been serving drinks to him for the past two hours was a spy in the employ of William Saunders.

Outside Will stopped in the cool night air and put on his hat.

'Sorry, old man, but I had the feeling you might revisit the cafe. Let's walk.'

He headed down Rue de Richelieu in the direction of the river Seine. Avery hesitated. Will turned and beckoned him on.

Before they reached the turn at Rue de Petits Champs, Will turned into a small, poorly lit alleyway. Avery followed, but with a growing sense of unease.

A few yards inside the alleyway, Avery could discern the figures of couples huddled in doorways. From the groans of the men and the giggles of the women, he realized he was in a local haunt of Paris's streetwalkers.

He stopped.

The idea of going back to his hotel suite and crawling into bed beside Lucy after seeing what was going on made him feel nauseous. In another time, another life, he might well have taken the opportunity to select one of these ladies to share his company. But not now.

'Why have you brought me here?' he demanded.

Will beckoned to one of the ladies of the night. After handing her some coins he escorted her over.

'I thought you might like . . .' He turned to the girl and spoke to her in a rough Parisian accent. She said something which Avery did not understand. Will simply nodded.

'Her name is Colette, but she said she is happy to be whoever you wish her to be.'

Colette sidled up to Avery and stroked her fingers down his arm.

'Monsieur,' she purred.

Avery took hold of Colette's hand and firmly pushed it away.

'I don't need this, for god's sake, Saunders, I have a wife!' he snapped.

Will shook his head and the girl backed away, still smiling. It was the easiest coin she would make all evening.

'Why have you brought me to such a place? How could you do this to Lucy?' he demanded.

Will rounded on Avery and punched his fist hard into his chest.

'Because you spend your days sulking in your hotel room and your nights drinking yourself to oblivion. Since you neglect your beautiful bride the rest of the time, I assumed you would be the sort to indulge in this kind of activity. I was merely doing you a favor by showing where you could find a suitable, clean girl,' he replied.

'Then you know nothing of me,' Avery bit back.

It was taking every ounce of his self-control not to grab Will by the throat and throttle him there and then on the spot.

He began to walk back toward the main street. He didn't need Will's help to find his way home.

Once he reached Rue de Petits Champs he turned and waited for Will. Anger coursed through his veins. He wasn't finished with William Saunders. No man branded him an adulterer without consequences.

'I should give you a damn good thrashing,' he said as Will caught up with him.

'Only if I can knock a bit of sense into you in the process. Subtlety does not seem to work on you, Avery. That girl was just a more direct approach,' Will replied.

Avery sighed. 'I am a Yorkshireman, we prefer plain speech. I don't understand your riddles, so out with it, man.'

Will nodded. 'All right, but not here. Not everyone on the streets of Paris at this time of night is as friendly or accommodating as Colette. We can talk back at your hotel.'

Back at the hotel, the night porter indulged them with a bottle of wine and the promise that they would be not be disturbed.

'I'm sorry if you think I misjudged you earlier. I was merely testing you,' Will said.

The anger still burned within Avery. No matter how things stood between him and Lucy, he would not break his commitment to their marriage.

Not now.

Weeks earlier, he had been ready to throw away their union, to give her the freedom she asked of him. But now, even as he stood on the verge of losing her, he determined to fight to retain what was his. Whatever lay between them, what he had with Lucy was more than he had ever had before in his life.

'Forget about it. But don't you dare make mention of this evening's misadventure to Lucy. I don't want to cause her further distress,' he replied.

Will replied to Avery's words with a derisive snort.

'You say you don't want to hurt Lucy, and yet from where I continue to sit, all you do is cause her pain. Frankly, Avery, you are a self-centered, selfish ass.'

'Well . . .'

Will slammed his fist down on the arm of the chair.

'I'm not finished! All you have done since you got to Paris is bellyache about yourself and your precious honour. You've allowed yourself to remain blind to the ongoing anguish you cause your wife. Damn it man, she loves you, but you surely don't deserve it.'

Avery put down his untouched glass of wine and slowly got to his feet. Controlled rage seethed through his body.

'Thank you for a most illuminating evening, Mr. Saunders, good night.'

'Avery?' Will said, still seated in his chair.

Avery turned. His mind vacillated between listening to Will's parting words, and punching him swiftly in the head.

'Yes?'

'You asked me a few days ago how you could ever repay me for helping to save your life. I've settled on my price.'

'What?'

Will closed his eyes and sat silent for a moment.

'Pascal Rochet is dead but you are not. Leave the past behind. Bury it here in Paris. Go home to England and make a happy life for yourself with Lucy.'

Chapter Twenty-Seven

Avery crept quietly into the hotel suite.

It was late. The clock in the hotel lobby had read three as he passed it on his way to the staircase.

He closed the door silently behind him and crossed to the chair near Lucy's side of the bed. Not wanting to climb into bed beside her just yet, he was content to sit and watch her. She had left the curtains of their room open and the moonlight shone on her long, flaxen hair.

He smiled. One thing he and Will did agree upon was Lucy's beauty. Her soft English complexion and rosy lips had him enthralled.

She snuffled in her sleep. There were so many unique things about his wife he was just beginning to appreciate.

Brushing his fingers over the top of the chocolate-brown felt of his hat, which sat in his lap, he pondered his lot. His clothing, finely cut, fitted elegantly to his form. He had more money to his name than he had ever possessed before. He was set for life.

He put the hat aside. To know Lucy loved him was a privilege beyond mere worldly possessions. Happiness. Contentment. Joy.

Even thinking the words seemed like speaking a foreign tongue.

He had spent his whole life hiding from any form of emotional connection. Until Lucy came into his life, he had prided himself on being able to exclude all but the simplest of emotions in his heart.

The loss of army comrades over the years had elicited the occasional temporary sensation of grief, but otherwise, safe in his heavily fortified castle, no-one had ever breached his thick outer walls. And yet here Lucy was, the beautiful enemy at his gate. A girl prepared to lay siege to his heart and starve him out. She didn't need a wall-wrecking cannon, she simply laid down her arms and waited.

William, damn him, was right. Lucy deserved to be loved. Any man who didn't love, desire and crave her heart was a madman.

But how?

How, after a lifetime of being alone, could he truly open himself to the concept of happiness? Dourness was at times his only trusted friend.

Lucy rolled over in her sleep. Her hand reached out across the bed. Searching. Yearning for him. Still held in the depths of slumber, she gave a small mew of disappointment.

In an instant Avery was up, out of the chair and hurriedly ridding himself of his clothing. He slid beneath the blankets and took hold of Lucy's hand, placing it over his heart. She snuffled once more in her sleep and he felt the warmth of her left leg as she wrapped it over his. She locked him in place, ensuring he would not be leaving their bed again this night.

He smiled.

She might have been the victor, but he was a willing captive to her army.

'Bind me in chains and never let me go,' he whispered into her hair.

Her hand slowly drifted down from his chest, over his stomach and came to rest on his manhood. Lucy shifted lower in the bed and Avery felt himself go hard in the knowledge that she was now awake.

She took him in hand and slowly began to rouse him with long, skillful strokes. As he lay back in the bed and allowed her to indulge him, Avery was struck with the answer to his question.

He didn't have to fight for happiness. All he had to do was open the door and let it in. He rolled over and filled her with one long deep thrust.

In the dark, Lucy raised her hips, taking him deep inside her body.

'Love me,' she murmured.

※

When Avery woke in the dawn light he rolled over and came to Lucy. Brushing her sleep-tussled hair from her face, he kissed her lips.

'Good morning, wife,' he said.

He was determined that today would be the beginning of something different. A new dawn for them.

'Come on, time to get up and head out,' he said, dragging his reluctant wife from their bed a short while later.

'Why?' she replied.

'Because you and I need to escape this hotel suite and see Paris together. The city awaits. There are churches and monuments to explore. And I'm certain there are shops you wish me to visit.'

She frowned and her gaze fell upon her travel trunk. She had had the hotel maids pack it. It was evident to her mind that their departure from Paris was imminent.

He snorted. They were not going anywhere until matters between them had been resolved. Until Lucy finally understood that she now possessed his heart.

'Are you sure you want to?' Lucy replied.

Avery pulled her to him, planting a hasty but sure kiss on her lips. When Lucy tried to pull away, he held her to him. Today he would counter no arguments. He was going to seize the day.

'Yes. I have much to atone for after the way I have treated you. Besides, when we arrived I promised to take you on a tour of Notre Dame. Having sat and stared at the top of the western facade most days since we have been here, it is time I made an effort to see it up close. We need to visit it together.'

Appealing to Lucy's love of all things historical was one way he planned to get on her good side. His wife was both beautiful and intelligent. If his luck held, she would soon understand what he was trying to tell her.

'Fine. We shall do a little tour of the city. I must admit I have been rather keen to see Notre Dame; I have read so much about it. Will offered to take me, but I told him I wanted to share it especially with you.'

Ever-loyal Lucy had kept something of Paris just for the two of them. Avery felt ten feet tall. He quickly dressed and put on his coat.

'Good, then that is settled. A day spent together sightseeing in Paris. I have an early appointment this morning, but I shan't be too long. I shall see you downstairs in an hour,' he said.

As he opened the door to their room he turned and gave her a hopeful smile.

'Thank you,' she said.

&

When Lucy finally met Avery downstairs, she greeted him with a warm smile. Hope flared in his heart. He quickly rose from the armchair and put down the week-old copy of *The Times* he had been attempting to read. With his thoughts now centered on Lucy, he had absorbed little of the news from home.

'You look so beautiful. I promise to make today very special for you,' he murmured.

As they passed the office of the hotel concierge, he gave the night porter a sly nod.

The man, who was just coming off duty, bowed deeply before rushing to the front door and holding it open.

'Monsieur Fox, Lady Fox. I hope you have a wonderful day today,' he said.

Stepping out into the September sunshine, Avery offered Lucy his hand as she climbed up into an open-topped carriage. She sat down in the seat facing toward the front and quickly threw a blanket over her skirts to keep warm.

Avery stifled a grin when she scowled at him as he sat beside her and pulled the carriage blanket over his knees.

'A gentleman is supposed to sit in the seat opposite a lady,' she said.

'You must remember that I am no gentleman, only an earl in training. Besides, I want to sit next to you; it gives me the opportunity to do this,' he replied, slipping his hand under the blanket and stroking his hand along her thigh.

Without a moment's thought for where they were or who could see, he pressed a warm kiss on her cheek. Let the world watch and say whatever it pleased. Convincing Lucy of the sincerity of his words was all that mattered.

'So where are we headed to first?' she asked.

Avery rapped his knuckles on the top of the seat in front and the driver instantly urged his horses on.

'I was thinking the Arc de Triomphe first, since it is a long way from the hotel. Then a picnic lunch along the river, before a visit to the cathedral. After that, who knows where the afternoon will take us,' he replied.

If matters went according to plan, their day would end with them both in a state of serious undress in their hotel room, Lucy hot and sated in his arms.

8.

'Did you know Napoleon had a wooden version of the Arc built just so he could parade under it? Foolish man' Lucy said.

She and Avery were standing on the side of the Avenue des Champs Elysées looking at the partially built stone Arc de Triomphe. When finished it would be a masterpiece of architecture.

Avery shook his head.

'He has been many things, but a fool is not one of them. There is a very good reason why he is held captive on the remote island of Saint Helena,' he replied.

'Really? He lost at Waterloo.'

'Waterloo was a near-run thing. Too many of the allies didn't take it seriously until the battle had actually commenced. While we were camped out in the cold and mud, the social elite were holding balls and parties.'

Lucy pursed her lips. She knew many of those who had attended the Duchess of Richmond's famous ball on the eve of the battle at Quatre Bras. In her youthful exuberance, she had once thought it all rather dashing. Now, hearing how the soldiers in the field viewed it, she felt differently.

He reached out and took hold of her hand. She trembled. All morning he had been so attentive and affectionate she didn't know what to make of him. Where was the angry, closed man who had shared her life for the past weeks? Making love earlier that morning she sensed something different about him, but she had lost the thought in the throes of passion.

He kissed her fingertips. Even through the fabric of her gloves she felt the heat of his mouth.

'I am just so glad you survived,' she murmured.

'So am I. Otherwise I would never have known you.'

The morning spent travelling the streets of Paris was one which would forever remain etched in her memories. For someone who had never before visited the French capital, she was surprised as to the amount of knowledge she had managed to accumulate through her reading.

Whenever they reached a point where the conversation touched on the recent war, she gently steered matters to a more neutral subject. Even as she attempted to maintain an emotional distance between Avery and herself, her thoughts continually came back to him.

When the subject of Waterloo came up once more, she stopped mid-sentence, and cast him a wary look.

'Go on, I am interested to hear about it,' he encouraged.

She made tentative mention of Will and his role during the war, stopping when Avery held up his hand.

'We must protect Will,' he said.

The carriage drew up at one end of the Petit Pont Bridge, close to Notre Dame Cathedral. Avery quickly opened the carriage door. As soon as her feet hit the pavement and she looked up, Lucy let out an appreciative sigh.

'I have managed to catch a peek of the rooftop from our hotel room, but to stand and see the whole magnificent edifice, takes my breath away. Have you ever seen anything so splendid in your life?' she exclaimed.

He chuckled.

'I prefer my magnificence in human form,' he replied.

She gave him a quizzical look. He was up to something, but she couldn't quite put her finger on it. There was an unexpected tenderness about him this morning, something which she had never seen before. Her heart stirred with hope.

'Where do you want to start?' she asked.

They began to walk toward the main entrance. A little way short of the main door, he stopped.

'I am happy for you to tell me everything, and I mean everything that you know about the cathedral. On one condition.'

'Hmm?'

'First, you have to come and share the luncheon picnic I have especially arranged for us. If the basket does not come back empty, I am certain the hotel's chef will be disappointed.'

He steered her toward the riverbank. At the bottom of a series of stone steps, a table and chairs had been set up. Standing beside the table was a waiter, liveried in the colors of the Hotel Le Meurice.

When she smiled, she saw her own joy reflected back in Avery's face. Her heart leapt with anticipation. Today had been one of constant surprises and delight.

'Avery, what a sweet gesture; you shouldn't have,' she whispered, her voice breaking.

'Actually, I should. And I promise to do more things like it from now on,' he replied.

As soon as they took their seats, the waiter poured them both a glass of champagne. Lucy held her glass in her hand, welling up with tears once more as Avery made a short speech.

'To you, Lucy, my wife. I hope that we are able to look back upon today and remember fondly that this was where our life together truly began,' he said.

Words failed Lucy as she sipped her champagne. Whatever had transpired to bring Avery to her, she was at a loss to understand, but she was filled with an overwhelming sense of gratitude. Were the gods finally smiling upon her?

❧

They sat overlooking the waters of the River Seine, enjoying the simple pleasure of watching the boats sailing by. After a wonderful lunch of poached salmon, served with *aligot* and green beans, the waiter produced a chocolate pudding, which made them both smile.

'I am beginning to think it would have been a terrible mistake for me to come and live in Paris. I should have been the size of a small cow within weeks with all this wonderful food,' Lucy said. Avery nodded as he licked the delicious, rich chocolate sauce from his spoon. When the last of the champagne was gone, they made their way back up the embankment stairs to the cathedral.

Avery watched as Lucy rattled off a comprehensive list of details about the cathedral. So detailed was her knowledge of Notre Dame, he wondered if there was anyone else in the city of Paris who knew as much as she did.

'Did you know there used to be a tall bell tower spire on the cathedral, but it was taken down in the last century? I've seen sketches of it. I wonder if someday they will rebuild it.'

When she turned and looked at him an easy smile found its way to his lips.

'What?' she asked.

'Nothing,' he replied.

Sometime during Lucy's dissertation, he had stopped hearing her words. It was his heart which had his full attention. It had finally spoken.

The realization that he loved her was not completely earth-shattering. He had suspected he was falling in love with her long before they set sail for France. At the Key, he had felt the first stirrings of what had been for him an unknown emotion.

His whole life he had stifled any thought of joy. Stuffed it back down inside, locked it away. A miserable childhood, followed by years of hardship and war, had left him wary of people who found delight in life.

But this girl, nay, this woman had given him the greatest gift imaginable. Freely and without reservation she had opened her heart to him. The merest touch of her fingers set his skin on fire. Lucy. His wife.

He chuckled softly, knowing she would always be surprising him.

'Avery?' she said.

'Come, let's go back to the hotel,' he said.

'But there's lots more I can tell you about the architecture of the cathedral. We haven't even gone inside yet,' Lucy said.

'As I said when we first got here, Notre Dame is still going to be here tomorrow. And so, shall we. There are more pressing matters,' he replied.

Once inside their room, he pulled her into his arms and kissed her deeply. She responded, as always, with warmth and passion. Her lips tasted of the honey and butter from the fresh bun he had bought her on their walk back to the Hotel Meurice. As he licked the last of the sweet honey from the corner of her mouth she groaned and he felt himself go hard.

When he finally released her from his embrace, he stood holding her hands, taking her in.

Lucy raised a quizzical eyebrow. 'Are you going to tell me or not?'

'What?' He knew she had been watching him closely on the walk back along the river to their hotel.

'Something has changed within you. I have never seen you smile as you have today. You almost seem happy,' she explained.

Avery took a deep breath, surprised at the degree of apprehension he felt over telling Lucy what was on his mind.

'I love you Lucy. I love my wife. And if that is what makes me smile, then yes, I suppose it is happiness,' he said.

He saw realization in her eyes as she beheld the truth.

He loved her.

'Oh Avery, I love you too,' she murmured.

She threw her arms around him and held on tight. He kissed her hair and pulled her close. Her body shuddered with sobs, but he didn't mind. He could deal gladly with tears of joy.

'I wish I wasn't such a watering pot,' Lucy said.

Avery lifted her face and he kissed away the tears on her cheeks.

'Never be ashamed of your open nature, my love. It's what makes you uniquely Lucy. I know exactly where I stand with you. There is no hiding behind a mask.'

If there was anyone who should be feeling a sense of shame, he knew it was himself. Lucy had succumbed to her fate and accepted her love for him long ago. Even when she agreed to end their union, it was because she had loved him enough to let him go.

'I sorry I held myself back from you for so long. I didn't know how to love you. I'm still learning, but I assure you all doubt is now gone.'

She offered him her lips. The hungry, needful kiss they shared spoke more than mere words.

'I have an idea,' he said. He took hold of her hand and led her toward the balcony doors. Pulling back the curtains, he opened the two large glass doors. Now they had an uninterrupted view of Notre Dame.

'Can you see the cathedral?' he asked.

'Yes.'

'Good, now keep your gaze fixed on it.'

Chapter Twenty-Eight

Lucy stood looking out over the rooftops at the two massive stone towers which reared up into the sky at the western end of the cathedral. For a moment, the room was silent as she took in the magnificent view.

Avery removed her coat. When she turned to thank him, he frowned and reminded her to keep looking at the cathedral.

A shiver of anticipation slid through her body, as his fingers painstakingly unbuttoned the back of her gown. He slid the bodice down over her shoulders, leaving her breasts bare to the cool air of the late afternoon.

He whistled.

'It's the French mode of dress. Nothing under the gown,' she said.

'I like it,' he murmured in her ear.

She swallowed. His words dripped with desire.

He placed a trail of long, hot kisses down her spine. Then, kneeling behind her, he pushed the skirt of her gown over her hips and it fell to the floor.

Apart from her stockings and slippers, Lucy was now completely naked in front of the doorway.

'Shouldn't we close the balcony doors?' she asked.

'No,' came the adamant reply.

He came and stood in front of her, temporarily blocking her view of the cathedral.

'No-one can see you, only me.'

He briefly kissed her lips, then his attention shifted to her breasts. He took the nipple of her left breast into his mouth. In the short time they had been lovers, they had discovered this nipple was the one which roused her most rapidly to a heightened sexual state.

He suckled hard and she whimpered. His other hand took hold of her right breast and began to gently twist and tease the other nipple. The mixture of pleasure and pain was exquisite. She closed her eyes as her body succumbed.

When he slid his hand up her inside thigh and pressed a thumb into her moistened heat, Lucy cried out. She clutched at him.

Her eyes flew open. Avery was still fully clothed! She reached for his buttons, but he pushed her hand away. 'I may be powerless against you in love, but in this sphere, I am in command. You will obey.'

Completely naked before the world and in full daylight, she should be feeling nothing but shame as her husband brought forth her wanton desire. Instead, she reveled in his hot, demanding attention. She would do exactly as he ordered.

He knelt before her.

She placed a hand gently on his dark hair as the first lap of Avery's tongue touched her pleasure nub. She shivered as her whole world shifted.

'Keep looking at the cathedral. Now tell me everything you know about Notre Dame,' he instructed.

A knowing smile crept across her lips. She understood the game. If he forced her to keep looking at Notre Dame while he pleasured her with his tongue she would have to cede her mind to him as well as her body.

'Construction of the cathedral commenced during the reign of Louis the Seventh . . . oh god.'

His tongue delved deeper.

'It was one of the first buildings in the world to use flying buttresses.'

She gripped tightly to his shoulders, sobbing as with every touch and thrust Avery brought her closer to the edge. He slipped two fingers inside her. The forceful strokes making her weak at the knees.

In the second before she came, Lucy managed one last glance at the cathedral. Then she soared.

As she returned to earth, her heartbeat slowing, Lucy chortled. While she had been staring at one of the greatest cathedrals in the world Avery had taken her to heaven.

'Good. Now for the next part,' he said, getting to his feet.

He led her over to the bed and arranged her on her knees, facing away from him. He threw off his coat and jacket before releasing his manhood from his trousers.

'Now show me just how willing you are to serve under my command,' he said, sliding his hard length into her from behind.

Lucy's still throbbing flesh welcomed him. His hands gripped her hips and he began to thrust deep into her body.

'Oh yes, take me,' she begged.

He groaned.

'Take me what?' he demanded.

'Take me sir!' she cried.

The pace of their coupling increased. She could hear the desperation to reach the end in the shortness of his breath.

'I want to hear you scream when I make you climax,' he said gruffly.

He shifted behind her, forcing her lower on to the bed. She was completely at his mercy. His hips began to rock her and the bed, slowly building the pressure within her once more.

With Avery pounding deep into her heat, Lucy knew the answer to the question of whether she could climax a second time in a matter of minutes was surely yes.

Avery slowed his thrusts. The grip of his hands on her hips lessened.

Head down, arms out in front of her, Lucy sensed a change in the room. He withdrew from her, but she knew he had not found his release.

The sound of his boots hitting the floor echoed in the room as he hurriedly undressed. He came quickly back to her. Strong, masculine arms wrapped around her body and lifted her upward, bringing her to sit facing him on his naked lap.

She brushed her fingers appreciatively over the dark curls of his chest hair. Then ran her hands over his broad, strong shoulders. He was a magnificent man and he was all hers. Avery cupped Lucy's chin in his hand and placed a fiery kiss on her mouth.

'This is how our wedding night should have been. How it will be for every night from now on. I need you to understand exactly what you have come to mean to me,' Avery said.

The passion in his eyes, the husky tone of his voice spoke of his highly aroused state. His thirst for her would never be slaked.

Lucy shifted, straddled Avery and guided his erection to her moistened opening.

'If this is to be our wedding night, then it should be for the both of us. I want you to know how much being your wife means to me,' she replied.

She had stood alongside him as he had bravely faced down the demons of his past; now she needed to show Avery that she was truly his partner in their marriage. That they could forge a strong future together.

As she lowered herself down, impaling her heated body on his erection, Avery closed his eyes. Lucy smiled when he groaned as she slowly began to ride him.

'I knew you would be a fast learner,' he said.

When Lucy reached behind her and cupped Avery's balls, he gave a deep growl of satisfaction.

'You have no idea,' she teased.

Images of the pictures she had seen in Millie's copy of the *Kama Sutra* came to mind. Now was the time to put those illicit readings into practice.

‚👁

The sun had begun to sink down below the other side of the city when Avery finally stirred Lucy from her post-coital slumber.

'Hungry?'

She nodded. 'Ravenous.'

'Good, supper should be arriving soon.'

He climbed out of bed and went to his travel chest. It still amazed him that a gentleman needed such an elaborate piece of equipment just to travel. His trusty old leather knapsack, now empty, would have to find a new use.

He had thought to throw it away, but Lucy protested. She refused to let him set aside his old life completely.

'It will be useful for fishing,' she said, putting the bag into the cupboard in their room.

He opened the top drawer of his travel chest and took out a small silk bag.

Lucy, warm and still sleepy, welcomed him back into their bed with a tempting kiss. He took hold of her eager fingers and held them at bay.

'Later, my insatiable minx. I have something for you.'

An expectant grin appeared on her face when he held up the small silk bag.

'Your father released some of your dowry funds to me person-ally before we left Scotland,' he said, chuckling when he saw her eyes grow wide.

'I had no idea,' Lucy replied.

'I think that was the idea. You were not to know everything.'

She gave him a playful punch on the arm.

'Beast.'

'Before I give you this, I need to ask you something. Be certain of your answer,' he said.

'Go on,' she whispered, hands held in prayer to her lips.

'Lady Lucy, love of my heart, will you be my wife?'

She managed a small but resolute yes.

Avery withdrew the ring from the bag and held it up to the pale evening light. The large diamond in the center reflected the fire of the rubies which sat ringed around it on the top of the bezel.

When he'd entered the shop of Fossin, the jeweler's, at Place Vendome that morning, William Saunders beside him, he had not known what style of ring to buy. Will had suggested a single diamond, but as soon as he set eyes on this particular ring, Avery knew it was perfect for Lucy.

He recalled how his hand had been shaking when he signed the bank instruction to settle the bill. He had checked the invoice twice. As they left the shop, Will had proudly patted him on the back.

Lucy said, 'It's beautiful, but you shouldn't feel obliged to buy me a betrothal ring, we are already married. Besides your love is more precious to me than any jewel.'

Avery slipped the ring on her finger. The delight which shone in Lucy's eyes told him what she truly thought of the gift.

'I need to make amends for the awful way I have treated you. You should have a betrothal ring. I want you to be able to show it off to your friends and family when we return to London. For everyone to know that ours is a real marriage,' he replied.

At the time, his refusal to hold their wedding at St George's or host a formal wedding ball had felt as if he was sending a message to London society. His life would not be dictated by others who thought themselves better than him. This union had been forced upon him, but only he would decide how proceedings would be conducted.

Looking at his tousle-haired wife, he knew his behavior had been petulant and petty. Against her better judgement, and her heart, Lucy had offered him his freedom. To his dying day he would be grateful she had not given up on him.

As someone of pure heart, Lucy deserved the very best.

'Thank you,' she said, choking back tears.

He brushed the first tear away with his lips.

'I promise we shall have a huge ball once everyone gets back to London. You will be able tell everyone all about our honeymoon in France.'

'Not all of it,' she sighed, wrapping her arms around him.

Some memories of Paris would only be for the two of them.

Epilogue

William Saunders closed the door to his small house and climbed the stairs. It wasn't actually his house; he simply rented a small garret under the eaves, but his landlady Madame Dessaint had always made him feel at home.

Stopping at the dining room on the first floor, he spied his evening meal. A ceramic pot stood in the middle of the rough wooden table, and a spoon lay next to it.

He lifted up the lid.

'Cassoulet, what a surprise,' he murmured.

He chuckled softly. It was Tuesday. Madame Dessaint always cooked cassoulet on Tuesdays.

'One has to praise a woman who keeps to a strict routine.'

He dipped the spoon into the pork and white bean stew and pondered his words.

Strict routine.

Putting the spoon down, he stared once more at the pot. Madame Dessaint had served up the same seven-dish repertoire every week since William took up his lodgings.

Three years, nearly four, since he had moved here from the house he had once shared with Yvette.

He wiped away an unbidden tear. 'Don't,' he urged himself. Tears would not bring back his wife. The assassin's knife had made sure of it. As he had done so many times before, he forced the memory of that night from his mind.

'I wonder how Lucy and Avery are getting on,' he said to the empty room.

When he had bid them farewell from Paris two weeks earlier, it was with the hope that they would find the secret to a happy future together. Avery would one day make a fine Lord Langham.

For the first time in a long time, Will suddenly felt a sense of overwhelming loneliness. His journey home to England earlier in the summer had been bittersweet. Once he had dreamed of happily squiring his lovely French bride home to meet his family. Instead he had worn the dark garb of a widower.

He smiled, recalling the look of unbridled happiness Avery had sported the last day he had seen him. Every time Lucy stepped more than a foot or so away from him, Avery had reached out and pulled her back to his side.

Will remembered that feeling. The warmth of knowing that you and another person were truly one.

He left the dining room, his interest in food gone. Within him a different hunger began to burn. The need for sustenance of another kind. Something he sensed he would not find in Paris.

Reaching his room, he pulled a large travel trunk from the corner of his room and placed it in the middle of the floor.

Apart from some minor business interests which he could easily manage from London, there was nothing to keep him in France. He had remained purely out of habit.

His parents and siblings would no doubt be pleased when he turned up on their doorstep and announced his permanent return to England.

'Madame Dessaint, I shall miss your culinary skills,' he murmured.

Kneeling in front of the trunk, he threw open the lid. It would take but a short time to pack all his things.

It was time for him to go home.

Time that William Saunders began to live again.

About the Author

Born in England, but raised in Australia, Sasha has a love for both countries. Having her heart in two places has created a love for travel, which at last count was to over 55 countries. A travel guide is always on her pile of new books to read.

Her first published novel, *Letter from a Rake* was a finalist for the 2014 Romantic Book of the Year.

Sasha lives with her husband, teenage daughter and a cat who demands a starring role in the next book. She has found new hiding spots for her secret chocolate stash. On the weekends Sasha loves walking on the beach while trying to deal with her bad knee and current Fitbit obsession.

Follow Sasha and find out more about her and her books on her website
www.sashacottman.com

Also by Sasha Cottman

The Duke of Strathmore series

Book 1: Letter from a Rake

Finalist, 2014 Romantic Book of the Year (Ruby)

Winner, 2014 Book Junkies Historical Romance

Book 2: An Unsuitable Match

Finalist, 2014 Australian Romance Readers' Awards (ARRA); Best Historical Romance; Best Ongoing Series; Best Author; Best Cover.

Book 3: The Duke's Daughter

Made in the USA
Monee, IL
05 January 2022

88141810R00177